"Tolstoyan in its sense of weighty importance ... Hemingwayesque in its taut terse language." —*Toronto Star*

"Evocatively told with spare, poetic elegance, this is a story of the love and life which can grow from a terrible loss. Henry is a man torn between escaping a past tragedy and embracing its implications fully within his own life. Set in rural Canada, where the reverberations of world events can both shatter lives and offer the potential for redemption, *Minister Without Portfolio* is an essential, modern, Canadian novel."
—Vincent Lam, Giller Prize–winning author of *Bloodletting and Miraculous Cures* and *The Headmaster's Wager*

"This isn't your typical war story, romance novel or tale of redemption—but a combination of the three that makes for one hell of a ride." —*Chatelaine*

"Michael Winter gives us the story of a man who suffers a shock, searches for a foundation, and rescues a home. This is a book about old-fashioned love, the very unlikely, smoking hot, so lucky you came across it kind. The lasting kind of love that blazes like a forest fire. In *Minister Without Portfolio* Michael Winter takes a ball-peen hammer to your heart and finds the veins of gold. Every sentence is an ungrounded wire, megawatts of ebullience, wonder and sparking-spitting joy. Electric prose."
—Lisa Moore, author of *February* and *Caught*

Praise for *The Death of Donna Whalen*

Shortlisted for the Rogers Writers' Trust Fiction Prize
Shortlisted for the Commonwealth Writers' Prize

"Extraordinary ... turning the spotlight entirely on this devastating array of intersecting lives and deaths, Winter has enacted some of the most powerful storytelling of his career."

—*The Globe and Mail*

"Winter fashions these disparate voices—children, neighbours, friends, family—into a compelling narrative that's like *As I Lay Dying* meets *In Cold Blood*. This is an endlessly fascinating glimpse into a side of St. John's that's seldom seen."

—*National Post*

"Winter has produced one of the best documentary accounts of a Canadian crime ever written." —*Edmonton Journal*

"[A] compelling reconstruction that gives a raw jolt to the conventional novel form ... Winter has done an exemplary job in this regard, orchestrating the various speakers into a tragic chorus over the short unhappy life of Donna Whalen." —*Toronto Star*

"A dark morality tale ... A brave work that showcases a stylist playing to his strengths, and it will undoubtedly reward the patient reader." —*The Walrus*

"*The Death of Donna Whalen* is well-crafted, a magic lantern kind of story."   —*The Telegram* (St. John's)

"*The Death of Donna Whalen* stands on its own as a literary effort that conjures a potent sensation of disquiet out of the grim details of an actual tragedy."   —*Quill & Quire*

Praise for *The Architects Are Here*

Longlisted for the Scotiabank Giller Prize

"A flamboyant gem of a novel … an intense, textured, tangled love story … puts [Winter] in a front rank of writers worth reading."
—*The Globe and Mail*

"Supreme originality, shattering insight … *The Architects Are Here* is proof positive that Winter is something special … One of the most distinctive voices in Canadian literature."
—*Winnipeg Free Press*

"Michael Winter's writing blows my mind—it's sharp and hard and beautiful and so completely original."
—Miriam Toews, author of *A Complicated Kindness*

"A soaring novel that breaks every rule … it absolutely soars with catharsis, resonance, and unexpected resolution … It is less a novel than it is a force of nature, a bloody, ugly, ultimately uplifting taste of life itself."   —*National Post*

"Mesmerizing ... Beautifully written, doleful and comic and heartfelt."   —*Edmonton Journal*

"Michael Winter redefines the Canadian novel ... Infused with tragedy and humour ... *The Architects Are Here* confirms Winter's reputation as one of Canada's most distinctive literary talents."
                                                                  —*The Vancouver Sun*

"[*The Architects Are Here* is] brainy and ambitious—just like its author."   —*Toronto Life*

"Blood-spattered and brilliant, troubled and tender ... Winter is a masterful stylist."   —*Fast Forward Weekly*

"It's a mature book, in Winter's mastery of his devastatingly effective prose style and sprawling, entrancing plot and in the concerns of his thirtysomething characters. It's big and ambitious and exciting."   —*Eye Weekly*

"The quintessential road-trip novel." —*Times Colonist* (Victoria)

PENGUIN

MINISTER WITHOUT PORTFOLIO

MICHAEL WINTER is the author of *The Architects Are Here,* which was longlisted for the Scotiabank Giller Prize, and *The Big Why,* which was shortlisted for the Trillium Book Award and longlisted for the International IMPAC Dublin Literary Award. His previous novel, *The Death of Donna Whalen,* was nominated for the Writers' Trust Fiction Prize and the Commonwealth Writers' Prize. His first novel, *This All Happened,* won the Winterset Award. He is also the recipient of the Writers' Trust Notable Author Award. He divides his time between Toronto and St. John's.

MINISTER
WITHOUT
PORTFOLIO

MICHAEL WINTER

PENGUIN

an imprint of Penguin Canada Books Inc., a Penguin Random House Company

Published by the Penguin Group
Penguin Canada Books Inc., 320 Front Street West, Suite 1400, Toronto, Ontario, Canada M5V 3B6

Penguin Group (USA) LLC, 375 Hudson Street, New York, New York 10014, U.S.A.
Penguin Books Ltd, 80 Strand, London WC2R 0RL, England
Penguin Ireland, 25 St Stephen's Green, Dublin 2, Ireland (a division of Penguin Books Ltd)
Penguin Group (Australia), 707 Collins Street, Melbourne, Victoria 3008, Australia
(a division of Pearson Australia Group Pty Ltd)
Penguin Books India Pvt Ltd, 11 Community Centre, Panchsheel Park, New Delhi – 110 017, India
Penguin Group (NZ), 67 Apollo Drive, Rosedale, Auckland 0632, New Zealand
(a division of Pearson New Zealand Ltd)
Penguin Books (South Africa) (Pty) Ltd, 24 Sturdee Avenue, Rosebank, Johannesburg 2196, South Africa

Penguin Books Ltd, Registered Offices: 80 Strand, London WC2R 0RL, England

First published in Hamish Hamilton hardcover by Penguin Canada Books Inc., 2013
Published in this edition, 2014

2 3 4 5 6 7 8 9 10 (RRD)

LIBRARY AND ARCHIVES CANADA CATALOGUING IN PUBLICATION

Winter, Michael, 1965–, author
Minister without portfolio / Michael Winter.

Originally published: Toronto : Hamish Hamilton, 2013.
ISBN 978-0-14-318780-6 (pbk.)

I. Title.

PS8595.I624M56 2014   C813'.54   C2013-907938-6

Visit the Penguin Canada website at **www.penguinrandomhouse.com**

Penguin
Random House
PENGUIN CANADA

But Love has pitched his mansion in
The place of excrement;
For nothing can be sole or whole
That has not been rent.

W.B. YEATS

PART ONE

1

She told him there wasn't another person. Henry watched her stand up from her kitchen table and push things around on a counter. She peeled up the foam placemats that made that satisfying sound. She was busying herself and of course he was in her house, he was the one who would have to physically leave. For three hours they talked it over and she told him how it was and he fled through the spectrum of emotions and they were both cleansed but she returned to what was not an ultimatum. I'm leaving you now can you please leave.

But I love you, he said.

He was quite proud of how he said it. He did not know he would begin a response with the word "but." He hadn't punched a piece of furniture or raised his voice and now he said this short sentence with mercy and with confidence and honour. It might have been the voice of a messiah, the little messiah that runs each of our lives. The statement was reassuring and he could tell it had some effect. But they were broken and she knew he was a good man but who can push through the hard times of the mundane life any more? The idea of not enough on the line, he could absorb that. But she had dismounted from the horse they were both riding. One of the things she said was she wanted to live a dangerous life.

He found his construction boots and bent his toes so the joints creaked and said so long in his head, not out loud, it would have been too casual. Also, he caught himself and understood that the previous words were the best words to leave on. But I love you. They would give him the high ground and he could really dig a good ditch for himself now and remain unshaven and unwashed and drink himself into a narrow hallway with no door at the end, he could do that and search for commiseration.

It was bright out, a very happy afternoon in the autumn. Astonishing. He put his heart on a little branch, hung it there, and then almost skipped into the street. He knew that if she was watching, that little hop would not be very attractive. But he was cleaving himself in two, something he did often for sentences at a time, but not for long days or weeks and that is how he spent his time now, split apart. A stacked cord of wood that should have been a tree.

Luckily he lived in a town that was built around a harbour and Nora's house was on top of a hill, so he had an easy walk down to the bars on Water Street. The roofs of buildings swallowed the hill and he would not have to walk past her house all the time if he just stayed downtown. That is the logic people use when they discover themselves drinking intensely. He had lived down here just after trade school in a one-room apartment on Colonial Street. He paused at the window now and the door where his mail used to come—his life before Nora.

He found himself in one bar called the Spur and a man in a corner was singing a country song which filled Henry with loathing. The man had no right to pollute the air with that song, a song from Nashville that understood nothing of a real life. He knew the man, of course, had spoken to him perhaps three times. Henry ate a pickled egg and chewed through the overboiled cold and dull yolk and drank down a pint of pale ale and came around on the song. Stripped of the production Henry was applying to the vocalization, the core of the song was ultimately true and as he left the bar he patted the old man on the shoulder. He was humming it now, Henry was. There was a line at the end where a man cuts off his lover's head and kicks it against the wall. He sang it the way the old man sang it and walked down further towards the polluted harbour and stared up at the green and marble monument to the war dead. The men up there with their bayonets and loose helmets and kneeling and dying and forever enjoying their patina. Was it brass? No one rubbed the nose of a soldier on a memorial for good luck. Live a dangerous life.

There was the dark harbour to end his land activity. The sleeping marine transports servicing the offshore industry and a coast guard search and rescue vessel and a military tug of some kind. Pure utilitarian boats all moored on very thick hawsers. He stared at the serious hulls, empty of men, and saluted. The stink of cooked diesel. Perhaps there is something here, he thought. The thought of war, or not war but an expulsion from civilian life. Or the hell with it, there is something noble in servicing oil rigs. Oil will be the end of mankind but to be in service of it is not without honour. What was it John's son had told him? Oil was the bones of dinosaurs. Civilization was something Henry had not chosen. He was born into good manners and a life sheltered from death. He could renounce it. What had it given him? What were the benefits but a broken heart?

2

He walked around the town all night and, as the sun rose over the ocean, he found himself back at Nora's door. He sat across the road and watched the house and street slowly wake up. The sun was a magnificent thing. He had to be back at the Bull Arm site Monday morning and he knew he'd pay for it, this being up all night. But he was thinking there might be early activity at Nora's house. He wondered if he had the strength and accuracy to fight a man and win. Anyone passing him by at that hour could see he was looking to break up what is called an aubade. But Nora was asleep and there was no man with her and the alert daylight made him stagger to the house of his best friend, feeling small and without a shell. He felt himself evaporating and it scared him. He let the sun warm his shoulders and kidneys and fill him up, the sun pushed him to John and Silvia's. He found the hidden key and let himself in and their dog, Wolf, did not make a sound but smelled his hand and knew who he was and followed Henry downstairs into the finished basement. Henry felt with his hands for any sleeping kids and fell into the guest bed with Wolf and hugged the big dog.

He woke up remembering Nora Power had broken up with him.

She had come into their bedroom about two weeks ago and, he realized now, tried to break up with him. Henry had been watching hockey on a small colour TV, with a bag of roast chicken chips on his chest. He had worked hard all week at Bull Arm and sometimes he just liked to lie around and be a table for a bag of chips. She sat on the floor with him and wiped away her tears and put her arm around him and he gave her a good hug and she ate his chips. She was wearing a white sweater with red sequins sewn into it and the chip crumbs clung to it. She had beautiful skin and she was a big woman with a gorgeous body that he loved to stroke.

He went to work. He drove his car to the site—it took ninety-five minutes—and every weekend for the next three months he tried to convince Nora Power otherwise. The word otherwise, he thought. Otherwise I will throw myself in the drink. It was edging into winter now and the drinks were frozen over. Sometimes, on a Sunday morning, he'd watch cartoons with John and Silvia's two kids while Silvia made pancakes. Clem: Did the milk walk away from my mouth? The boy was using a straw in a small glass of milk. His sister Sadie explained the milk was running back down the straw. Then they ran around the house with their Star Wars lifesavers.

3

Henry's buddy John Hynes had a contract with Rick Tobin and was gone to Fort McMurray for three-week stretches. It was mining, not oil. Henry had been thinking it was the work at Bull Arm that had made Nora stray from him, but Silvia didn't mind John in Alberta. They managed to foster a love at a distance. He examined his friend and his friend's wife. Fostering, he thought. I will foster this love. He spent the money he made and attempted to convince Nora. He found himself one evening pressed up against her frosted window pane saying please, Nora, please until her father's waist arrived and said Henry, Henry. Her parents were over for dinner—it was one of the family things Nora did that Henry loved. He stared at her father's belt through the window that Henry had caulked the year before, the yellow wool vest Nora's father wore in winter—Henry knew her father loved him but her father also understood his daughter. Or at least—because no one can understand Nora Power—he backed her up in her dismissal of Henry Hayward.

It took five failed efforts for him to turn the corner on Nora. The corner was tall and sheer and almost so acute it might have been an eighty-eight-degree angle. It had taken a hundred days to have Nora agree to go out with him in the first place so he felt another campaign of a hundred days would convince her to let him return. But it was Christmas and no return occurred. John Hynes and Silvia took care of him. It was John who asked Rick Tobin to hire on Henry for an overseas contract. John was home for two weeks to get his buddy back in shape. John, his hair dark and thick and cut short and his handshake arriving just before a generous hug, his lanyard ID still around his neck, the little slap the lanyard gave as he walked towards you, touching him under each armpit in a self-affirming manner. John loved people. He always found something in you to love. That nose that had been broken on the job several times, set by John himself. This job isn't an Alberta job, he said. It's in the Middle East. You're through with Nora now you need to break your relationship with the land. The land is her land or it's your land together and you can't walk it any more alone.

The contract started in March. Springtime, Henry—start anew.

This logic of land and season reminded Henry of those Sunday school sermons of ancient times when men walked with giants. The only thing keeping you standing, John said, is fresh air. Get that out of your system and you'll be set to go again.

John, not a big man, but with strong shoulders who had been in construction his entire adult life. A man used to turning slowly. He spoke of Henry as if he were an old shed built with found wood. Which he was. Which we all are. Henry had worked with John out in Kelligrews hauling busted cinder blocks into a rolloff container. They had lined up at coffee shops covered head to toe in spackle. If you sat in a car with John you realized his torso was long (his head touched the ceiling). He was telling Henry that Rick Tobin had won this contract in Afghanistan. It's a big one and it'll be hilarious and we get to hang out with Tender Morris. Tender Morris was in the reserves and now he's stationed in Camp Julien. Oh my god Tender Morris. They had gone to trade school with Tender and then Tender had joined the reserves.

Henry returned to work in Bull Arm and took an elevator every day down the leg of a module four storeys underwater to conduct stress tests on the concrete being poured there. It was a routine and he enjoyed how busy he was and how distracted he felt and insulated from the truth of Nora Power having left him. This enormous pillar underwater protected him from that truth and he could lick his wounds. It was when he came back to the surface that he was vulnerable. Sometimes on the weekends, when he could not sleep and he knew he was deeply alone in the world, he'd check Silvia's computer and there'd be an email from John out in Alberta telling him of the crazy things going on in the mining sector.

Henry spent his weekends in St John's. He continued to have drinks in bars, but one early morning a man next to him called for a pint and the bartender told him there was none left. Can I take the keg home on my bike? No. Okay let's have five tequilas.

Tequila's the only thing that's true, the bartender said.

Man: She is hard and cynical about everything except a deep sentimental attachment to anything dealing with animals.

Henry paid his bill and left. He promised himself not to hear that type of language again: caustic truths with no self-mockery. He did push-ups and vowed he would get his life together. He remembered the man who had lived in this finished basement for a few weeks during 9/11. Noyce was his name. A stranded passenger that John and Silvia had befriended through Colleen Grandy. This man Noyce fell in love with Newfoundland and bought a house around the bay near John and Silvia's summer home in Renews. Noyce was strong in the way a bird is strong, big chest and hollow-boned. Ready for perky flight and a ruddy, round, sunburnt head with just a horseshoe of golden hair at his ears, hair that he kept a little long. He wore torn T-shirts and necklaces children from the Amazon had made for him—strings of wood and feathers and beads and strips of black rubber from sandals perhaps.

Henry would receive strength from the walls of this basement just as that man Noyce had. Noyce is a spiritual man and so will I be. On Saturdays Henry played with John and Silvia's kids and took them to lunch at a diner downtown. Over hamburgers and pea soup he saw a woman in a gallery falling a hundred times in three hours, one time for each Canadian soldier dead in Afghanistan. She did this in a gallery with a window onto the restaurant where he was eating his hamburger. He did not like art particularly, but there was something in the woman he liked. Henry was not shy. He was a guy who handled polyethylene tubing and connected electrodes to cured cement but he was not flummoxed by a performance artist. He crossed the street with the kids and opened the door to the gallery and asked the artist where she got the idea. She told Henry about this residency with the military. They have artists who accompany the army to the Arctic or, in this case, Afghanistan. She returned and felt compelled to become each soldier that had fallen.

He never saw this woman again but it made him think about John Hynes's notion of a contract in Kabul.

4

Rick Tobin was three years older than John and Henry and Tender Morris but they knew him growing up in the west end of St John's. Little Rick like a bantam cock in his blue coveralls, all hundred and forty pounds of him bounding into things. Rick had energy that bewildered Henry and he was not the first to realize Rick could channel this force into ambition and drive and learn how to connect labour with materials and funnel them into the delivery of services to small towns along the shore. It floored him, how successful Rick was. He had married Colleen Grandy and moved into her town which was down the road from where John and Silvia had a summer house. Renews. Tender Morris had been left a house there too by a great-aunt, a house Tender Morris was going to fix up some day if he ever got out of the military. Henry asked Rick if he worried about leaving the city for such a small place.

I'm never home, Rick said. If Colleen is happy then I'm happy.

Henry had visited Renews a few times, but living in a small place was not something that had appealed to him. He appreciated a city giving you a movie to watch, rather than having to constantly make your own movie. Rural areas were for excursions.

Henry and John and Tender, in their twenties, had gone to work for Rick. One time they set some dynamite to blow up virgin land in a new subdivision that was being cut out of the woods. There was concern for the fallout, so Rick had everyone park their vehicles around the perimeter of the blast site to act as a buffer. Rick pressed the button and the earth lifted a little. There was a whump and the sound of tinfoil crumpling. The surface of the denuded land was torn away and all was silent, and then soil fell on them, entire root systems, and when they got up off the ground they could see that the windows in all the vehicles were blown in. The performance metrics on this job, Rick said, are a little askew.

A few years ago Rick had bought nine second-hand dumptrucks from Alberta and shipped them here. He went halves on a sawmill in Horsechops Lane and became principal owner of a lounge in Fermeuse, the Copper Kettle. He snapped up two big boats from the classifieds, forty-footers, when the snow crab fishery collapsed. John explained that Rick Tobin was constructing an old folks' home up the shore, and he'll take the senior citizens out in the wilderness area on the crab boats and then, if all goes well, they'll lose all their money on the video lottery terminals at the Copper Kettle.

Henry was in this bar once and Rick called him over. Hey Henry. Rick bought him a beer. Then said Henry there's a man at the door I have to have a word with. He went over there. Rick obviously a small guy. It got loud, and Rick wiped the floor with him, then took him outside and kicked him down the handicapped ramp. That guy owed me three hundred dollars.

He's buying land in Costa Rica, John said, to grow trees. Teak wood, he said, you can't get your arms around it. He wants to set the sawmill right here and ship the teak up. He asked me to supervise the mill. You can have all the teak you want, he said. Teak is twenty-seven dollars a board foot, Henry.

5

You can say no to Rick and that's okay, he'll find other people and other plans. Such is what happened with John, and the sawmill and Costa Rica went bye-bye. Tender, oddly enough, moved to Nova Scotia and stayed in a Buddhist monastery. Then he returned and joined the reserves. Some kind of spiritual vexation, John said. And this Kabul gig—the money is good and Silvia is behind it.

She's not delighted but she's okay with it, Henry said.

They have family to help with the kids. You sign on for a year with one trip home and four-day stints touching down in the United Arab Emirates. Health, dental, a seven-hundred-thousand-dollar insurance policy—put down one of my kids, Henry. Security provided by her majesty's government. Tender Morris will take care of us.

Live a dangerous life. The one unsmooth element in the story of Rick's life around the bay was the rumour that his wife was having an affair. Colleen Grandy. That spiritual American who had lived in John and Silvia's finished basement and bought the lightkeeper's house in Renews. Noyce. Everyone seemed to know about this affair except Rick. Or if Rick knew he did not let on and, like the fight in the bar over three hundred dollars, he wasn't the type of man to absorb nuance. Who is to know how couples arrange their lives? On financial matters Rick had life solved and he wanted to share that solution with his friends. He sent the international paperwork and Silvia printed off the forms and spread out the duplicate papers on the dining room table while the kids ate a bucket of chicken on the carpet with paper towels and root beer. John and Henry initialled each page of the agreement and signed their names and Silvia witnessed it. Airplane tickets arrived as a PDF on Silvia's laptop.

6

They flew west to Toronto and then east to Frankfurt and south to Kabul. In the airport in Toronto they saw a woman with a golden retriever on her way back to Connecticut. John asked her about the dog—John will talk to anybody with a dog. She was bringing the dog to a family. She was blind and the dog was eleven years old and starting to fail, so the dog had to go and she would get another dog in two weeks. But she was heartbroken about the dog.

The only thing interesting about the Frankfurt airport was a ceramic fly that told you where to point your stream of piss in the urinals.

Tender Morris met them at the airport in Kabul. He was in a green jeep called an Iltis. I'm to escort you to barracks, he said. Tender a tall, rangy man with red hair and long, involved tattoos. His real name was Patrick, but he'd been called Tender since high school—he'd been their hockey goalie. You'll stay where the tradespeople camp out, Tender said. A secure area, inside the wire. A separate facility from the army station but protected by our Canadian compound. He smacked the steering wheel hard when he said protected. Beds are better, food is better, wages: better. So fuck you and fuck your benefits. I'll tell you the one thing before you get all superior on me: you're not as safe. Tender's eyes patrolling the small houses and gates and vast blank areas of sand and rock and garbage. He was a reservist who volunteered for combat and was enjoying every minute of it. He was alive. On the safety issue I got to show you something, he said. Under your seat, John.

John pulled out a heavy padded envelope. Inside, wrapped in clear bubblepack, the shapes of flat heavy things. John tore off the tape. Two dull metallic Sig Sauer automatic pistols slipped onto his lap.

I couldn't find ammo and I want those back when you go home, Tender said.

The gun was heavier than it looked and Henry shoved it in his jacket pocket and made sure the velcro flap was sealed.

Tender drove them into Kabul. There was a pig's head on the ground beside a shaded cart and boys on skateboards zipped through the white rubble of an old government building. Tender drove through this into a quieter neighbourhood with high metal gates and the tops of established trees, their leaves covered in dust. He stopped the jeep behind a line of new black cars and climbed out and rapped on a gate made of galvanized metal. It was very loud. The sun was just setting. A rusted slit opened in the gate and Tender told them he had two civilians who'd like to eat. They're looking for Chinese food, a voice said, just the top of a lip available at the slit in the gate. The gate pulled open and they walked into a cement courtyard. Razorwire on the walls. The lip of the man was not there.

Look, Tender said, and took Henry in a headlock and rubbed

his head. I heard about Nora. This is a good spot to forget about Nora.

I need to get her out of my head too, John said.

You, Tender said, have to be good.

The building was stucco and inside it suddenly got dark, men at small tables with white tablecloths, a music in the walls, men from various non-governmental agencies and tourists, Tender said. There were guns on the table. Two men studying the steel tang in a big knife, passing it back and forth almost in wonder as to how the metal got in there. A string of lamps shone over a buffet table with stainless steel trays full of vegetables and meat. The light bounced in a dazzle off the food but the food itself was dead. Around the buffet were perhaps a dozen Chinese women in tight tops with bare arms collecting white plates. They had red bows around their necks that somehow kept their dark hair pinned up and they were listlessly bending over the food to prepare the plates and then delivering these plates into corners of the darkness with some accelerated urgency.

They took a table near the back wall by a hall to what was the washrooms and one of the servers came over. Her fingers touched the edge of the table. In English that was both bright and bored: What would you like, a drink? She was wearing a simple black and white outfit and you saw her midriff directly in front of your eyes—there was a lively rhinestone stuck to the bellybutton—and her shoulders were bare and a number of buttons undone at the cleavage. She was serving the food and opening up tabs on cans of beer and glasses of crushed ice and soda and small plastic bottles of hard liquor like you get on an airplane.

This man here needs a full service, Tender said about Henry. And we're his friends who will take care of his bill.

I might need a little dessert, John said. Tender shoved him.
Or watch some dessert.

They ate and drank and Henry asked about the barracks and
Tender said it was not a problem.

They were all suddenly ravenous and they ordered more
food. The crushed ice and little bottles kept arriving. The ice was
almost the same as the ice of home but there was no doubting
that everything was different here. The air rubbed the surfaces of
things in a different way. He slammed her with a beginner's zeal,
John whispered. There was a burr to everything. Henry drank his
drink and another little bottle arrived and the screw caps required
elbow work. The cap she is very small. Henry, the next day, could
only remember being led down that hallway past the washrooms
where the quality of the paint and the cleanliness of things seemed
to become less interested in convincing you the establishment
was high grade. There was music in a grate. Lie down here, sir. A
ceiling and the top of a heavy curtain that he guessed covered a
window. Perhaps it gave you the comfort of a window but there
was no window. He was taken care of on a rubber mattress and
a cloth on his belly and then his friends brought him back to
the jeep and the compound and to a bed with a thin camping
mattress, the sun was already hanging over the low, flat city.

7

Rick Tobin came over for the first three months. He was part of a larger contingent—SNC-Lavalin—that repaired water and sewage and revamped wiring and took care of waste management for the Canadian forces even as they were participating in the draw-down of operations at Camp Julien. They provide warehousing, Rick said. Transportation, bulk fuel management, vehicle maintenance, food services, communication services, electricity, water supply and distribution.

Rick used up all his fingers and he hadn't even gotten to the Nepalese who took care of the cooking and cleaning.

Everything, he said, to operate this facility and maintain it.

Rick Tobin, believe it or not, was also a mini-soccer coach. He organized Afghan and Nepalese children on the army base, and dribbled out free soccer balls inflated by his own tire pump he'd packed in his checked baggage.

They had to wait to use the computers to skype home. It was one of the services the trades and soldiers shared. Tender was talking to his girlfriend, Martha Groves. Stripped to his waist with dogtags on his collarbones, a tattoo of some kind across the back of his neck, Tender sat with other soldiers in the dark at blue screens manoeuvring the cursor over to the panels that allowed their loved ones to see their faces. John Hynes sat next to him, his face turned from concentration on figuring out the connection to a relief at seeing the top of his son's head too close to the built-in camera, Silvia grabbing at Clem's shoulders to get him and Sadie steady and then all of them synchronized to a connection no longer staggered. Tender's girlfriend on the screen now, a beauty. The beauty came from a confidence to be on a screen projected over eight thousand miles. Henry knew Martha. She was a physiotherapist—that's how Tender met her, a hockey injury. She wasn't from St John's, was she. No, she didn't know Colleen and Silvia and Nora the way they knew each other from school. But they had included her. How vulnerable they all looked sitting on steno chairs at the little booths inside the tent that reminded Henry of a time when he took John's kids, Clem and Sadie, to a jumpy castle.

You want to grab this one after me, Tender said.

It's okay, Henry said.

Say hello to Martha.

Hello Martha.

She waved at Henry while she looked a little up, into the green dot he guessed that made sure you were being screened properly. My god, Henry thought, how can it be I have no one to talk to.

THE TOILETS WERE AT the far end of the compound and these too were prefabricated and there were instructions in several languages about how to sit on the toilet and how to keep the toilet clean. Henry Hayward realized that these two sections of the compound were the most important to keep functional. Although bedding was crucial and the canteen too. But you did not think of these because there was enough to eat and the cots were adequate.

The screen and the toilet were the furniture he would sorely miss if he were off compound overnight or on an extended sortie. If he was a soldier. Of course he did not have to worry about this, he was a subcontractor with Rick servicing the structure put in place by SNC-Lavalin. He had to push tubes full of wiring through tunnels in the ground and thread them under rivers to connect up the busted grid and listen to sonar equipment for a clear contact. But they did all sorts of work. One time they had to rewire an Afghan house. He was surprised at how modern the house was, there was not a traditional bone in its body. He was with John and Rick one afternoon when they had to cut through a door with a reciprocating saw and enter a hallway while Tender Morris, attached to their civilian unit, kept a lookout for Taliban. Got your pistols, he said. There were tea sets and some plates and small pieces of furniture that looked like they had been handed down from someone old but the rest of the infrastructure was brand spanking new. A set of particleboard bunkbeds and three teenaged Afghan boys in windbreakers dancing to a stereo and playing bongos and electric keyboard.

8

They worked through the spring and into the hot summer until there was trouble in the southern provinces and, after a security assessment from Ottawa, funding was restricted for the services Rick Tobin provided. A civilian support worker had been killed in a rocket attack. They were violating the mandate, Rick Tobin said, that they be used in a stable environment. It was the first of July and the minister of defence had flown into the base to celebrate Canada Day and told them directly their revised plans. The minister had served wild turkey burgers and hotdogs from a train of barbecues with red maple leaf flags on toothpicks punched into the buns. He was celebrating the draw-down in troop allocations as if this was something to be positive about. It was one of those ceremonial dinners where the minister makes sure the national papers have photographed him wearing a festive apron while doling out maple-custard ice cream.

The minister explained to Rick that their contract was being adapted to meet the desire of operational deployment. We have to achieve mission success while operating within an imposed troop ceiling, the minister said. Certain hybrid situations for support trades were being considered. Would they ride with the military? Dressed and armed for robust situations?

What do you think about that, Rick said to them. He had John and Henry alone in a bubble corridor. Either that, or we go home.

Henry Hayward looked at John. You have to live on the edge, John. Or you're taking too much room.

Easy for you to say, John said. He was serious. You don't have kids.

Henry had never heard John play this card before. And he didn't like how humourless he was. But they got on board. The powers that be pencilled in Rick's request and that's how they lingered on at Camp Julien. Tender Morris thought it hilarious that they would be coming out on patrols after they did small arms training and a twenty-day soldier qualification course. You have to be issued new apparel, Tender said. And a beret that needs shaping. Tender showed them how to do the shaping.

You get a razor, he said, and you shave all that fuzz off. Use a single-blade razor and draw it over the inside and the outside. Do it lightly. Now, put the beret on and pull the string so it's snug. Tie it off and cut the strings at the knot.

John: Why not burn the strings?

Tender: Trust me you don't want fire next to a beret. Now you're ready to shape it. Put it on and hop in the shower. Turn the water on warm and just let it run over your head. No stay in there. Ten minutes. Okay get out now and dry off, here's a towel. Keep the beret on. Let it dry on your head. Keep pulling it over and combing it down. Leave it on until suppertime. And keep it in that shape, don't fold it or flatten it.

I'm going to wet mine and put it under my mattress overnight.

Tender Morris: Wet it and blowdry it. You can shave it close and put it in the freezer, that works too.

John: Then tie it and burn off the strings down to the knot?

Jesus no fire. Shave it until it's flimsy but don't get any bare spots.

Tender showed them how. John stood in the doorway with his wet beret on his head, pointing it at the sun.

It's like wearing a solar panel on your head.

You got to remember, guys, it's an ongoing process.

Why not use a straight razor.

Soldier, this is a don't ask don't tell army.

It doesn't matter if the razor was straight or not, girl.

I use a razor that cuts both ways.

What about a grill lighter.

Your beret will stink.

They received ammo and a clip for their Sig Sauers. They started going out in the jeep.

9

Kabul River runs from the mountains of the Hindu Kush into Pakistan, north of the Khyber Pass, where it joins the Indus River and then flows south to the seaport of Karachi. Halfway through its drift to the sea the river weaves into the city of Kabul where women bring baskets of washing and crouch in its water. Tender drove into the river, almost dry in the late summer, and up past the ruined shell of Darul Aman Palace. He gunned it around the refurbished Ghazi stadium where buzkashi competitions used to be held in the traditional days and then, when the Taliban were in power, a woman was shot in the head on the perimeter of the eighteen-yard box in front of thirty thousand spectators. Henry remembered that footage. She had killed her husband. The surface of the field was being removed now by heavy equipment as though the soil had been contaminated and new artificial turf installed and soon men with artificial legs will run here and wheelchair basketball was occurring in a cement court nearby. There are women training to be amateur boxers.

They drove through a refugee camp and parked the jeep and children ran up to them. Rick had long wiggly balloons. He

threw out a soccer ball and it bounced towards Nasem, a man
Rick could trust to oversee the ball and make sure the kids shared
it. The tents were set up with canvas tarps over ridge poles, the
walls fired mud brick three feet high and the tarps held down
with boulders tied to stays. There was a blue hand-drawn sign
telling you the tribes that were in the camp. Nearby a well that
was just a pipe coming out of the ground. Several families with
blue plastic containers. A man carried a tower of twenty-two
bricks in a tether on his back, he was hauling them out of a chalk
field where lay the shells of old Soviet tanks. A brightly painted
truck was covered in dust.

They overtook bicycles and tricycle handcarts made with
wooden wheels and had to show their papers to an anti-mortar
platoon. Sheet metal workers hammered tin for portable stoves. A
kiosk with a man braziering meat and waving a big woven straw
fan in the shape of a hatchet fed the stove little slats of wood
from fruit crates. Tender stopped the jeep here to eat. There was
a café with open windows to the street, a brocaded tapestry of a
freedom fighter on the cement wall. The air smelled of toasted
sesame seeds. A boy who had survived a landmine and had no
arms begged for money. Their kebabs came on an aluminum
plate with naan bread in the shape of a split fish. The people here
knew Tender.

We need greenery, John said. I need to rinse the dust out of
my ears.

I'll take you over to Lake Qargha. We can drive through
Shakar Darah—you'll love that valley, Tender said. It's a bit like
home.

Out of the dry chalky desert rose a plain that Tender had
visited many times, a valley of lush green unlike anything Henry

had ever seen in Newfoundland—Tender must be out of his mind. The jeep descended into the green and the humidity rose like a soft moist brush against the face. There were flowers here and an oasis of green that the mind encouraged to creep over the land, to perhaps—in some wild biology—be released across the homeland of the soul. We're here to assist, Henry thought. He could not articulate the idea, but he felt a compulsion to counter the devastation he had been witnessing on the ground. Tender yanked on the handbrake.

10

They came upon Americans doing recon—they knew they would intersect them in the morning—and they compared themselves to these units. Tender was annoyed at the marines, how they don't wear unit patches. The only patch a marine needs, Tender said, is the anchor, globe and eagle. That screams elite. And John Hynes hollered this out into the hot thin desert air. Yes sir, the self-centred, cocky, overbearing marine!

Tender: And the marine recruiters, they all wear dress uniform to international events.

Landpower, baby!

Tender Morris: The professional ethos of the corps.

What does the corps sell?

All three of them with fingers in the air: Commitment, honour, integrity!

John: And elitism.

No education, no bonus.

Go pound sand, man.

It sets them off from the air force at least.

Who show up in coveralls.

More fingers: Many are called but few are chosen.

You left out the thousand and one ways to annoy everybody in the room with grand tales of how great the marines are.

I got to say I like this beret over their patrol cap.

It could be worse, we could be wearing the blue helmet.

Hey the UN motto: where there are genocidal dictators we will be nearby doing nothing.

THAT WAS HOW THEY TALKED. Once, just before Tender went on leave in the fall, he drove them beyond backup helicopter surveillance. It made them all feel alive to the raw possibility of being killed and there being no one to help them. The sergeant in charge at Camp Julien had said you must have Patrick Morris supervise you at all times. You hear how stringent the rules are for engagement—it takes four or five signatures for a piece of paper to leave the building—and who can leave the forward operating base, but the thing that is true, too, of all human occupations is that familiarity leads to a loosening of procedure and the trust of those in positions of power to sense when to let the line remain undrawn. So for a month, while Tender returned home with Rick Tobin and relaxed and made love to Martha Groves, Henry and John stayed close to a desk. But the day after he came back they went on wild patrols and moved through a quadrant to dispense food rations and inflated soccer balls and deliver education supplies to small one-room schools with large black chalkboards that seemed from another century—Tender Morris hovering at the perimeter with a C7, ready to engage. Afterwards, on their way back to camp, they sat in the jeep and spoke of things like boot blousing, how the pants are easy to blouse when it is wet but when it's hot there's no ventilation at the bottom of the cuff.

Tender was against blousing, then you don't need a camouflage boot as the pantleg covers the boot. That string you tie at the bottom of the tunic, Tender said, is useless. There are pockets on the chest that the flak jacket covers, so you have to sew pockets on your arms. And the fabric was designed for infrared protection, but aren't the enemy using night-vision goggles?

They detoured around a Leopard tank blockade and an infantry company shoring up a bridge with chicken wire and rock. They ate rations that you heated in a bag with a chemical that was activated by water. They were living a life.

11

There was a Labour Day disco at the base sponsored by the Dutch. They were bored so they invited a couple of servicewomen to shoot pool in Kabul. A television bolted to the ceiling with Al Jazeera. Hammered, they were hammered, and they were being pressed by some American servicemen to finish up their game. A chopper had landed and the Americans had poured out of it and they were tired of being polite. One of them, Henry heard him, said this is a takeoverable operation.

What if we were Americans, Henry said, so he could be overheard.

Let's not be Americans, Tender said. Let's be outlaws. Except for Henry—he's our minister without portfolio.

What the hell is that.

You're not committed to anything but you got a hand in everywhere.

Henry accepted this. He didn't know what it meant but he accepted the position, the honour, the judgment. He didn't have a wife or a house and he was an employee. He was enjoying, at the moment, the presence of a Canadian female soldier but they were not allowed to kiss or even hold hands and this limitation suited him. He was quietly growing back his pinfeathers for love. They were drinking rum.

Orange Bliss is my favourite, the servicewoman said. Deadly, deadly. I'd drink that straight up. I wouldn't put nothing in that.

John: It tastes like medicine.

Servicewoman: That's banana.

The names of the drinks are all sex names. Panty ripper, pink pussy, blowjob, sex on the beach, screaming orgasm, slippery nipple.

Tender: You must work in a shooter bar.

John: What's your strongest rum. You don't have any Martinique? I just want to see if it's as bad as it used to be.

Every guy I got to try Orange Bliss loved it.

Performance in the world is full of fakery, John said. He was staring at the Americans now who were not paying him any attention.

You and Henry, Tender said quietly, you're not soldiers. You're drinkers.

That's not what I'm talking about, John said. The Americans were staring at the TV and waiting, it seemed, for the table to get knees and walk away from these idiot Canadians and position itself over them.

We're drunk here, guys. We are enjoyably drunk.

One of the servicewomen: All anyone is ever trying to do, deep down, is be loved.

Her friend, the one Henry liked, the Orange Bliss lady, said, You are way lost here. Let's get back to the important things. Another round.

Curfew, said Tender. We have curfew to maintain.

That's when the Americans moved in. They pushed the last balls in the pockets and instantly had the cues and had absorbed whatever resistance was in John and Tender and Henry.

You guys are the soldiers, John said. But we're the convincers.

They're convinced they want more money for doing the same things as us.

Give that up, Henry.

For Tender was like the Americans on the pay scale.

An American tapped the butt of the cue stick, very polite, and said perhaps you shouldn't raise your voices so. He stared at the women and asked them if they were okay.

We have to get back to base, one explained.

There's a Sikorsky leaving from a pad, you can take that. We'll trade you a ride for the table and no hard feelings.

Let's turn our voices into marches, Tender said. Let us pass by the injured and those that throw stones (he motioned to the Americans) and alter a law through a circuitous route. Come on guys.

Henry and John had no idea what Tender was talking about. Obviously, he had time to read, like a fisheries observer.

Take the Black Hawk, the American said. It's a coalition chopper. We're on leave and this is a no-nookie zone.

You can drink in here but no rendezvousing.

Not with military personnel.

Hurt those you mean to help, Tender said. We'll take your ride and be a member of the steering committee for the marketplace of ideas that fights against the very same structure put in place by your bilderberg group!

They found the helicopter and Tender Morris unfolded the sheet of military paper and handed it to an ISAF lieutenant who made a hand signal and they piled in while the rotors churned and the heavy lift and yaw of this eight-million-dollar machine came to life and suddenly all of Kabul stretched below their knees as they followed a strip of lights towards the Canadian base. They made curfew.

12

They had to be careful with their drinking as sometimes they were up in the morning before the sun—a jeep full of Newfoundlanders. They were hitting the road at six hundred hours, a regular patrol outside of Camp Julien, so it was bad form to get drunk on illicit rum and Russian vodka supplied in mouthwash bottles and play crib at ten dollars a hand until two in the morning. Henry was riding up front with Tender Morris. Tender had been telling them about life with Martha, the house he had around the bay that had to be fixed up or knocked down. Martha wants to save it, he said, and I feel pressure to save it.

Family pressure, John said.

Henry: Is it worth anything? You could sell it.

It requires a little work.

John: Shit man fresh air is keeping that house up.

I tarred the roof.

Yes as long as you keep the moisture out of it.

For John knew the house in question. He owned the house next to it.

I've got a year left in the army, Tender said. Then I want to have a kid with Martha and get some work with Rick Tobin. Do what John is doing—John's figured it out.

Each man's shoes, John said. Walk a mile.

Henry listened to these men betray a spirit of making a family and owning something old, of cherishing the past and digging your feet into soil that other generations had also been digging in. Henry admitted he was nervous about that kind of commitment. Was he a strong enough man to pull it off. You like kids, John said. Tender: But it requires growth—it's called seeking roots in a rootless tradition.

John and Tender spoke quietly using these types of words in this type of place, a country landscape completely redesigned by the fact that western countries were occupying it. Henry had none of this attachment to the past or to old things. He was recovering from a hurt brought on by broken love. But he recognized John possessed a judgment of a house that was the same judgment he had once used on him, fresh air keeping it up.

The jeep seats were still cold from the night. John Hynes in the back. There was an erratic disturbance in the road ahead and Tender Morris slowed a little to size it up. Go have a look, Tender said. John and Henry piled out of the jeep and they hesitated at the side of the jeep for a second. They were hungover and empty and knew they weren't supposed to be doing this. They had obeyed Tender and then realized they had no training in reconnaissance. But what the hell, let's do everything. They looked around and then they fanned out to examine the disturbance and scan the horizon. They were civilians embedded in the army, non-combat personnel in their early thirties. Within another set of rules neither of them were supposed to even be in Tender's jeep. And here they were, scouting! The morning still had a variety in the pattern of light, in an hour or two the sky would be a dull white and very distant, but now the sun was in front of them, it felt like it was about ten miles away. Not a good place to be. The jeep, not following procedure, sort of gunned over the disturbance and Tender Morris made to leave them there. The jeep halted on a rise and Tender leaned over to laugh at them, letting the jeep's weight roll it back towards them. He was only kidding, Henry realized. Tender is a little crazy. Then a shape leapt at the windshield. Henry couldn't see the particular shape except it was an animal lunge. It made the interior of the jeep dark. Is something going on, John called out. His tone of voice was encouraging rules to maintain their order. Henry could see John. It looked like Tender had hit a civilian. Where's my fucking gun, Tender yelled out. The jeep's brake lights were on now and then the horn. Tender was hitting the horn. That guy was crawling around up there in his big grip boots on the wide hood, he was trying to connect two artificially coloured adhesive stickers by his armpit. Someone called out, Cleared hot! It was John, in a panicked voice. Henry took up his pistol and realized it wasn't his, he was carrying Tender's Sig Sauer from the coffee holder by the stick shift. That's where Tender kept it because it got in the way of him changing gears. Henry's own pistol was still in its holster on his leg. Neither of them had a shot at the man and so Henry ran off the road into a gulley full of torn plastic and wire and empty water bottles. John was doing the same thing on the other side and John shouted with some urgency now that Henry was putting them in a crossfire. Henry was thinking more about setting off an IED, what things felt like underfoot. He had never been in a ditch in Afghanistan. He wasn't sure what the ditch was meant to carry as he had never seen it rain here.

The man had bands of plastic explosive taped to his chest. The windshield caved in and a loud crack jetted out a hundred feet from the jeep and made his head split open, the jeep buckled backwards into itself and then blew apart into ribbons of metal lighter than air.

13

At first it was a cloudy day, the sky just ten feet above him and then he knew this sky wasn't open air at all but a ceiling, those grey panels of what looked like tin moulding in John's house but he couldn't be there, he was in Afghanistan and this building wasn't old enough or permanent enough, though he liked the idea that at death earlier rooms were transported to you. That's what happens when you die: vistas visit. The building wasn't a building at all but a prefab unit that could be deployed in three hours. Rick Tobin had told him that. It was fabric. Henry couldn't move his arms or legs though he sensed resistance. He was strapped down. A thin new canvas strapping they did not issue during basic training. He moved all of his bones and nothing was broken. Tender, he said. Henry pulled his head up and looked around the ward. Where's Tender Morris. An arm went up. It was the arm of John Hynes. I've known that arm for twenty years, Henry thought. John was down by the tall brown canvas door—he was sitting up now. They didn't mind having John be able to kneel up on his elbows. Tender's dead, John said. And Henry noticed he'd said it very quietly. The only thing of the jeep they found was the spare tire.

No, Henry thought. They found him. Or I found him. Henry had crawled over to Tender, the trunk portion of him. His face and shoulders and chest. Tender ended at the points of his white hips. The rest of him they couldn't find. But Henry had crawled over to what remained and Tender was alive. Hiya minister, the mouth said. Tender could sense someone near him. It's Henry, Henry said. Do you want a minister. Do you need a religious man.

You'll do, he said.

You're going to be all right Tender. We'll get you out of here.

Yes, he said, I'm getting out of here. I'm going to meet my maker.

As Tender spoke his jaws moved independently, the bottom of his face was broken up under the skin. Henry held the hand. He had all of Tender's fingers and they were solid. The tattoo at his neck, he saw now what it was, an eagle and the words HOUSE OF GOLD on a banner carried in the beak. Then the fingers relaxed.

Henry said to John, I had Tender's pistol.

The next day Tender's superiors visited and received their statements and they went over carefully how contractors on a three-month tour managed to extend that tour indefinitely. They allowed Henry and John to elaborate on the ease in which they drifted from restricted access into sorties out in desert towns rimming the perimeter of Kabul. They went away and Henry was left to lie down and stare at the panel of plastic window behind him and how the birds landed on a temporary power line. The birds were catching the orange light as the sun set, the sun directly on the chests of these birds, and Henry wondered what the birds did when there wasn't a camp here and no wire to perch on. They probably stood on the highest knoll or rock to soak in the sun. They did that back home, barren hills full of seabirds. He could not see these birds clearly because the plastic distorted the view, but he understood they were together on this project, storing up some heat for the cold night to come.

The authorities returned and at one point they separated John and Henry and spoke to them individually in small white cubicles. He could hear John in the next room. His body ached like bruised elastic—he felt the bends his limbs made. Henry spoke at a level of description that both interested the superiors and made them impatient. He could tell they judged him much more than he judged them. He did not know what they were, but they were very sure about what they had on their hands. When Henry read back what had been written there was a very different story which he did not mind, he knew he had done something wrong, but there was nothing in there about his possession of Tender's Sig Sauer. The superiors said he wasn't remembering that part correctly; Patrick Morris's pistol was blown up with the Iltis. Tender Morris, Henry said, he could have taken care of himself, but he'd reached down and grabbed ahold of an empty coffee holder. They said they found Tender's pistol near his body.

Where'd you find mine?

It was in your holster.

That was the end of the mission for him right there. They convalesced at the hospital and took walks outside in the bright dry air and looked for those birds but could not see them during the day. He closed the big brown door that was like part of a barn and he drank a lot of fluids and hot meals on plastic trays. They talked to Rick Tobin. They were done with contracts for the army. It has to do with the jeep, Rick said. The Americans won't work in an Iltis. Bombardier got the contract to build those German tin cans. You know what the Germans call them? Ferrets.

John: We were driving around in a ferret.

Tender didn't have a chance and it was only because he was crouched behind the radios that he didn't get his face blown off. Tender was a greybeard and Henry had heard other soldiers call him Old Man. Tender was good at learning things but he refused to move up, he'd been in the reserves for nine years, a lieutenant in the Purple Trades, he read books on political science and sociology and somehow got boosted into the theatre of war and transferred from Newfoundland to New Brunswick to Germany and then Afghanistan where he was meant to be merely assisting a clerk but found an enthusiasm for the outdoor life and got himself on successful scouting missions in the region. Then John and Rick and Henry touch down and he's ordered to back up these subcontractors and man a weak jeep.

14

They flew home tethered to the gutted frame of a Hercules drinking warm bottles of water. It was a series of junkets, first landing at Camp Mirage in the United Arab Emirates. Tender Morris's casket in the belly of the plane with them. In Canada they met Tender's girlfriend, Martha Groves, on the tarmac as they wheeled the casket into a special terminal. They'd flown her up to Ontario for this reunion. John Hynes and Henry Hayward rode in a convoy with her as they took the Highway of Heroes south from Trenton, the solemn civilians standing at attention inches from the gradient and the overpasses three deep, full of bunting, the sumac a blaze of orange on the flared hills that stretched back into November orchards and Dutch farmland of middle Ontario, back to Toronto where the casket was slipped aboard the belly of a domestic flight out of Pearson and flown, with Henry and John Hynes on board, to Newfoundland to bury him. Tender's family at St John's airport. There was some outcry because the casket was delayed and had to be picked up at oversized baggage. They found Tender next to a crate of oysters. Letters were written (Henry wrote one) and a locally televised interview with the girlfriend went national and that changed military procedure. They drank the night before the funeral and things went on so long and hard that at ten in the morning Henry had to kick John's bed and beat him with his pillow to convince him that he had to get his suit on, that he absolutely must make an appearance at this funeral.

They drove out to Renews, where the family was from. There was a hill of dirt with an artificial green carpet over it and a portable gazebo from the funeral home as the forecast called for rain. They did not lower the casket during the service, but they all walked down the hill to a reception at Rick and Colleen's where the cars were parked.

They all hugged one another, Colleen Grandy and Silvia and Martha, the women looking out for each other. The kids were with John's mother. The Morris and Hynes families have all known each other for generations. Across a field from John's was the old house that Tender Morris had inherited, that he'd hoped to fix up some day with Martha and maybe have a kid out there. Seeking roots in a rootless tradition. Well that was all over with.

THEY STAYED THE NIGHT in Renews. Henry needed air and he walked around the Morris house. He walked out to the frozen brook and let the sky darken. He stood on the clear ice and the water ran under the ice. Bubbles of air. And then something spectacular, the flush of fur, a wide tail. A beaver swimming under him. The torso and tail of a beaver.

You could hear the wind splitting itself in two on the corner of the eaves. The house was dark and the clapboard had been blown clean of paint. The house utterly dead and Henry felt like he was standing at the House of Tender Morris, the snuffed candle, the end of a line and he, Henry Hayward, had caused that end. He patted himself on the arms, trying to relieve himself of the upset he felt at being exonerated from blame. How the army had scrubbed very hard at his story and made up many new bits of language that Henry hadn't said to make Tender's death the result of an ambush by irregular forces. What a terrific minister without portfolio I am. Way to handle a case, buddy.

Then he turned around and screamed into the wind: Well I lived a dangerous life!

15

Snow fell horizontally and the plough raced past and curled up a brown wave of sand and slush. Silvia was standing on the porch wearing John's clothes and old boots as John and Henry shovelled the driveway. Snow, wind, sober.

John and Henry were wearing new steel-toe Kodiaks and quilt-lined flannel shirts. They were dressed for Alberta. John had talked to Silvia about it while Henry shovelled the driveway. John spoke it over his shoulder while she stood on the front step in his old parka and boots. Henry looked at her and realized when John was away she became him, and this parka and boots was the start of it. Then, when they finished the drive, they stood in the kitchen by the open fridge and drank the elderberry juice and popped the birch and juniper pills. They were flushing out the system—Rick runs a dry camp.

Silvia drove them to the airport.

They worked twenty-eight days straight. Rick had seventy-two men in his crew. They were employed on scoops and pumps and diesel engines half a mile underground at thirty dollars an hour. A guy Henry had never met before, a guy from Cape

Breton, came up to him on his third day and said, You give me motivation.

Henry felt something missing. It was one thing to be away from home in a war zone, but another to be away only because you are working. It's been a year now, he realized, more than a year—without Nora. Surely to god he was over Nora. What was it John had said? He had to break the relationship to the land.

On Christmas Eve they flew to St John's for ten days and there was a party. Silvia warned Henry that Nora would be at the party, and he remembered this was the town that Nora owned. Snow was melting in the hall. There had been no inkling of a party, no one had really thought to have a celebration, but trust John Hynes to begin the suggestion and the cars had to park on both sides of the street and around the corner in order to get into the Hynes house that night. The kids were upstairs in one corner bedroom watching a movie and other kids were with them for there wasn't time to get babysitters or all the babysitters were at the party and so, during the loud dancing to retro music in the living room, the kids would stream downstairs in their pyjamas and wriggle around the adults under a disco ball made from a pink buoy with squares of mirrored glass glued to it, something John had made with the kids one Sunday afternoon out in Renews. All you had to worry about was stepping on little toes as the kids were barefoot and the adults had left their wet boots on. They were all, mainly, in their thirties. There was three feet of snow touching the windowsills outside and snow traipsed into the porch and halfway down the hall to the kitchen with only the dog taking care of the snow by wolfing up chunks when he felt like it. A big dog that some said was part wolf, now that wolves were back on the island. No, John would say. Coyote maybe. But we call him Wolf to encourage his prospects.

The snow drifting against the house sheltered the bass of the party and allowed the people who were recovering from the mourning of Tender Morris to really let loose. The heat was turned down for the rooms were hot with bodies. This was not a summer party. It was a party that requires grim conditions, the short days and the bitter cold and a death in the family and a dark night and very few reasons to go on but you do go on. Having kids was not enough. A party like this was necessary and John Hynes knew it. If life were to continue on this bald rock in the ocean, if a laugh were to be had, then this party at John and Silvia's was the dream that disturbs hibernation, that wakes you into a spring thaw.

Henry Hayward lifted six cold beers from the vegetable crisper and hoisted them with both hands high over the heads of the women who were drinking red wine (Hayward watch it with the beers, said Nora, being as warm as she could) to a voracious clump of men. Rick Tobin had begged the men to work for him in Alberta. His wife, Colleen, a hand taller than him. The men and women in this kitchen knew that Henry and John had been with Tender in Kabul and understood their role in the jeep when Tender lost his life, but you could not talk about these things. The event did not communicate itself well. Military tragedies were difficult to explain. There was no teaching model on the experience of modern warfare. Henry knew this about civilians even though he could not see the men for the wall of women in sheer tops who stood between them.

Silvia was talking to Martha Groves and Colleen Grandy and Nora Power and Henry sort of shifted his shoulders into their conversation until Silvia drew her arm around his neck and pressed him up against a new sheet of drywall that had been replaced and only plastered but not sanded or painted yet. The drywall rasped on his shoulder and left dust on his sleeve as Silvia said Henry Henry Henry. Then over came Martha. Where is Henry these days, Martha said. She was dressed all in white. She was the opposite of mourning, or perhaps this was the new mourning. Martha had said, earlier, If you threw me in a snowbank you'd lose me. And John Hynes had replied, It's the belt that makes it. Henry told Martha he was on a flight in the morning back to Fort McMurray. He said this while Nora Power had forgotten about him and was absorbed in a man's description of a marine ecosystem. Martha had been Tender's girlfriend, partner, wife. What do you call it when they are not married. Tender is dead now, so what is she. Widow. He tried to listen to Martha while Nora's head was visible over her shoulder. Nora, who had broken up with him, paying attention to this biologist friend of Silvia's. The women were talking in that high positive tone that can break any depression from your shoulders. It gives you strength. Rick, in the middle of John's solutions for the local economy, said: I don't want to hear about aquaculture in Virgin Arm or mussels in Dildo Run or crabs in Backside Pond.

Martha: It's good to meet you.

Henry: We've met before.

I don't remember.

You don't remember?

John, interrupting: This is your chance, Henry, to say you don't remember me with all your clothes on.

Henry: Friends with a beginning but no end.

Martha: You were covered in flakes of cement and wearing a woman's fluffy slippers when I met you.

Nora's slippers.

John: Rick's looking good.

Henry: He is. Except maybe the vest is a little too much.

I meant physically.

Martha: You're all rough-hewn men.

Is that what the women are saying?

Martha: Colleen and Silvia are planning a women's evening in bikinis and drinking.

It's a spa for women, Silvia said, leaning in.

John: You're not going off the cock, are you?

No we're not going off the cock.

Martha: It'll be like the YMCA change room, John.

With drinks.

Henry: Take it on.

I'm taking it on, Martha said. One day at a time. One week at a time, actually. She rolled her hair up behind her neck, as though tying it.

Silvia (to change the subject): I used to have real vivid dreams—killed five times in one night, but now it's just ahh new shoes.

John and Silvia peeled away and Henry repeated to Martha he had a plane ticket to lay fuses for Rick Tobin and he appreciated how well she listened to him given her utter grief that he could read in her face. Martha was warm, she was pulling up the hill any sort of social manner that allowed her to talk to people without breaking up and falling on the floor in tears. She gravitated towards him because she saw, too, that he was having to deflect his attention from Nora Power. It had been a year, but still. He had flinched at the mention of her slippers. They talked and stood close to one another. Martha put a hand on his arm.

Silvia was reeling a little now, saying aloud that she was annihilated—five glasses of wine and no substantial dinner.

Martha put her face near his shoulder, he felt her hip touch him while she studied Silvia, as if trying to remember how to be a woman who has not lost everything. How to enjoy abandon without feeling abandoned. She turned a little and understood the fabric of Henry's shirt. He felt her belly, she had a full figure. Her face was all one colour, a hazel colour, even her hair. She was like some minor animal that devotes its genetic material to cunning and can only provide itself with a simple coat and complexion.

She was looking at him because he'd been with Tender. She was looking at and holding on to Tender.

You're a capable man, she said.

Most people are capable. At something.

Martha was a physiotherapist and worked at the Health Sciences Centre. She treated a number of work-related injuries and, in the past few years, soldiers. She described this stainless steel tool she used for superficial tissue work. And then she got tired of explaining work.

That house around the bay, she said. Now that needs work.

You know how to make an attractive offer.

It was Tender's.

He's got family.

No one wants it.

Then knock it down.

Exactly.

Here's my advice: let them knock it down. Be done with it. Never think of it again.

Come on, she said, and grabbed him by his shirt buttons, where's your sense of adventure.

16

They fell into bed and rolled around and Martha asked him to be careful. She pushed him away and told him, sternly, to go and then grabbed for him and said please stay. She punched him in the chest and cried. She kicked him. They had called a cab and gone back to her place. They were not fully undressed and they held each other and both felt the alarm of serious damage and swept through the vast fields between desire and loathing. They kissed each other deep and hard. It was the embrace they both needed and with the pressure of a body they both managed finally to sleep.

A taxi hauled him to the airport in the morning and thank god he'd phoned for a wake-up call. After the phone rang he'd said to Martha I have to go. It was still dark out. Her eyes opened and she took her own bottom lip in her teeth and then with that wet lip pulled herself up to kiss him. You know where the key is, she said. They rolled together again. A fondness. A delicate prayer to the loss of a love. She closed her eyes and was very loud. She was absorbed in grief. She was crawling towards some physical release of her pain. Don't forget that, Henry. Do not fucking forget it. She had been at the Hynes party working out an anger over the loss of Patrick Morris. And he was too, working out his guilt at Tender's death and a bad impression women had made on him—Nora Power. A new way to see the world.

On the plane he decided it was perverse. It sickened him, what had happened with Martha. It was a degradation of something sacred. What a fuck-up he was. He looked down at his own knees and was disgusted with where the knees had been. He was still dressed in the clothes he'd worn at the party. John, in the seat next to him, understood this.

If the world were not round, John said, we'd flee. We'd run. We'd just head west, buddy. We would always drive hard to the left.

They both had major hangovers and were quiet and doing their best to preserve their structures, sitting there on the plane, maintain the centre or if the centre be lost form a new centre and honour it. The king is dead long live the king. But Henry could not banish the truth that he was perverting himself. He had slept in Tender Morris's bed, with Martha. Had seen his bookshelf with a *History of the Machine Gun* and *The Tet Offensive*. I am a good man, Henry thought, but I'm not a good man. I'm following kinky side routes that do harm to the moral fabric of many lives. What was it Tender called me—a minister without portfolio. What a disparaging comment. Let me get a portfolio.

They were sitting in the emergency aisle and were relieved for the extra leg room. I'm going to do an over-wing briefing, the flight attendant said. Do you know you're sitting at an exit today? The window will fall in.

They flew west and settled into the basement apartment John rented in Edmonton and did their work for Rick Tobin just outside Fort McMurray. They delivered pre-fab materials and threaded tubes underground and listened to hydrographic data on big earphones while a meter blipped on a laptop screen. In the mornings and evenings when they left the mine Henry could see the flares from natural gas and the caps of hills torn away by heavy equipment that circled down into pits to eat and truck out bitumen. He thought about Martha. How raw it was, what had happened, how out of the blue even though it felt, on another scale, inevitable. How wrong it was. A dead man's woman. A man he had helped kill. He shook his head. And what was it. Had anything happened? You know where the key is. House of Tender Morris. Instead of running away he had run directly for the centre. No, that wasn't Tender's house he was in. That was Tender's bookcase. His house was in Renews. I've been all around that house too, a beaver swam under my feet. And then something startling sat in the front of his mind: Martha was the house of Tender Morris. Of course. Upon his neck a house of gold. I have rubbed the exterior walls of that house but thank god I did not enter. He hadn't stripped the house down. Well, at least Martha didn't let him. Martha was sensible.

They ate cafeteria food and slept in a dorm with fifteen other men and spent the weekends in John's apartment in Edmonton. They shared it with two guys they hardly saw who worked a different shift. A woman ran the apartment and complained about how much hot water they used. She saw evidence of wastage everywhere. She would be happy, John said, if they did not use anything. It would save her washing the sheets and wiping up the toast crumbs.

They took two lifts to work, the first lift descended and the light of each floor how it passed in a streak, first every second and then a flicker of lights as the floors sped up. Then the second lift and the flicker was even faster and the intervals between it darker and it reminded Henry of that nighttime American helicopter ride, the way the streetlights in Kabul zipped beneath them as they bulled north to the army base.

One day a drilling machine lost power in a tunnel by the jewellery box, which is a face of rock in a room that's full of precious metals and stones. Every mine has a jewellery box— you're told to leave it alone and specialists come in to harvest the rock. The drilling machine fills the entire tunnel so the only way to inspect the engine is to crawl through it. The machines don't turn around, there's no room, they just venture in and out. There were no mechanics on duty. It will take ninety minutes, John said, to fetch one from the surface.

Let's go have a look, Henry said. While we're waiting.

I say let's leave well enough alone.

I'm coming with you.

It was Jamie Kirby. And Jamie called out: This is the man who motivates me.

Jamie Kirby, John whispered, is half crazy. They packed their pockets with spare parts, a can of air, small tools strapped with flexible cord around a shoulder. You go first, Jamie said. And John gave Henry a look but it did not stop him. The men crawled into the hole and through the bowels of the broken-down machine. Henry twisted his waist inside the chassis to reach the hydraulics. He shone a flashlight on the area. He heard Jamie behind him clunking his wrenches. A rubber housing had snapped off its mounting so he replaced that and engaged the connector but he had forgotten the machine's batteries were still running. As soon as the pressure returned the driller started up automatically and twisted its central axle. It was alarming, it could have snapped Henry in two and he turned his head into the noise to tell Jamie but all he saw of Jamie was a mouth open in agony—he couldn't hear him for the noise of the driller and there, in front of them both, the jewellery box lit up. It shone, this gold room, like some underground temple to wealth while Henry reached beyond himself to tear at the connectors, to shut it all down.

Jamie Kirby had broken both of his arms.

That was it for Henry Hayward.

I am cursed, Henry said later. I shouldn't be with people. I shouldn't work with anyone. I'm going home out of it, Rick. I can't bear it.

He packed his tote bag and John drove him to a mall in Edmonton. He bought a little tin whale that rolled on a string. Should I get two? John: They can share it. No, I'll get two. John drove him to the airport.

Give my best to Silvia.

I'll explain to her how you're a complicated but good man.

Don't be too hard on yourself, Henry. These are accidents.

My hands are responsible for these accidents.

17

Nothing was said of Martha. John had ploughed two roads for them to meet at an intersection but he was no police officer supplying directions. What a guy. The terrain of Canada moving below Henry's shoulder. Window seat. Three tugboats towing an offshore rig in from sea. He had stood in the ballast of that rig. Was bad weather coming? He recalled the flight home with the body of Tender. Christ what a dismal scenario was that. The realization that he had Tender's gun. The immense error because he was in a situation he was not trained for. Judge the metrics of that performance, Rick.

He rolled his shoulders and fished out his earphones and distracted himself with a movie. Henry often went away to work but came back. Now he would have to stay and resolve a few things. He knew why he was leaving work but he wasn't sure why he returned to Newfoundland. Home. It held a gravity, some kind of atmospheric orbit that spiralled him towards the centre whenever he exhausted things out there in the world. Jesus I sound like a salmon. Like a lot of Newfoundlanders, though, he pictured an acre of land in his head that was his land. The picture has no location, it's a floating acre with a perforated edge like a postage stamp that hovers slightly above the land, though there is, of course, a view of the Atlantic. He understands this image to be romantic and unrealistic, and yet sometimes in foreign beds, rather than imagining a woman to keep him unlonely, he will think of this two hundred by two hundred view. He was thinking of it now, just weeks after that party at John and Silvia's—an acre of land that belongs to Tender Morris, and Martha worried about what to do with Tender's heritage—as his plane flew into a dark blizzard, the airplane pounded by weather, a bright snow flurry against the tracking lights on the wings and the woman next to him, who had watched a movie with a two-dollar headset she'd had to buy with her credit card. She pulled out a black plug from the armrest and said she was prone to panic attacks and, if it came to it, would Henry hold her. Henry removed an earbud to understand her. They made a descent and the plane shuddered and the tarmac zoomed up a little too fast in the plastic porthole and the landing gear jerked out of the frozen wings—they were inches from the runway and the woman next to him grabbed his arm and gripped it tight. The seams of the plane groaned as the fuselage twisted sideways a little and Henry thought whoa so this is it. The belly of the plane lifted and the landing gear tucked itself away again under the wing and the captain on the intercom, in a voice touched with receding panic, said the computers would not let them land in this weather. They flew a thousand kilometres back the way they had come and it took every kilometre for the alarm to melt away. They touched down at three in the morning in Halifax where, as they deplaned, they were all handed a 1-800 number to rebook. The woman who had sat next to him said what do we do now. She was a novice of the airways. We get a hotel room, Henry said. And let that hang ambiguously. They took their bags and had a drink in the lounge and Henry ate a chicken souvlaki while she made a phone call and told him about the local documentary film business and her two kids and her husband. He was surprised to hear she flew all the time. I guess she doesn't fly strapped to the bulwark with a nylon cord in the hull of a Hercules with no seats, he thought. They talked and Henry realized this woman loved her husband. He explained he had just quit work because he helped break a man's arms. Not just one arm but both of them. The man has to go back to Cape Breton to live with his mother. He can't even open a door.

They spoke about their lives. The woman was good at prying him open but it was also the circumstance of knowing he'd never see this woman again. I don't know to what I'm returning, Henry said. There is a woman, he admitted. But he didn't know. What he did know was he might be giving up on airplanes.

The next morning he found her with a cup of styrofoam coffee in the lobby and they shared a taxi like old friends out to the airport and flew again over a white clear land and underneath the plane Henry saw the contour of the land he was to love, the little bird islands he'd kayaked around with Nora Power years ago, the little cove where Tender's summer house stood. Could he see Tender's house. No, that was a roof he could not pick out. All the houses looked like heads buried in the sand. What is this compulsion to see a house, he thought. What he wanted to see, he felt instinctively, was Martha Groves staring up at him, giving a big wave.

They landed in St John's at midday. He watched the woman he'd almost spent the night with as she strode quickly away to meet her husband who had the kids, still with their winter hoods up. No, he hadn't almost spent the night with her—he'd turned the corner on women. He was faithful, as this woman is. I'm a changed man, he thought, and allowed the cab manager to shepherd him into an orange taxi that drove him downtown to John and Silvia's where he was still renting that room but not for long.

18

He phoned Martha.

That house, he said. Let's go look at it.

She couldn't that day as she had to be in town to finish up with a patient who had hip dysplasia—she was helping the man with his adductor squeeze. Henry waited for the weekend. He drove her down the shore to Renews and they spent the night in John and Silvia's summer place. In separate beds. It was freezing. There was a darkness in some of Martha's silences, a realization that things could not go on between them because of what had already happened. It was almost misery, is what he saw in her. But there was something brand new too, like the swipe of window wipers refreshing the glass. Her eyes pushed away the darkness and she was with him again. He was ready to give over even though the idea of sleeping together seemed perverse. One thing had led to another which led to the beds and they were both relieved about the beds and their easy independent access to them. I want to be good, Henry said to his own stomach as he undressed and climbed into the sheets.

In the morning they walked over to the cemetery and visited

the new grave. It looked ugly. Cold and wet and the snow didn't even cover things. The soil had settled and frozen and heaved up again. He was buried in there like an improvised device. They would have to groom it in the spring.

Then they visited Tender's house.

The doors were locked and Martha did not have a key. Henry sized up the interior the way Tender trained him to do reconnaissance. The house, from the outside, looked to have good bones. He stepped back and stared at the eaves and the corners of the house were plumb. He fell back into the snow and stared up at this thing that someone he had no connection to had built. The front and back porches, the sills were gone and the porches were falling away from the heart of the house. The electric service cut off. The doors and the porches made it easy to defend from the inside.

Tender wanted to do this place up.

He had ambitions, Henry said.

I've been inside.

You've walked through it.

I like it.

Henry turned around. To be next to John and Silvia, but I don't know.

He tried to touch her shoulder the way a friend would, a caring person. He thought of the woman on the plane. Someone not sexual. Martha was overwhelmed with what had occurred and what her life was now to become. She needed and enjoyed distraction. Henry tried his best. He was exercising new ways of arranging his limbs. It is possible to be someone else, or the portion of you that doesn't get exercised often. He thought too about that artist and how he should return to her and tell her that the way she was falling was not anything like how a soldier's legs break from under him and soldiers rarely are killed in open fire. Soldiers are blown apart, their uniforms are shredded at the site of wear, and the stomachs are pierced, the neck ripped and the feet torn off as are the hands. What you find are torsos in full battle rattle and the torsos will collapse if run over, a body will dry out very quickly and turn into flattened rags.

19

John came home and dancing broke out at three in the morning—a spontaneous call for a taxi to deliver a forty-ouncer. Silvia woke up at dawn with the kids, exhausted and accepting, and said they wanted to go skating. It was Saturday. Henry fell into a car with a bag of cheese sandwiches on his lap, a car that drove to Dead Man's Pond. Martha was driving as she hadn't been drinking. John held an open jar of green olives between his knees, shoving his fingers into the wide mouth, trying to fish them out and hand the olives over to any mouth that would open. You mean, he said, you put up with all of us all night long completely sober? It was trying, Martha said. The jar was empty when they got to the pond and John poured the brine out on the snow. Henry helped shovel off the pond, hungover, and just lay there next to the aluminum shovel with John Hynes still drinking American cans of pilsner as there was some brewery strike across the country. It felt like anything he looked at was made of aluminum. They watched the women in their white leather skates flash in the dull sunlight. We used to do this, John said, with hockey sticks.

With Tender Morris in goal.

Tender Morris, John said, was a loyal man.

A deep sadness crept into Henry's shoulders as he realized his own tendencies made him a shit. A shit but hell he was doing the best he could.

Tender accompanied them when they hit the red light district approved without paperwork by the generals. He oversaw things. Tender Morris loved the army life though he did not partake in the tender vittles.

Martha overheard them. He loved it more than he loved civilian life.

They made a bonfire. It was heartening to see Martha's friends circle around her and include her in the social gatherings to make sure she was not alone. She was distracted and liked to laugh and was game for anything that came up. Henry counted off three fingers. But it was almost like she was religious or had some secret pact where she had to live a righteous life

She's involved, Henry realized, in some impossible truth. Tender has been dead, what, three months. It was something else in her that was giving off a physical manifestation. Sometimes you see loyalty in the air like that. When things are hard you adjust the dial on your emotions and learn new, complicated emotions that work over the scar tissue of torment and allow the face and hands to convey a manner of grace. Thanks be to god for that.

Martha, skating backwards—trusting the surface. After his breakup with Nora, Henry's friends had taken care of him and now that Tender Morris was gone they were doing the same for Martha. That was obvious. But what suddenly occurred to Henry was that his friends were impatient with him, urging him to pursue a scenario with Martha. He thought this was a private instinct but he understood now the visible traces of intent in the air. They had allowed Martha and Henry to leave that party together at Christmas. The knowledge of this stalled him. What was romantic about an arranged marriage? But he liked looking at her mouth. She has this fine hair down from her navel and she was self-conscious about it. Tender had an idea of airbrushed beauty. Tender, in Afghanistan, had once discussed his perfect woman while they played crib. But what about Martha, Henry had said. Martha's going to get fat, he said. It was a quick remark that blurted out of Tender and ran against all the grain of what seemed to exist on the ground between the two of them. And that struck Henry as a hard and salient fact, and it worried him, that all the beauty in the world could be ground down by emphatic, cruel statements like that. It made him feel loyal to the things he'd already done with Martha Groves, if Tender felt this way. But perhaps ten percent of a man's thoughts run this way—can you still blame him for them? Henry was alone, but he'd seen Martha in all the ways that nominal virtue allowed, and he felt guilty about it. He did not know if he could ever get along with a woman, to be honest.

20

The trees were covered in glitter ice and orange taxis slid around on baloney tires. A school bus full of kids braked on Kenna's Hill and slipped sideways through the intersection using all three lanes of road. The driver looked very calm about it. Henry walked a mile in cold weather to the YMCA and worked on the conditioning weights. Sometimes he did that, walk instead of taking the car. He looked at the car and remembered the jeep and could not bring himself to open the door. That was how Tender Morris ended his life and the idea of voluntarily harnessing himself into that position repulsed him. He'd seen a counsellor on his return and did not tell him about this aversion. The army physiotherapist had given Henry a routine to eventually loosen out the kinks from the impact he received from the exploding jeep. Martha had looked over the routine—it was printed on a two-sided laminated sheet that reminded him of scuba diving positions and eastern yoga. She said do this one and this one and not to do the exercises on the other side of the sheet. They've all been overturned.

He watched the news on a flat TV bolted above the running track. The news had no sound, just the anchor interviewing the minister of defence in high definition, their conversation in closed captions. You could understand in ten seconds the power and the status quo of the media and government by studying the national news with the sound off. He thought about Tender Morris and John Hynes. They had all met this minister of defence at the base in Kabul. Tender Morris was in extremely good physical shape at that dinner and then, within three months, they were attending Tender Morris's funeral.

He did thirty minutes on the rowing machine and then the exercises Martha recommended. He thought about what she had told him about Tender Morris's house. A house like that and he could row every day. Martha wasn't drinking. They were all drunk but she wasn't. Her righteous life. It was a bit of a drag this no drinking. Could he live with that. There is no telling if it is a truth or a fleeting truth but Henry saw that pervading inertia can take hold. Passive people think the world doesn't change, but it does and there are forces out there rolling stones and rubbing off moss. Inertia, if you recall, applies to acceleration and deceleration, not to change. Perhaps it was that impulse in him that first started to turn Nora away. Yes, he can see it now. She had loved how different from her he was. He was physical in the world, active, building things, and he used his shoulders and legs. She read books and sat at tables talking with colleagues. She attended meetings. And she realized that, along with the animal pulse in him, he possessed an independent drive to go public with his devotion. A willingness to be slayed, which is what war is. The biggest meeting of all.

He exercised until the taekwondo class ended then he boosted himself off the equipment and took a shower and dressed and reminded himself of the perversion of his thoughts: try and steer a safe course.

He walked home in a rifling wind and, instead of heading into Silvia's house, he shovelled out the car and jumped in and warmed up the engine and drove past Martha's place. Her car was gone. He knew where the key was. He could let himself in and put the lights on so she'd know someone was there. He could read one of Tender's books and get educated. Well, his car would be a clue right there. There is no need to frighten her.

He drove back through town past the new wings of development on the old city—subdivisions he had helped build with John and Tender back in their twenties. As he slowed he saw Silvia sitting in her car in the driveway. She looked like she was crying. Or at least, she had her hands on the wheel in a way that made it look like she was trying to hold on. The wheel was giving her anchorage. Keep driving. He drove to a coffee shop and had a coffee and an old-fashioned donut and read a section of a newspaper from the day before. It was sort of cheerful to know all the news before reading it. An insert with real estate. Illustrations of a house with a saw through it: under construction. John had told him, before heading out west, that the kids were growing and they needed to expand into the finished basement. Would Henry consider, you know, finding his own place.

I should call first, was his thought. Silvia answered. She was inside the house now. He explained he was moving on. Come over, she said cheerfully.

The dog helped him open the door then sidled over to him and presented his back. Wolfy. The kids weren't home yet from school, and John was delayed in Fort Mac. Rick had asked him to stay on another week. They were short men with Henry gone and Jamie Kirby in arm casts.

Sometimes I'm so involved with my own life, he said, I forget what other people are doing.

The women around me, Silvia said, they all comment on the day as it's happening. They say they're having a wonderful time and isn't this great. I just want to live it. I want to think about it years from now, and judge it then. But I'm with a man who does this very thing, and it's made me realize I'm the man and he's the woman.

I'll not mention that to John.

I miss him, she said. He's loyal, and he loves. He's a generous man and he reminds me to be generous. She laughed. It's like feeding a lion. If I buy a roast, a big eighty-dollar prime rib for us and the kids, he won't go to bed until that roast is gone. He'll sit there at one in the morning with a jar of mayonnaise.

I've seen him in the meat section, Henry said. His nostrils flare at the steaks.

I've never seen anyone quiver with such excitement at meat.

Henry stroked the dog. He remembered how they got Wolf. John and Silvia and the kids had been swimming around the bay at their summer house when they saw the dog low in the water. The dog had come around a headland and was struggling. The dog's nose went under, just his ears left, and it was Silvia who waded out to the dog and grabbed him and yelled out to John for help. He was too heavy. There was a cinder block tied to his paw. They got the dog ashore and cut off the rope. They found the owner—an old guy out in Fermeuse. John went up to him, said if you ever do something like that again I'll come over and ram your teeth down your throat. I ain't got no teeth to ram down. Then I'll get a set made for you and ram them down.

Silvia: Martha told me Tender's house is for sale.

It came out of Silvia's mouth before she knew what she was saying. Henry must have looked puzzled.

We all know about your night with Martha.

You don't seem entirely happy about it.

I've known you too long, Henry.

He was mainly a friend of John's and the way Henry was in the world was something she disputed. Silvia was fond of Tender Morris. John had said to Henry once, Have you ever noticed how Tender and Silvia talk?

You have to forgive the strong love and never speak ill of it, John had said. But John hadn't told his wife about that conversation in Kabul, where Tender described his ideal beauty. Surely he hadn't.

Henry explained his idea about Tender's house in Renews.

Silvia took the keychain off a pegboard in the kitchen and tossed it to him, the key to their summer house.

Martha's pregnant. Did you know that.

He caught the key and stared at it, afraid to look at Silvia again. If a promise can be a cube of sugar then he felt this cube dissolve in him. He could not look at Silvia but he knew she understood how he must feel. He was betraying that feeling in his face.

That makes sense now, he said.

I doubt the house is locked, just go in.

No it is locked, he said. We tried before to get in.

I meant our house. You should think about what you're doing here. You and Martha. I told you because I thought you should know.

The key dangled from a plastic Labrador dog. He was astonished at the situation. Martha was pregnant. Tender was on a month's leave and she got pregnant. Tender had turned the key on a new life and then Henry had shut the door and locked it.

He cleared his head. Are you okay taking care of things on your own, he asked.

Are you kidding me? Silvia laughed. I was upset when you drove by—you don't think I didn't notice you? I have a big life, Henry. A life without John. I get lots of things done and have friends and family to help with the kids.

You're becoming different.

You get different, don't you find.

I'll get us some dinner, he said. It's too late to be driving out there now.

The kids came home and he ordered pizza. They had those toys, the tin whales that you wound up. As it rolls along, it gobbles up a smaller fish. One was smashed but the other still worked. He put the kids to bed. He told them a story of a bear that had come into his cabin when he was a boy and the only evidence of the bear he found was a pawprint in the bacon fat in the frying pan.

I like cabins, Sadie said.

We could roast marshmallows over the sun, Clem said.

You could have really long sticks, Sadie said.

No, you climb on a cloud.

But when it's cloudy there is no sun!

When they were asleep Silvia had already gone to bed, so he found his way downstairs to the finished basement. Wolf was waiting for him. He woke up in the middle of the dark night, bewildered. Then he got his bearings. But these were only bearings for where he was, not when he was.

He turned on a light and read a magazine. There was not a sound in the house.

He must have fallen asleep again for Silvia's face was waking him up. At first it felt like Silvia was someone he lived with, that he had ended up with Silvia and the rest of his adult life had been a dream of the night before. He could have, he guessed, ended up with Silvia. Stranger couplings have occurred. There was light around the bedroom curtains. Six in the morning. I'm making breakfast, she said. He put on his shoes. She saw him to the porch and must have read his mind. You don't have kids, she said. It's hard, having them, but they've made me understand who I am. And soon they'll be old enough and another life will return.

That's not what I was thinking.

Silvia had to tidy up the kitchen and get the kids off to school. She was late for work. She has a modern job where she works indoors on things that have happened outdoors. There is a wafer of electronic data that courses through her day and she gets to talk to other people and that part of her job she likes a lot.

Another life. The sun pulling itself out of the Atlantic.

He ate breakfast with the kids and before leaving he helped Clem lay his parka on the floor and watched him bend over and push his arms into the sleeves and lift the coat over his head and don it. It struck Henry that this is how the search and rescue technicians slip on their helicopter vests.

He got in his car and decided to find that performance artist and tell her about soldiers dying but the gallery was not open. So he drove up to Signal Hill. He watched a limousine pour out a wedding party in a blizzard. The bride in her white gown and two men almost on their knees grabbing at the hem. My god, is the world going to rub it in? Someone getting married, not him. But he had enough reserve to cheer. Behind them, down at Fort Amherst, the white lighthouse and below that the old fortifications from two world wars. The lighthouse is a seagull and the grey fortifications are its young, camouflaged against the rock. What did that suggest? The fledglings of our own birth arise from a militaristic past.

21

An hour up the shore in wicked snow conditions. In Newfoundland, south is up. Henry had the radio on for company, stopping in the Goulds to fill a grocery cart and withdraw cash from a bank machine. When he got back out to the parking lot the afternoon was dark.

The radio helped him drive the slow road out to Renews. The wind lifted the car off the road. This driving in the winter reminded him of touring through Afghanistan, the road our convoys took south of Kabul towards Kandahar. Not that he's an expert, but one does experience things even when one is in a foreign situation ever briefly. Sand and snow both obliterate a landscape, turn it into something artificial, or a borrowed place. It does no harm to pollute this sort of landscape. Renews in winter was the Kandahar of Newfoundland, if you can think of the island as a Pashtun province and the Atlantic ocean standing in for Pakistan, which was a thought right up Henry's alley. Tender died at home. The difference in the world rests mainly in moisture and latitude.

He saw then lost the lighthouse beacon out on the head. The

snow and the dark. Being driven to a place is much different than driving there yourself. The world involved in its own copulation.

The side road was ploughed and the headlights lit up the high banks of snow along the road. There'd been a lot of weather out here since the funeral, or at least a lot of snow had drifted in from the sea. There was no place to park except on the road. He left the car running and knocked on a neighbour's door. The house front encased in a new brick veneer. An elderly man in a clean shirt leaned himself up in the doorframe and Henry remembered John telling him that this was Baxter Penney. He could feel the tremendous heat from a woodstove barrel out the open door, the heat had a density to it. Baxter Penney looked over at Henry's idling car, the confident shafts of headlight catching the descent of snow and said he could store that car in the lee of his barn. Baxter's house and barn and driveway were lit up by a five-hundred-watt outdoor lamp that beamed a cruel anti-criminal light on the neatly shovelled lot and the brick veneer siding. How did you come to settle on brick?

The answer to that, Baxter said, wears a dress.

Henry parked the car and shut off the engine and, for the first time, realized he was now at the mercy of the sound of weather. The ocean was roaring. He crossed the road to John's summer house and jumped the snowbank and plunged into darkness and noisy wind. He'd never been here in winter, only a handful of times in summer.

He waded through hip-high snow to the storm door and knocked the ice from the padlock. The key. He had it in his pocket. The shackle of the lock leapt out of the chamber and that was very satisfying. Inside he tried the porch light but it did not work and he reached into the kitchen and that switch did not work either. He kicked off his boots and felt around for the fuse box and it took ten minutes to discover it out in the front porch. He pushed on the main breaker and the lights came on. Artificial light that you have no part in creating, the system of deliverance of light is one of the cheeriest joys of the past hundred years.

The floors were cold in his sock feet. Henry set the thermostats on several baseboard heaters and grabbed a handful of splits from the back porch and crumpled three sheets of newspaper in the kitchen woodstove. He struck a match while jumping up and down on the cushion floor and bent his elbows and laughed at the fierce conditions he was volunteering to be in. Make a cup of tea, he yelled out, but the water was shut off and the blue container that had water was frozen. He had not thought ahead. What he needed was a few packets of self-heating food. The active packaging in the army. He enjoyed that, pouring water into a bag and sealing in the meal and allowing it to heat.

He filled a pot with snow and melted it on the electric stove and found powdered milk in the cupboard along with half a bag of cookies and scraped the frost from a window and stared across the dark white field at what must be Tender Morris's house. Dark against a dark sky and field. It was hardly there. It wasn't there except he knew it to be there. Drinking John's tea and eating his cookies made him feel like he was John looking out at this house he'd only heard of while on manoeuvres in Afghanistan. There had been a woman living in Tender's house, right up until she died a dozen years ago. An older woman. All alone—like me, Henry thought. This was Tender's great-aunt. John had seen her a few times when he was a teenager, walking down to the back of the property with a bucket. A house promised to Tender Morris. These houses all along the shore had been lived in for a hundred years by families but now they were being torn down by the dozen or only used in the summer because this generation has gone soft. John Hynes only came out to turn off the water in October and then maybe once more to fire up the snowmobile and say, bravely, that he'd been skidooing. The house—Tender's house— was probably a wreck but his family wanted five thousand dollars for it, which is what the land is worth. He was buying land.

22

In the morning he found a pry bar in John's shed and hooked it into the tongue of the yellow padlock but the lock wouldn't give. What he ended up doing was wrenching the latch and screws from the frame of the storm door. Tender's house, inside, smelled good. You could see your breath. He stood there in the kitchen, wondering about being there. He felt like an intruder. Over the back of a chair was a woman's wool coat. In the parlour a sifted hill of snow—it was part of a larger snowbank that had come in through the front porch. The wind had blown snow particles under the door and into the parlour. It was pointing itself towards the chimney. Snow lived here now. Tender Morris had never spent a night here. He had inherited this house and, while he had plans for it, the truth is he wasn't going to get around to those plans. Tender had admitted that himself. This house required an energy too large for the type of life Tender Morris was planning on living. Martha Groves lived in town and Tender would be in the army until he turned fifty-five. There was no chance of much attention finding its way to this place. Unless they had a kid.

Pregnant. Silvia said she's pregnant. What do you think of that, Tender Morris? Dead three months now thanks to me and your wife pregnant.

He opened the hall door and swung it in his hands. A heavy well-hung door. He walked to the staircase and stroked the varnished newel post. He took the stairs and they did not creak. He had to lower his head to enter the bedrooms. The ceilings were low and the wallpaper was peeling off in thick sheets.

He was trying to connect to the impulse he had to be here. He felt like he was starting a new life, venturing into new but old places.

Newsprint and flour paste sleeping under the wallpaper. He searched for dates and found them, between the world wars. He read of fashion and baked beans and the religious judgment of loose behaviour. There were beds that were thirty years old and expensive when they were new. The aunt had a taste for the modern. The laminate bubbling off because of the damp. On a hook behind the door were hung three dresses. A pair of lady's pumps. Under a seat cushion a leather pouch. A letter. It was typed, from an American military fellow on board a ship docked in St John's: Dear Nellie. Her name was Nellie Morris.

On the back of the pale blue paper a red mark—lipstick. It was a mouth. He read the letter. The letter was asking for a walk.

He stood there in the room, utterly alone, and looked out the window. Others had looked out this window but how long ago and who. What was a window doing, framing how you look at the world. What you saw was a hill with not a tree near it. He got up close to the window and his breath fogged it. And in the breath he saw something grow: the print of a child's hand.

HE SAT DOWN AND FOUND other letters in a drawer and read them. There was an old radio and he turned the knob and it leapt alive. Batteries that still held power. It was an oldies station. He turned the knob to get some modern music and then he remembered the old man in the Spur singing that song of the woman whose head he kicked to the wall. He turned the raspy knob back to the oldies station and listened. This is what Nellie Morris had listened to before she left the house. The station was run by volunteers in their eighties and they spoke gravely of religion and there were public service announcements that warned seniors of the dangers of identity theft and the commercials were for dentures and funeral homes—Muirs has been carving monuments since 1841. Tender has a monument from Muirs on the road to the lighthouse. They call them monuments.

Henry figured out, through the letters, an entire family. The structure of the family involved a widower, Melvin Careen, who had married the aunt, Nellie Morris, but the aunt already had a girl—out of wedlock is the term—with the serviceman on the ship anchored in St John's harbour. When Melvin Careen died the children from his first marriage had tried to push the aunt out of the house—there were legal letters, threatening her. Henry thought of the aunt, all alone here, perhaps her nephew—Patrick Morris—had helped fend off the legal threats. Henry stared at the pumps and her dresses and her letters in the drawer and the notes she kept in the leather pouch. He was letting all this affect him.

I am concerned, he realized.

He bent down to smell the bedframe and there was a rank scent of mould. He surprised himself with this motion: his own reflection caught in a bureau mirror. His torso hovering over furniture. He realized, in a fussy instant, that this figure in the mirror was a bully. He had bullied Nora into leaving him. He didn't know how to be himself. He found he was shouting at Nora Power. When you shout you don't know you're shouting. But it can ambush you later and that was happening to Henry now. He never liked that Nora was being herself. He confused her being herself with disloyalty. And now he knew she was right— she had been bewildered and surprised. Why does he think this way. Think ill of her motives. Think of her as judgmental. It had driven him insane with a rage he couldn't gauge for he had no mirror, no one ever looks in a mirror when in full fury. Perhaps all the mirrors fold away on little hinges. Until she left him. Or asked him to leave. And in that sorrow, or realizing he did not know how to be himself without being angry at others, he had decided to capitulate.

But I love you.

This man in the mirror has never owned a house, all he's owned are contents. I've never owned people, and people have never owned me.

He turned off the radio and walked downstairs. He looked out the window to see if anyone was watching him. The glass in the windows was the old kind that warbled. His breath fogged the window but there was no child's hand here.

The woman's coat on the chair. Tender had been late so Nellie took off her coat and laid it over this chair. This was her last afternoon in the house. She had collected a teacup and her slippers and a pack of cards and stowed them in a green box made of papier mâché and then Patrick Morris arrived and took her by the elbow and helped his aunt out the door and around the house to the car. They got in the car and reversed up onto the road and he drove her out to the Aquaforte seniors complex Rick Tobin had built where she lived until she died.

But she had forgotten her coat. Her coat lay over this chair. It was a light yellow wool coat and the lining was exposed on one sleeve, a pale pink sheen to it and half of the maker's label, the white buttons down the length of it stopping five inches from the floor.

Henry whipped open a contractor's garbage bag and plunged the coat in. He laid it on the seat of the chair. He left the house and walked over the field and slept the night at John and Silvia's summer home. In bed he thought about the house across the field holding hands with this house under the earth. Their heads above the sand. The people who had lived and died in these houses. Why does this matter to me, he thought. I am no kin. Kin, he thought, an ancient thing.

23

He got a lawyer in the Goulds involved. The lawyer, Bill Wiseman, said who owns this house. He said it rhetorically. What he was saying was a lot of people owned this house. It was left to Tender Morris by an aunt, Henry explained, and I'm buying it off Tender's wife with the blessings of the Morris family.

Bill Wiseman rolled about the carpet in a black steno chair, with a ballpoint pen between his fingers.

Yes, he said, you're buying a house off this Martha Groves. You're to give her money, a wife you call her but there's no marriage in the books and a woman who hasn't even stated on a tax return she's common-law. She's to hand you a key to a lock on a door. I'm unfamiliar with the term widowed girlfriend and so too, I'm afraid, is the registry of deeds. That's like me selling you that field where my Impala is parked. Bill Wiseman pointed out the sheers with the ballpoint pen, as if he needed to. I can sell it to you, but is it mine.

Henry explained that Martha Groves was acting as agent for Patrick Morris's bereaved family.

Bill Wiseman shook his head. That house, that aunt. What about Melvin Careen?

Melvin Careen? He had not thought of Melvin Careen.

Bill Wiseman leaned in now and put the pen on the table, for he had information. There's two families, Henry. I know you're dealing with Patrick's immediate family, with a girlfriend he was to marry, and she means well. But the blood of family spreads further than brothers and sisters.

The aunt, Henry said. And he remembered the letters. You're talking about that man she married.

I'm talking about Melvin Careen.

I don't know the Careens.

Married the aunt like you said, Bill Wiseman said. And that's your problem right there.

Bill Wiseman pushed his short fingers together, gathering up Melvin Careen and corralling him between the two families. Melvin Careen wouldn't move into that house he didn't own half of it. Trouble is, he was married before. Had a wife and child and that child has family now, three sons, and those sons are not five miles from where we're sitting, hating Patrick Morris's guts.

It was impossible to follow this lineage without a diagram. It was impossible and absolutely boring to try and relate. No one in his right mind, Henry said, can hate Tender Morris's guts.

Bill Wiseman picked up the pen again and rolled away on his steno chair. Patrick Morris, he said, died in honour for the sake of our freedom but that hardly makes up for robbing the Careens of a birthright.

It was Tender's grandfather what built the house (Henry said "what built the house" in a gesture of idiomatic camaraderie).

Bill Wiseman checked his papers. Aubrey Morris, he said. Bill Wiseman did not acknowledge Henry's word choice.

Aubrey Morris, yes, he built it for Tender's great-aunt.

One letter separates aunt from a swear word that labels what women do to the records of possession and inheritance, Henry. It don't matter who he built it for. No will, no deed, nothing. She only has a right to hand down half the house.

Bill Wiseman severed his connection to the pen with one finger. The pen, and the house, were set adrift in the cosmos. How on earth did he come up with that swear word business so quickly?

Who's to say, he continued, one of those men ten years from now will come walking into that house and ask what the hell are you doing sitting at his table. A man who in the previous thirty years didn't have a single thought about the property—no sir this deal is not going to fly.

And with that the pen landed back on Bill Wiseman's desk.

24

Henry sat in the car, bewildered, and turned on the old-timer station and listened to music that actually skipped—they still played vinyl records at this station. He stared at Bill Wiseman's office window blinds. He rehearsed a little monologue. He counted off his fingers and corrected his language. Then he drove to a payphone outside a coffee shop and phoned the home of each of the three Careen grandsons and said he understood their loss. He did not want them out of the picture when it came to selling their grandfather's house. He hung up between each call and enjoyed the weight of a payphone receiver, payphones that were now being ripped out or added onto with screens for some reason he had yet to figure out. He phoned Martha Groves on his own phone and said look what am I going to do here, can we split the money between the families. I'm talking about the Careens. She wasn't there, he just left a message on her machine. He made out a cheque to her for three thousand dollars and bought a stamp and an envelope at a postal outlet and found her postal code and mailed it.

He drove back to Renews and walked into John Hynes's backyard and stared at the low hills and the community pasture where nine cows were standing in the failing winter sunlight. This is what you saw from that bedroom window. Cows, hill. He thought about what would be the best approach to get Tender's house. He turned to face the house in question, sitting in its own shadow, and realized how often he'd seen houses falling in on themselves and wondered why no one fixed them up. Now he knew. Bill Wiseman is right. I can't mention Martha or Tender or the Morris side of things. It has to be the Careen house entire. He laughed at his own consideration, the amount of energy he was channelling into this house and to the past. For what purpose. Do I plan to live in this house? Am I, he said aloud, doing this for Tender Morris? Tender Morris had no intention of living in this house. It's all a muddle, emotions and intentions, I could be living in London or California. How often will I see Argentina, living in this house. But what isn't refutable is you only have one life and you better make the most of it.

The next day he used Baxter Penney's phone and asked the three Careen grandsons to get together. They could do it Thursday, Harold Careen said. It was poker night.

25

He walked across the field and set himself up for the night at John and Silvia's summer house. He was preparing for bed but realized he wasn't tired. He had broken out of routine, and cheered the decision to give in to momentum. He tore off a bun of bread and cut through two inches of hard cheese with his pocket knife and pulled on cold boots and zipped up his jacket. It was freezing out. He waved over at Baxter's and, further along, Rick Tobin's house. Rick's wife was in there, a woman who liked a good urban party but was living on her own out here on a rural road. He remembered her face on a computer screen as she talked to Rick Tobin at the base in Kabul. The yellow house at the end of the road was closed up for the winter. That belonged to the American, Noyce, a man who fell in love with the place after 9/11. What was it John Hynes had said of him? A man more loyal to the culture of this place than its own citizens. Spent his summers in Renews. But there was a light on now, so someone was in there. The old lightkeeper's house. No car. Visiting, like Henry, during the coldest part of the year.

The road forked, a quad trail down into Kingmans Cove and a wooden footbridge over a noisy frozen brook and then a path used by cows and sheep, so the rock was smooth and bare of snow and the grass very hard. This was where the cemetery was. Where Tender Morris was buried. He left the sheep trail and the frozen grass was hollow and broke softly underfoot. The lighthouse flashed and arced a flare of light over the water and he zippered up the top four inches of his jacket so his mouth nuzzled against something warm. It got dark quickly here. When he was near the headland he realized it was not a lighthouse but a new, three-storey automated signal. People still called it the lighthouse and there were photographs of the original, magnificent lighthouse—John and Silvia had one in their hall in St John's—that stood near the same spot. He was disappointed but that's progress.

He walked further into the valley, fifteen minutes by his watch, and found an old grass-covered cellar. He climbed down into it. The stone arch of the doorway. It offered some shelter and blocked the noise of the sea. He stood there, staring into the deep darkening distance that he had decided was Pakistan. Snow fell. He felt moved by this place, this little alcove in the landscape, although he had no idea what it looked like in the daytime.

Suddenly the distance moved, or a piece of the dark vista broke off and clarified and moved towards him, a slant of shape approaching fast and the sawing action of colourful nylon, a figure, head down. He climbed out of the cellar and called out, instinctively. It was a woman, lean, walking very quickly and she looked up and said hello back. It was Colleen Grandy. Silvia Hynes had called her, she said. I saw you walk out this way. Silvia had been worried you wouldn't know how to turn on the electricity, or where things were put, or if you had water. Colleen was breathless from walking, but she walked a lot, she said.

She was Henry's age and friendly and she was Rick Tobin's wife. Henry had spoken to her through the years but had they ever been alone once like this, talking directly? He was uncomfortable talking to women. They walked back to Renews and he was surprised at how easy she made it to enjoy her company (although she was walking at a clip). She explained in the manner of a tour guide how the broken slipway had been torn out by a hurricane last fall and the fishermen no longer used Renews as an anchorage. The rocks angled up sharply as the day they first emerged ten thousand years ago after the ice sheets melted, the slanted blue slate like the stern of a broken ship on its way down.

They got to the dark American house and Henry remembered the small niggling rumour of her and this man. There was a light on earlier, Henry said.

His son is here, she said. I can't wait for him to get here.

The son?

No, Larry.

Larry, he thought. Larry Noyce. Such an unspiritual name. Which livened him to the possibility. To be with a man named Larry.

He has this meditation every week, Larry does. When he's here. It's a meditation and a discussion. Silvia has gone to it.

There's no car.

The boy hitchhikes in from the airport. I told him I could pick him up but he said no he prefers to thumb it.

A son. Colleen with no children. But John and Silvia had once suggested adoption and Rick had been interested.

They passed the empty slipway—the only fishermen that went out were the mussel farmers and the sentinel fisheries officers who canvassed the seas to judge the groundfish stocks which were in decline everywhere but especially here along the shore road. The fishery is a community activity, there are no fences for fish and everything that was shared was gone now, armies and fish were all privatized.

They reached Colleen's house and she said she had an empty container that he could fill from her kitchen sink. I'll drive it over to you, no need to walk it up the road. Twenty gallons of water. She filled it in the laundry room and Henry waited in the porch. Rick's house. Modern. Everything in the house is new. Rick was sinking money into a castle.

He put the container in the trunk of Colleen's car and they drove the four hundred feet to John and Silvia's house and she came in with him to look around and she realized he knew how to take care of himself. She said goodnight and Henry watched her get back in her car and drive down the road. He slept in the second bedroom and he found he was thinking about Colleen Grandy. It helped, when he was alone, to think of a woman. He wondered about her and Larry Noyce. Did Rick know or was it even true. She was just a woman alone, there is bound to be talk. He held her in the bed and was intimate with her and it helped put him to sleep.

26

They called her the walker and Colleen accepted it, her rural persona.

Years ago, when she first married Rick, she took him back here to Renews where she was from. She missed this cove. They laugh here. She was Catholic and people keep an eye on you. At first Rick worked with her father, Emerson Grandy, and then her father had the accident that lost his hands. He had been guiding, overhead, a cement pipe to link up with another section of pipe. He laid his wrists on the bottom pipe and turned to hear something Rick was saying. Rick felt responsible. He helped him with the rehabilitation. He gave her parents money. Colleen's aunt had muscular dystrophy and lived with Emerson and his wife, Carol. Then Rick found work in Alberta and it paid well. It could take care of all of them. Colleen had to stay to help her father and mother. But she felt alone. She kept up the house and watched television and preferred the large bag of Lays chips and started putting off the housework until she got the word from Rick that he would be home in three weeks. And then when it was down to three days she hauled out the vacuum cleaner and soaked the dishes overnight in the sink and made a trip to the grocery store and tried to remember the condiments he liked to have in the fridge. She found it difficult, when a grocery item was finished, to remember that it was gone. She walked down the aisles looking at boxes and jars and tins and stared at them to see if they ever had been in the fridge or the cupboards. She studied the contents of other grocery carts. This helped her.

The weight came on in increments. A few pounds. Then she had to buy new pants anyway and the bigger number felt better. She sat on the sofa and watched the quiz shows, but only when Rick was away. She gave a small amount of money to an online evangelist and felt embarrassed as none of her friends did this. It was an old-fashioned thing to do but giving the money made her feel good. She listened on her computer to the weekly lectures given by a southern female Baptist.

One afternoon she was about to go to the post office to pick up the mail and found it hard to get off the sofa, just pushing herself up. It was this bolt of alarm that her legs were not capable. She found a way where you fold a leg under yourself and you push up from that leg. Rick didn't say anything but one night they were down at darts and he came over to the table with their drinks and he said, They're all wondering if you're over in Alberta with me. They don't recognize you and you don't go out. What's up? What's going on?

She went to see Martha Groves at the Health Sciences Centre. Martha knew people who studied obesity. She got a referral and she talked to Martha about their trying all manner of having a child but it didn't take and she couldn't talk to Rick about it. We love each other, Colleen said to Martha, the spirit of each other.

We have good chemistry and we like to laugh at simple things. Martha too suggested they could adopt.

Rick listened to her. Colleen was a better storyteller than Rick was and Rick admired it and he was glad he didn't have to keep up his end of it. Rick coasted on his wife's ability to hold up the family's side of the conversation. In the end, that's all you need, is a few laughs, make love and listen. Isn't it? Martha agreed and Colleen hesitated, as if the list she'd blurted out contained a few things more than what they had.

Then Larry Noyce arrived. Colleen told Rick about him. He's a spiritual man.

Are you going to fall in love with him?

She laughed and said only the spiritual bit in him.

That bit's okay with me.

When Rick was back in Alberta she cried because she didn't deserve him. But also she felt marooned here on a dead-end road where no one cared for her. Guilt turned to resentment. They didn't miss her and no one invited her over to play cards.

Move into town, Rick said.

My parents. My aunt.

Colleen put on a lot of weight. She knew how to cook. She can cook for large numbers of people. Her mother said she should have a large family the way she cooks. Cooking is how she met Larry Noyce.

She had enrolled in a two-week technical college cooking school. It was Martha's idea that Colleen should focus her skills on something she was already good at. It was in the fall. Rick was in Alberta and her mother gave her this coupon that expired in October. They had been receiving orientation in the kitchen, they hadn't touched a piece of food, when someone said there's been an accident in New York. They watched the footage on a television in the pantry and then a phone call came in from the president of the campus. You need to cook supper for two hundred people. There were planes landing at the airport. They drove to the grocery store and filled nine carts with food and they cooked two hundred dinners of stuffed chicken breasts. They spent the next two weeks cooking food non-stop, sleeping at the campus and working night and day in the kitchen.

Larry Noyce was aboard one of the planes. I need a dog, he said. I need to pet a dog. Colleen drove over to Silvia's and borrowed Wolf. As he stroked the dog a woman arrived with a dozen pairs of fresh underwear.

The women here, he said, sure know how to take care of the men.

After three days in a gymnasium they put him up at John and Silvia's. He slept with Wolf. Larry was moved by the whole experience. He was on his way back to New York, from Peru, and they rerouted him to St John's.

He was here for ten days and fell in love with the place. One thing led to another, John drove him out to Renews and he saw that yellow house for sale and he snapped it up. The lightkeeper's house. Pure speculation. But he came every summer. Colleen, being the closest neighbour, got to talking and she did some meditating with him and something switched in her and she adopted a walking program.

It was a ceremony Larry Noyce conducted that made her feel worthy. She can't speak of it now but the ceremony spurred her walking which triggered a new vision in her head. She was going to Peru.

I don't even know where Peru is, Rick said.

It's the centre of all being, she said.

I'm not impressed with spiritual matters, he said.

Colleen laughed.

You can be here but it's good to visit the centre too. That's what Larry says.

The centre, Rick said. The centre moves.

Colleen weighed herself every morning and every night, and she had the digital scales that took it down to a tenth of a pound. She wanted to be one hundred and forty-three pounds for this trip to Peru.

27

Henry made sure he was wearing the arid-region camouflage jacket he had been supplied with and drove into the Goulds. He used a computer at the public library to draft a sale of land and print it off. Then he headed to the mall and waited in line at the bank and withdrew thirty brand-new one-hundred-dollar bills. He asked the teller if she knew of a justice of the peace. She looked at him and turned to another woman counting photocopied papers who had a rubber cup on her finger. The finger stopped counting. Linda Hillier, she said. Is Linda still doing that? She's in the Anthony Insurance building across the road my love.

He walked over the road and opened the door to Anthony Insurance and then another glass door for motor vehicle registration. He asked for Linda Hillier. A small woman with short dark hair arrived and she tried to be friendly but her feet hurt. She was walking on marbles. Could she drop over to Harold Careen's tonight at six o'clock to witness some papers. She knew Harold Careen's wife and indeed she could do that, she just had to dart home first and put some dinner on and then she'd be right over. Six-thirty would suit her better.

Henry stopped by a gift card shop and bought three white envelopes. Next door was a homestyle cooking restaurant. He sat down and ordered a hot turkey sandwich and a cup of coffee. He thought, this will be my restaurant when I'm tired of cooking. The restaurant had no windows for it was in the mall but it had a mural of a window and the view was a canal in Venice. The waitress propped the handheld credit-card device on her belly and set her feet and said what the specials were. This is how I will holiday in Italy when I buy this house.

It was quarter after six and he drove over and parked opposite Harold Careen's driveway. He still had his hands on the wheel and he could see the sleeve of his army jacket and how he felt, pretending to be a soldier. When Henry first arrived back in Newfoundland he was still in issued clothing. His outfit was dark green with spots of mustard and black—temperate woodland they call it—his tight helmet in fabric of the same colour strapped to his waist under the right arm. He wore shades and carried a small knapsack, the same pattern as his suit and helmet. This was the outfit that had taken him months to collect, as Rick extended their contract past the original limits and ended up hooking up with Tender Morris. He recalled his first afternoon home when he was walking to the YMCA and he got to talking to an off-duty bus driver, the driver was with two other drivers, all in maroon coats and grey slacks in line waiting for a bus and this driver asked him where he was stationed and when he was set to go back to Afghanistan and, even though Henry was wearing no stripes, the driver did not suspect he was merely a civilian parading himself off as military. As they spoke a snowplough operator swung his yellow blade towards them, crossed a lane of traffic aggressively and jolted to a stop and turned the front wheels hard to straighten up again. The driver leaned over the passenger seat and stared straight at Henry and slowly saluted. Then he snapped off the salute and drove off with one long honk.

The bus driver stopped talking to allow this attention, and this sort of civilian respect moved Henry. There was gravity here and, as they resumed their conversation, he tried to think of another occupation that offered such dignity. There was nothing. He was not like the man operating the snowplough or even the bus driver, Henry wasn't their type, but they did not perceive his individuality—they regarded the uniform and the uniform offered the epitome of service and their own services were climbing a ladder towards the apex of putting one's life on the line for one's country. It made him feel like a fraud. Henry had done a statistics course in trade school and knew that more snowplough operators and bus drivers lost their lives than Canadian troops in theatre, and just last night a bus driver T-boned into a cherry picker that was servicing a utility pole on Rennie's Mill Road and killed the spotter. A week earlier a rogue highway snowblower chewed through a police cruiser on Elizabeth Avenue, killing the officer. Perhaps these men knew the real risks and were unprepared to leave their families and shave in large stainless steel bowls and drink warm bottled water eight thousand kilometres away.

But now that he was involved with Tender Morris's house he felt it was wrong to be dressed in army kit. John told him what Tender Morris had said when they shipped him from New Brunswick to Germany to Kabul. I want to see if all my training works out—but I don't want to kill anybody. Tender, a few years out of trade school, had shaved his head and lived in a Buddhist colony in Nova Scotia. This was before he turned to the army and the social behaviour of men.

Henry was, technically, still associated with Rick's contract with SNC-Lavalin but his head was concerned with other things. He followed a man he liked the look of into a clothing store and bought the clothes that the man lifted up and discarded. Occasionally he saw a movie and he rowed at the gym watching the news. About once a month the minister of defence came on—he was always jumping out of a caucus meeting or highlighting a list of hot points to cover with the news anchor. Both men leaned into the conversation and the top of their buttoned suits bowed out a little, like flexible armour. When that happened Henry couldn't help but think that a few months after the minister of defence had delivered their turkey burgers, the majority of Tender Morris's body was flown to Camp Mirage for treatment and the majority of that body died at the hospital after portions of his heart suffered congestive heart failure. On the ward, he read the news release from the minister of defence that was posted: Our thoughts and prayers are with the family and friends of our fallen comrade during this very difficult time. We will not forget Lieutenant Morris's sacrifice as we continue to bring security and hope to the people of Afghanistan. The next day Henry read the printout of what the prime minister said, reacting to the death: It is with utmost sorrow that I extend the condolences of all Canadians to the family and friends of Lieutenant Patrick Morris, a brave soldier who died due to injuries sustained in Afghanistan. Our thoughts and prayers go out to you at this time of loss. Lieutenant Morris served Canada valiantly and deserves the gratitude and respect of this nation.

Tender Morris was killed because of a washing machine timer, a cell phone and a garage door opener. Tender Morris was killed because his coffee holder was empty of a Sig Sauer 9-mm pistol.

Henry had sprayed a towel and wiped the handles of the elliptical. He went off in search of a rowing machine.

28

He opened his car door and walked over to Harold Careen's. They were just after pulling up the supper plates from the table and there were children in the living room playing on a computer. Two decks of cards on the counter next to the phone. Harold's wife wiped the table and he waited for the table top to be dry and he accepted the cold beer Harold handed him and then he said to the three grandsons that what he had to offer for their grandfather's house wasn't much but it was all he could afford— he was interrupted then by Harold Careen's wife who called out, from loading the dishwasher, that house could fall into the ground before Harold would sell out his grandfather's legacy and Harold said Joan that's enough. Henry said he was sorry about that, he understood the passing down of things and the loss of things, but that this house had a hole in the roof the size of a wheelbarrow and the porches were sagging and after the next big wind that house probably would cave in like Joan says. I understand, he said, that if the grandsons of the man who built this house want an acre of land with no service to it then I will honour that, but perhaps a man's wishes take a detour and the promise of a home is cherished by a stranger just as much as the blood of the family and there is something both humble and generous in allowing the passing of a house to someone who wishes to care for it and no amount of money could equal that wish of those upon which burdens are handed down.

He placed the three envelopes, each with a thousand dollars, on the table in front of the men. He couldn't tell if they looked at one another first, he was still recovering from his speech, but they all picked up the envelopes and took his pen and put their signatures on the sale agreement he'd printed off and just then is when Linda Hillier arrived in a coat and scarf and Henry realized while she knew the Careens she had never been in their house before. She signed and stamped the documents and it was a service for which she was not paid, it was part of her civic duty and she was there all of ten minutes, she had to get back to her three children and her own husband. After she left the Careens continued on with other things as if the subject of the meeting was something else entirely. The kids came in and one asked why the Canada flag stitched on Henry's arm was green and he said it wasn't stitched on it's velcro and the green is so he wouldn't get shot. He left with handshakes and a hug from Joan and the next day he drove those papers over to Bill Wiseman and by then the lawyer had already received the letter from Martha Groves returning Henry's cheque and declining the three thousand dollars for her share of the house.

She seems to have had a change of heart, Bill Wiseman said. The lawyer, who had been rankled by Henry's steamrolling ahead and having gotten, miraculously, the three Careen grandsons on side, seemed satisfied that somewhere along the line a roadblock had halted the sale.

Could I use your phone, Henry asked.

He called Martha Groves and she was startled to hear his voice and said she was really sorry but she had something in mind and she'd like to drop by that weekend if it was okay with him. That weekend. He handed the phone to the lawyer, for it had a strange cradle to it. He got back in his car and pulled up to Bidgoods and tramped the aisles for groceries and then a hardware store where he filled a cart with a foam pad and two pillows and a duvet and a cooler. Then he bought beer and ice and two disposable flashlights, a can of white gas and six pairs of work gloves. All this he squeezed into the trunk and folded-down back seats. He needed the lights on by the time he hit the small road that ran into Renews and he felt both vexed and excited. The little houses were all lit up but Tender Morris's house still had its eyes closed.

He walked over the snowdrifts and opened the back door. He used the new flashlight. The house smelled good. He carried in the provisions he'd bought and, as he went back to the car for a second load, Baxter Penney came over. He was lugging a heavy kerosene heater. It was in the barn, he said. He showed him how to light it right there in the snow. It was finicky to get going but it helped cut the chill in the Morris house.

But don't you want a heater in your barn?

Forty years I've been meaning to put a stove in that barn. You want to know the reason I don't? He lives in Fermeuse.

I don't know anyone here.

My brother-in-law. The constant visitor. He'll never leave that barn if I put a stove in.

They bent over the machine figuring out the knobs and the lever for the wick ring. Colleen Grandy walked by, on her way around the cove, and they exchanged hellos. Do you know her, Henry asked.

That's my wife's niece, Baxter Penney said. The man I was just telling you about—I married his sister, a Grandy.

And he drew himself up to connect the dots on the tips of his fingers.

But we're also related by blood if I'm not mistaken—our great-grandmother floated into this cove in the 1800s. She was a servant to the third Napoleon. A French woman. Baxter pointed out at the water, as though some remnant of her might still be floating in. She was shipwrecked, he said. Only survivor. She had one of those whalebone hoop skirts and the air was like a lifeboat. We're from the one lady. His hands touched and then split apart. But now Colleen is his daughter. You know her husband.

Rick Tobin.

They're like you, no kids. For a long time she had nothing to do but get a bit heavy.

I know the story, Henry said. That's the one thing I know from this cove.

She couldn't get out of a car. That's when she started walking.

Henry tore open the box of beer and offered one to Baxter and Baxter twisted off the cap and threw it into the snow and followed him, with the heater, into the house.

I used to come in here as a child, he said. Haven't been in for sixty years. There used to be a piano in that room and there was a partition wall they must have tore that down.

Baxter looked hard at the dark rooms as Henry got the heater burning and then filled the Coleman lantern with white gas. It was fascinating to think that sixty years had gone by since this man had crossed the street and come into this house, that he used to be a boy and those days weren't that long ago and the word Napoleon had been uttered, as though he was sitting in the parlour polishing his sword.

We're looking forward, Baxter said, to seeing some lights on in this house.

They finished their beers and Henry pumped the lantern and lit the mantel. He could see the insides now and they were exactly as he'd left them. The heater gave off a plume of odour he associated with the machines they'd operated a mile underground in Fort McMurray. Henry made a bed on the floor in the parlour and Baxter said, You're not going to sleep in her in this condition. Henry said that was the plan. He asked about power and what he was to do for water and Henry said, a little beleaguered, that he'd figure all that out in the next few weeks.

Well, Baxter said, if you need anything we're across the road, and he pointed out the window as if Henry would not know the direction. He was off then. He crossed the road back to his snug little home that had in it a wife who was at that moment moving from room to room turning on more lights.

Henry made a little sliced deli sandwich and put the lantern with its throaty glow on the table so he would have something to look forward to on his walk home. He was going out to visit Tender's grave, and the cellar in Kingmans Cove.

29

That night he tried to sleep in Tender's house but small animals were near his head. His ears judged the varying acoustic weights and, as the night marched on, his mind weakened. The idea of quick animals with teeth became hysterical. He was once in a tent with Nora by a river that had a beaver dam. They awoke to splashes and then, slowly, heard beavers brushing by the tent. The beaver were chewing on birch trees and it did not seem outlandish to think one could mistake their heads for the trunk of a tree. It was a feeling similar to this one, but now there was an urgency of numbers. Not one shrew or three mice but dozens and perhaps animals a little heavier. The sounds were not consistent. He was aware of the danger of a weasel. They used the house for shelter just as they would an alcove of brush. They lined their nests with the pelts of their prey. He looked at his watch: two o'clock in the morning. Okay let's solve this.

He willed himself up and found his boots and coat and walked across the field with the stars above him. He stopped to look up at Orion and salute his little belt. He laughed at the animals that had trespassed and forced him out. What was he but a trespasser.

Up to his old room in John and Silvia's. Baxter was right. It was crazy to try and sleep in Tender's house in that condition.

30

A car woke him, the engine shutting off. He didn't know where he was. He looked out the bedroom window. Kids, independently pouring out of the rear doors. It was Silvia Hynes. She had come out with Clem and Sadie for the day. She popped the trunk and pulled out the wooden toboggan. They climbed the hill. While she was up there Silvia used her cell to talk to John. It was a scheduled time. That's what people did on this hill, climb to the top of it and use their phones. There was a hill like this in Kabul, Henry said, but no one ever climbed it. They lived on it, little fired-brick houses wedged into the rock. A shanty town built by the widows of Kabul.

Henry, to Clem and Sadie: Watch yourself, don't run up there or you'll fall and break your head and we'll have to put you in the ground.

Silvia: Man, guy babysitters.

Henry walked the kids home and helped them roll three sections of a snowman. Then they reached the eaves for icicles. The house in town has no icicles, Sadie said, because of insulation.

Henry found a piece of kindling with a knot in it and split it with an axe. Frosty's pipe, he said.

They sang songs and made snow angels and got cold and Henry built up the woodstove and pulled off their wet socks and had them run up the stairs to the second-floor bedroom—the bedroom he used—where there was a grate in the floor. He fixed them a snack. When Silvia came in she stared up to see their bare feet on the grate.

They discovered old toys in the back pantry, toys they'd had when they were younger. They were bored so they resorted to using them. Kids play with smaller kid toys in complicated ways.

I'm going to do a few things over at the house, Henry said.

HE WANDERED ABOUT Tender's house imagining himself in it. One time Baxter Penney, near his own car, waved at him. It surprised him—people can see me in here. What on earth do they think of me, rummaging through a dead man's house, staring at bracketed plates of Jesus and small union jacks from an early jubilee.

He made sandwiches and saw Colleen in her bright windbreaker walking up the road and she stopped in to say hello. Her hair was tied back savagely and she was excited about Tender's house and what did he think.

Well come in and have a look at it, he said.

I'm in the middle of my walk, she said.

You'll be walking the entire time. You can march on the spot, like a soldier.

But she stood still and soon understood the condition of it. With her hair pulled back it gave her face an abnormal intensity. Yes it requires a little work, she said. She turned and, guiding

Henry's elbows as though pushing a toy boat in water, stood him in the middle of the parlour.

I feel like some photograph from an earlier time.

She said, You could live in it until it falls down around your ears. She clapped her hands together then and twisted her wrist to the face of a watch.

What a walker, he thought. And wondered about her and Larry Noyce in bed. The thought shocked him. He felt a fizzle in his skin when he realized he was alone now, a condition he often wished for. But as soon as he had it another force arose from the hills: a sense of dread at his own company.

He watched Colleen head over the road and, two hours later, after he'd ripped a wall down to studs, he saw through the window that she had returned to drop in on Silvia. So he went over too. He was, he realized, becoming a busybody.

Look at him, Colleen said. He wants to stay home and take care of his hundred people.

Henry looked at her. What does that mean, he said. And how do you know.

It's written all over you.

Colleen marched off to her house, the snow recently ploughed from her frozen yard so it could be graded by heavy machinery, ready for a spring sowing of grass. The Poole brothers from the Goulds, men Henry was trying to get to okay the wiring in the house, were out there right now stringing a roll of ten-two through a new shed that had been built over the winter. They watched Colleen's arms pump hard as she turned into the concrete path before her house. What do you call that, Henry said.

Silvia: Her constitutional.

31

Take care of my hundred people. Was she mocking me? Am I a fraud? All he was doing in Afghanistan was escaping a city that had become Nora's city. It was John's idea—a good idea.

He drove to Wilson Noel's to buy traps and steel wool to plug holes in the Morris house as he found them. In the spring he'd have to cut away the grass sod from around the house.

On the way back he slowed down for a young man with a gas can hitchhiking. He pushed the paper sack with the traps from off the front seat for him.

Henry: Where are you broken down.

I don't have a car. It's a lot easier to get a ride if you have a gas can. I'm going to saw this baby in half and screw two hinges to it so I can carry my sandwiches.

You've got it all figured out.

He realized who the boy was, the American's son. He had long blond hair and blue eyes. He was staying in the lightkeeper's house. He was wearing a snowboarding jacket and had a stud in his ear. He smelled of pot.

You're Keith, Henry said.

I'm taking a pause from school, the boy said.

Henry thought about what that meant. This kid isn't going back to school. He has nothing with him in the way of supplies. Living on his own is the beginning of his manhood.

They talked about where Keith was from and what he was doing here in the middle of winter—hunting with Justin King, he said. Hunting what, Henry asked. Birds, Keith wasn't sure. Henry tried to sew together what might happen in the woods with guns.

It's been a while since I hunted, Henry said.

You want to come?

There's no room on one skidoo.

You can take the one next door to you, Keith said.

You know John Hynes?

I know what he's got in his shed.

The boy moved, with his leg, the bag of steel wool and traps. You got a couple of mice living with you?

You have to kill the enemy, Henry said. And stop their movement—that's what they taught us in Afghanistan and you deal with rodents the same way.

You were in the army?

Henry told him what he did.

If you don't mind me saying sir that's a pretty radical description of human life. That comparison to a mouse. I mean, you're back in civilization now.

Henry drove him into the cove—they passed Colleen walking and he waved—down to the lightkeeper's house.

Thanks a lot, the boy said.

I tell you what, Henry said. If you see a skidoo tomorrow morning you'll know it's me.

The boy didn't wave, just walked into the house and turned on the electric heat. There was a note under the door from Justin King. He'd come by with the truck in the morning.

THE BOY SLEPT THAT NIGHT in his father's bed. It was a better bed and you could see the ocean from this side of the house. He slept in his socks and T-shirt. He woke up with Justin King staring down at him. It was ten in the morning.

Before we go, Justin said, let's have a bowl of cereal.

It was two o'clock before they got their gear together and loaded the machine. Justin was eating one of his prepared sandwiches when they heard a snowmobile bombing down the road.

Who's he? Justin said. And Keith explained.

I'll follow you guys, Henry said.

No odds to me. You got some grub?

I made a lunch, Henry said.

We're staying overnight.

In the open?

In my uncle's cabin.

Let's roll.

THEY DROVE THEIR MACHINES into Kingmans Cove and turned into the soft powder of a woods trail through a cutover that was filled with new snow. These were Wilson Noel's woods. They had to be careful with the snowfall about getting out again. Henry followed the boys. He hadn't, in the end, set the traps. The boy had gotten to him. He realized he had to be careful how the world shapes your opinion. He'd spent the morning hauling the heavy tarp off John's machine and checking the oil and rocking it out of the ice and dry-starting it in the field between the two houses. It was a good machine. That decided things.

They pulled in where the power lines cut through a hillside. Snowmobiles had used the power line into the cabins. Some families even walked in on snowshoes with canvas sacks of provisions and dogs and their wives and children, Justin said. After this hunting trip he was on his way to the Burin to do his second block of sheet metal.

Keith cracked open a box of Black Horse beer and pulled out three bottles.

Having a few rips of horse, Justin said.

Henry joined them in a beer. And he got in tune with his younger self—the man he'd been before Nora Power. When he went to trade school with John and Tender and they all worked construction for Rick. But these boys were not like John and Tender. They were a new generation and they were preoccupied with different things. They started up the skidoos again and Keith got on the back behind Justin. They had to keep to the trail other machines had made, with the two of them on, Justin said. Too easy to get bogged down in the powder. They slung their machines under the wide branches of fir and spruce and across a frozen white bog and up a little incline. They stopped to ice-fish at a pond, and when it was starting to get dark, they turned on their ignitions. After about eight miles they lost the fresh track and had to push through, hoping they had kept to the high part of the trail. Henry got a little worried about the dark. John's snowmobile had a headlight, but barely. Justin was good, though. He knew the way. After an hour he called out over the engine and said the cabin was up ahead. And then on a rise Henry saw a hut sheathed entirely in realty signs. The signs lit up as their headlight passed over it. That's Wilson Noel's cabin, Justin said. We're almost there.

It was a blizzard now but there was hardly any new snow underfoot. It was as if snow only flew horizontally in this region and came to rest in other places. They zipped up their jackets and tugged down their hoods and Keith lit his pipe.

Take one last hoot on this, he said.

Henry: That stuff is too strong for me.

Keith passed it over to Justin who had his flashlight out trying to find his uncle's cabin. The flashlight was dazzling: big fat flakes that confused his eyelashes. There was a smaller, flakeless snow too that did not melt and then what felt like a third type—a hail of pellets that beat against your jacket and legs.

It's back this way, Justin said. It's terrible to be cold, travelling in the dark, and tired. But Henry had a pound of bacon in the knapsack and he knew how happy the boys would be to hear it sizzle in the camp, best sound in the world. His knapsack was full of food and he could feel a can of corned beef nudging his shoulder blade.

We're going to get tangly as fuck tonight, Justin said. And then remembered Henry. He stepped down from the grade of the track and fell through a shell of ice into a brook of water.

Justin was up to his waist in water and he looked a little shocked at the cold. His face was pale. He wasn't dressed for wind—denim is one of the coldest things you can wear.

Get his arm, Henry said.

He and Keith pulled him out and Henry was worried about hypothermia.

Where's the fucking cabin, he said.

The storm was constant and you got used to it. If you looked up, through the stream of snow, you saw the stars and the milky way. The storm was living in the first twenty feet of air.

They walked until Henry felt, in the darkness, the side of something. That's the cabin, Justin said, and Keith let out a little hooray. It was not a cheerful sound, he was cold too, and had gotten wet pulling Justin out. They were all a little discouraged. Henry was going to have to pull up the slack for the rest of the night. But it's Justin's turf. We'll get in there, light the stove and oil lamps, Henry said. Strip down and warm up and get that bacon on. Have a munch-out and after you guys can enjoy a few pipe tokes.

The door was padlocked but Justin found the key hanging on a nail in the eaves. Henry warmed the key in his mouth and banged off the padlock and tried the door but it was frozen shut. He pushed at it and it opened a crack. Henry shone the flashlight at the crevice and it looked like someone had pinned white canvas around the door. But Keith saw what it was. He'd been checking through the window.

The entire cabin, he said, is blocked with snow.

They pawed at the snow with their hands. The shovel was behind the door, Justin said. They were going to have to carve away the snow and get the door open and find a way around the door to the shovel and spend an hour or two just clearing out the camp. The snow was hard packed. That was when he heard a little wail coming out of Keith. He sounded like he was crying.

Wait, Justin said. He put a shell in his gun.

Henry: What the fuck are you doing.

Justin shot twice into the snowbank. The snow broke into chunks and Keith revived himself and tumbled them out. The shots alarmed Henry. He felt out of control and he knew Justin was doing something insane. He was loading the gun again with birdshot and Henry asked him, sternly, for the gun. Justin handed it over, but as soon as Henry held it he shared in the vengeance they were having now on winter—he fired from the hip and the boys cheered and pulled out large boulders of snow. He fired again and cried out loud and tears harmed his vision. He stopped shooting and the boys did not go at the snow but stared at him in wonder. Here's some more shells, Justin said, but Henry Hayward was on his knees, sobbing.

Justin: Wow man the war kind of fucked you up didn't it.

Oh, so that was the story on him. It felt, to Henry, like they had cornered an animal and were killing it bit by bit.

The cabin door wide open now. I'm sorry boys, he said. Just a little overwrought here.

He broke the gun to make sure it was empty. Then they heard, in the wind, the low chug of a small generator. Off to the east, Wilson Noel's cabin, the windows flared up from a dull orange to a bright white. Parts of FOR SALE signs, houses that had been bought and sold for many years on the Avalon. Wilson's here, Justin said. And Wilson Noel's door flung open, the shape of a man. Who's shooting at the Kings?

It's me, Justin said. Justin King.

As he said it, it registered in Henry that Wilson Noel had asked the question almost in a jocular fashion, as if he'd like to join in the fun of destroying some Kings. But Wilson Noel was only trying to understand what could prompt anyone to start firing into a house packed with snow.

32

I'm sorry, Martha said, it's so early I know I just woke up at dawn and I like to drive when no one's on the road so I came straight out but the storm door was hasped and I thought you might be in there overcome with carbon monoxide so that's why I banged until you woke up.

It was Saturday morning. Henry had spent the day before in bed. Wilson Noel had taken them into his cabin that night and, after a glass of Canadian Club and water, he'd slept in a bunk, head to foot with this man he had just met. The boys shared the other bed. The boys were embarrassed by the whole experience, the getting wet, the cabin full of snow, Henry's reaction. They did not hunt but turned back to Renews, exhausted. Henry had left his gear in the porch and climbed upstairs. And now a knock on the door.

Henry looked out the window, expecting it to be Silvia with the kids warning him she was there, but it was Martha Groves.

I have not been overcome, he said.

He let her in and put on the kettle. He could see now the pregnancy. He wasn't sure what to do about this foreign element and his own knowledge of it but he felt a loyalty to Tender and he would defend this loyalty although he had no idea how it would be employed.

It was cold and the water was still shut off so he was refilling the blue container Colleen had given him.

I know that's bizarre that thought about the asphyxiation but when you work in a hospital you see everything and so every possibility gets into your head.

He decided to keep things light. Nothing about pregnancy or the house. He must have appeared very distant.

I've come about the house, she said. I heard you got through to the Careens. I'm really sorry about the house, it just come to me when I saw your cheque I thought, three thousand dollars, for what. I'm not saying it should be more and I know you and Tender were close—

We weren't close. Tender was close with John Hynes and I know John. Me and John go way back.

You went to trade school with Tender.

I know Tender but I wouldn't say I was familiar with him.

You were over there together. You were the one he last saw.

And suddenly a moment returned to Henry. This was years ago. They were required, for their underwater welding, to take a scuba diving course. John was paired with their instructor so Tender was Henry's buddy in the water. They pulled on their neoprene suits and hoisted on the air tanks and masks and stepped backwards in their fins and fell ass-first into the sea. They swam out to meet their instructor. The OK to Tender. Then something happened. Henry met a ledge in the sea floor and sank towards it. He felt himself accelerate and the sea darken, he was falling but could not tell which way was up. The sea was black. Then something tugged his arm and it was Tender Morris pointing at his chest. Tender had followed Henry down, grabbed him and gave the proper hand signal: add air to your buoyancy compensator. They rose together.

It occurred to me when I saw your cheque, Martha said, if you want a place for the summer then you can have the place but maybe I could come out here now and again. When you're not here is what I mean.

So it was all out in the open. She blurted out her intentions and he realized he was conniving. He was using cunning against Tender Morris's wife. You want to own half the house, he said.

And you're wondering which half.

He laughed. My god she was young. And yet how far from that youth was he. She was, in fact, older than him by six months. We're all youthful.

The truth is, she said. And couldn't say it.

Animate. Words in a kitchen not his own. A woman telling him this—she was trying to let him know.

Silvia, he said. She let me know about your situation.

Okay good, she said. Then you'll understand that this house is all I have left of the baby's father.

Various parts of this shocked him alive and held him against the back of a chair.

It's absurd, she said. She had refused to think it could be. You were there when he got leave.

I was, he said.

I knew as soon as it happened, she said. Tender left and I knew I wasn't alone. Then when I heard from John I just couldn't believe it. I was waiting to tell him and then two officers come to the door with a priest like I need a priest, and this feels like something from another century. My first thought was this isn't real. He was injured, I can deal with injury. I work with it every day. You're not here to tell me what you're here to tell me.

Henry was astonished at this candour.

I'm sort of going out of my mind, she said.

Why didn't you tell me.

When would I have told you.

Perhaps before the night we had.

I didn't know that was going to happen. I mean nothing happened. Okay something happened but we were flailing with grief. Well, I was.

It was very moving.

I know it was, Henry. Everything's been so crazy.

I love you, he said. I mean, if that helps. I could love you.

She looked at him knowing that he had spoken honestly.

What about Nora, she said.

It's been a year. More than a year.

I don't think you can love me and her at the same time.

Do you still love Tender Morris?

Tender is dead. And I've seen the way you look at me.

I'll say it again, he said. I could love you.

It was as true as the way he had said it to Nora when she asked him to leave. Something he was proud of saying, but also surprised by.

I'm not sure we know what we're doing, Martha said.

So let's just be honest. Let's be disciplined and vulnerable and absorb punishment and try to be generous.

She breathed out. She was taking little breaths in but mainly expelling air. Then she looked across the street and got up. She straightened herself out.

I'm going to keep the house, she said. Or a part of it. In case you change your crazy mind.

Because of the baby.

Letting it go feels wrong. Perhaps we can split it.

I'll take the kitchen and the parlour. You can have—

He pointed up the stairs.

He pulled out his pocket knife and punctured a can of evaporated milk. He put his body in between the puncturing and Martha. She had those grey eyes and fair hair and she moved with fast gestures and she was nervous and she was mentioning Tender without emotion. She was four months pregnant. You could tell, now that you knew. She carried high. She wore boots with felt liners. She had big feet or the boots could have been Tender's— Silvia did the same with John's clothes. Had Nora ever worn his clothes? Martha took care of herself with what she had nearby. He didn't even know if they'd moved in together but what they'd done was move towards each other.

Silvia likes it out here, Henry said.

Martha didn't answer that. Martha would know Silvia's opinions on Nora and himself. Instead she asked a question of her own. Why wouldn't you say you were close? she said. To Tender.

Because it's true.

You didn't like him?

It's not that, he said.

Tender was waiting for a furlough, she said. You get a deferment or I'm not sure what it's called you'd know better than me. He was a reservist and he volunteered. He didn't have to go over. He wanted to get a medal and then work for Rick Tobin. He got me pregnant and went back to finish up his service.

I don't know any of the terms, he said.

Because you're not a soldier.

Tender Morris named what I am.

She kissed him. Then said, We shouldn't shut the curtains or Baxter Penney over there is going to talk it up.

That startled him. He told her how much help Baxter had been, and friendly. Baxter was in the police force, Martha said, he was one of the first cops along the shore here and he's very good at putting two and two together. Anyway I'll sign whatever you want. I wasn't going to live out here, not without Tender.

She left then. It was getting to be a nice day out and he walked her to her car.

33

How would he do this. Who was she to him. What did he need and what did she need. Do we need people. Parents, offspring, census reports. Marry her. It felt reassuring, that he could muster up the protection a child would need and he would be fostering love, creating something that was not his own, but marshalling up an inner strength to help what existed outside of himself. Not a hundred people, but two.

He worked on the house and thought about Martha as a mantra that lay in his jaws. He wasn't living a dangerous life, but taking care of his hundred people. Minister without portfolio!

It was spring now and it rained for eight days straight, killing all the snow. The roof leaked. Everything should be made of plastic, including the birds and animals. The cows were calving.

John had arrived, home from Alberta. Still operating a mile underground. He came up to Renews to see how Henry was doing at the house. He was cooking sausages on a barbecue in the rain.

John: What I love about that liquor store in the Goulds is how the woman at the cash she takes the neck of a whiskey bottle and tips it upside down, flaps open a narrow paper bag, and slides the bottle in.

He paused to indicate the erotic nature of this act.

Henry: I love driving a car on the shore road. There's no anxiety. Gas. Wiper fluid. Radio. Knowing where I'm to go.

Everyone wakes up at three in the morning, Henry. No one forgets the small hours. War is just the small hours and no bigger hours.

It's always three am in the army.

Go ahead be sarcastic. I enjoy being disturbed. It makes me alive.

Henry: Are you saying everyone is at war?

Not everyone is wearing a three-point chin strap but they're still at war. They are, in fact, more vulnerable.

Because they think they're behind the front lines.

Now you're talking. Minister without portfolio right there.

Don't fucking call me that.

John was hurt.

It's disparaging, Henry said.

You don't even know what it means.

It means I have no purpose and no moral compass.

It means you're so capable you're to oversee everything.

Tender was judging me.

He judged you to the good.

The rain made the sausages sizzle. Baxter came over and said he needed a hand. If you have a couple of minutes. Henry got some bread and mustard and made three sausage sandwiches but Baxter wouldn't take one so they followed him in the rain to the barn. He said his cow had been labouring all yesterday and last night he went to bed, convinced she wouldn't give birth, but in the morning the calf was hanging half out of the mother.

John: You left her there with the calf half out of her all night?

Baxter: I should have stayed up. We pulled the calf out and it was dead so I got her in the back of the truck here.

There was a shape under a canvas tarp.

The barn was dark inside. The cow lying down in the corner. She lost power in the back legs.

They finished their sandwiches and ducked into the low door. There was a man at the rail and he had hooks for hands. This was Colleen's father, Emerson Grandy. Henry remembered the story Rick told of him losing his hands. You heard, loudly, the rain on the roof. The wood rails and walls for the pens had a polished oily sheen as if many animals have brushed up against this wood over the past century. The lack of electricity made it feel like you were walking into a timeless zone. The rafters were dry and clear and the floor was dirt and Emerson Grandy was sucking on a cigarette and staring at the cow with no affection. The cow was sitting on the ground. She won't get up, Baxter said. I'm afraid she's after cutting off the circulation. We got to move her over but she's heavy.

John walked around the cow. Have you milked her?

Didn't think to, Baxter said. John knelt down and lifted the hind leg away and the udder was swollen and sore.

Her milk is in, so that's painful.

He started milking the cow. The milk sprayed seven feet out towards the men standing at the rail. Get me a bucket, John said. Baxter left the barn and came in with an empty riblet pail from the house. Emerson kept smoking and not looking at what was going on in front of him. His cigarette and the riblet pail were the only modern things. John held the pail and aimed the teat at it. The cow was interested for a second and then returned to staring straight ahead. John pushed on the udder and pulled the teat in and out and got the milk flowing and filled up the pail and that got Emerson's attention.

Let's try lifting the side of her, John said. Henry came in the pen with him and they knelt and John said to Emerson, Take her head. Emerson spat out his cigarette and took her head with his elbows and Henry and John lifted and Henry could feel the man's elbows near his head and he thought of how he'd lost his hands with that five-ton cement pipe coming down onto his wrists, the hands must have sat by themselves somewhere like a pair of gloves.

The cow repositioned her front feet and lowered her nose. Let's try the other side, John said. The trouble was the long hind leg splayed out like that and you couldn't lift her without it acting like a lever against them.

You got a rope, John said.

Baxter searched his head for rope.

They looked around in the barn, into the rafters, looking for ten feet of rope. I'll check my shed, John said.

They walked across the road to John's. The shed was full of tools from when John worked construction. His sledgehammer at the door—what Rick called John's persuader. He's got nothing over there, John said.

What do you mean.

That barn, there's not even a stick of wood. They're poor people.

Baxter gave me a kerosene heater.

That's the last thing he had.

They tied a pulley under a beam and threaded a rope through and used a come-along to winch up the cow around the midriff. Henry and John under one of the haunches and they'd convinced Emerson Grandy to push in the extended hind leg as the cow was raised. At first the rope sort of tightened and was collected through the come-along to no appreciable movement. Then the cow was lifted. Baxter yanked the cow's tail. They had the cow half up but she still wasn't on her feet and the winch rope was tied into her gut. The cow's eyes were bulging with shock as she teetered, her hindquarters high in the air with no purchase. Boys you're busting her up, Baxter said, and it was true, John had to let her down but at least she was sitting now on her other leg. She looked like she knew what she was doing.

I'm going to have to kill her, Baxter said. He was disgusted with himself for having slept through the night.

You can't shoot an animal that still eats and drinks, John said. A hundred-dollar fine.

Emerson: I lost a horse once in a barn. Had to tear the wall out to get the horse through.

Baxter: And they won't use her for beef. Have to bury her in Aquaforte. You're not allowed to bury her on your property.

Feed is twenty dollars a sack, Emerson said. Seven sacks all winter I fed the goat. Now they want me to give it away.

Baxter: Nothing's no good no more. You can't make a living in animals.

He threw an armload of hay at the cow's head and she started munching. As they left the barn John stopped and turned and rubbed the bridge of his broken nose and launched himself once more at the cow. He slid on his knees into the soiled hay and slammed his face into the cow. With a tremendous heave he lifted the cow up singlehandedly onto her feet. She staggered and fell against the back wall and righted herself and shook John off her legs and steadied her bearing. John's face was purple, his chest hoovering air. He held the rail and caught his breath. His fingers were trembling. Emerson Grandy laughed and shook his head. That was something, he said.

Henry took John by the arm and walked him out of the barn. At Baxter's truck he stopped to gather himself. He laid his wrists over the side of the truck bed, exhausted, and his fingers grazed the blue tarpaulin and Henry saw that something stirred. He flipped over the tarpaulin they had laid over the dead calf. The calf's clear open eye.

John, look at this.

This animal is alive.

Baxter: What's that?

Get this calf some milk. Get that beef bucket over here.

In a week, both the cow and calf were walking along the hill into Kingmans Cove.

34

Henry stripped the house to studs, then wired and insulated it and stapled in a six-millimetre vapour barrier. He left the walls open so an electrician could inspect the work. He printed off his bank balance and realized he needed work. He emailed Rick in Alberta. You got your class one heavy truck? I drove the bobtail for you didn't I, Henry said. You can drive a dump for Wilson Noel.

It was one of the trucks Rick Tobin had shipped back from Alberta. Rick had a piece of Wilson Noel's operation. It came with a grey credit card in a pouch on the windshield for fuel. The one advisory Wilson gave was don't go shooting shotguns inside the truck.

Henry sat there while Leonard King operated a front-end loader and dug out a basement and filled his tandem. Leonard adjusted the gears and steering while flipping a white beard up and over his free hand. Henry had an order sheet for customers looking for fill along the shore and, while he waited for Leonard, he arranged the deliveries to avoid a dead head. At four o'clock Henry drove the empty truck back to Wilson Noel's and got in his car and headed to Tender's house.

He hadn't done much upstairs. There were still bags of garbage beside the bed Nellie Morris had used. He looked into one and there was a religious book—a study guide to scripture. In the book a small photograph, an old studio shot of two men in military outfits. One man sitting and the other standing beside him.

Brothers.

Henry couldn't tell but the style suggested an era from eighty years ago, or during world war one. Impulsively he searched the garbage bags. It was mostly clothing and bathing products—shampoo and soap and shower curtains, all of which seemed strange for a house with no running water. There was a magnifying glass with a compass embedded in its handle. The compass was so small you needed a magnifying glass to see it. Which created a problem he thought about for some time.

In a small leather pouch was the photo of a girl. She was about five years old, standing outside at the corner of a house. Henry recognized the framing of the window as the type used in Tender's house. So he walked to that window. He stood where the girl had stood and felt a bend in his dimensions. The girl Nellie Morris had. The one out of wedlock that died of consumption.

He used a wooden ammunition box to keep anything that seemed valuable and threw out the rest. He was going to use Wilson Noel's dump to haul this all to the incinerator.

EACH NIGHT HE TURNED off Baxter's kerosene heater and walked over the field and ate his dinner in John and Silvia's electrically heated house. Meat and liquor, come ahead. He played crib solitaire. They played a lot of crib in Afghanistan and he remembered Tender with his head of red hair and the Russian vodka they drank. He drank to the men, to Tender. If he had the energy he walked out to the abandoned community of Kingmans Cove and stood in his root cellar. The roof of slate covered in grass sod, so it was like a Viking house. Wilson Noel had told him he planned to put a vegetable garden out here—he owned family land on the hill that was all trees now. The trees he had skidooed through. It would have to be cleared. Henry stepped down into the cellar that pointed out to sea. My secret place, Henry said aloud—so it wasn't a secret that he kept from the land. He wanted the land to know.

35

Wilson Noel, after work, was leading a volunteer group to help foster sports within the municipality. The Poole brothers would be there—they're the ones who pass wiring. In Afghanistan they had power and water within seventy-two hours of occupation. And here Henry had gone two months without electricity.

He said he had a bit of time.

He got to the arena early and watched a goalie tug on his skates. This was Wayne Poole. The man's son was with him, studying his father's accurate hands on the thick white laces. Wayne Poole had pulled on blue hockey pants and the wide shoulder pads and chest protector. A black canvas bag of gear he was donning, and his son rocking on his heels, his belly sticking out, his hands under his armpits, resting.

You're in Nellie Morris's old house, Wayne said. He stood up and, in his skates, looked about seven feet tall. We got a call from Martha.

His son handed him his goalie stick.

The house belonged to a goalie, Henry said.

We know Tender Morris, Wayne said.

Henry asked about passing code. Don't worry, Wayne said, we can wire your house. You're a friend of Rick's.

I got it wired, Henry said. I just need the panel hooked up and the connections in the boxes.

You need an okay from a licensed contractor—Rick told us.

The son was running back to the door in the boards and Wayne Poole, in his goalie skates, tiptoed after him. Henry followed them. The zamboni honked as he curled the machine out of a corner. That's my brother, Wayne said.

It looked like it was powered by steam and Henry had forgotten a zamboni had a horn. But the driver saw the boy—his nephew—and his manners were the polite ones we think workers had back in the days of steam power.

Wayne was adjusting his white helmet with its plastic-coated visor cage. He stepped onto the ice and stumbled and caught himself on his arms, the goalie stick slapping against the ice. His son was shocked at his father's slip.

Henry watched a bit of the game. The zamboni driver, Mark Poole, came over with Wilson Noel—they were eating hamburgers cooked in a truck near the skating rink. Henry waited for Wilson Noel to tell him what to do. They were unrolling the winter tennis court out over the soccer field, heaters forcing in air, stuffing the giant tent like a turkey. Wilson gave him a big maroon-hooded coat. It takes three hours, Wilson said, for the roof of the tennis bubble to teeter into the night air. The floodlights came on. The roof staggered up and the work crew affixed the doors. Heavy steel doors with locks but no windows. The doors were the only substantial thing about the tennis bubble. You need a password to unlock the door, a metal door you could not break through and yet a lazy person with a kitchen knife could carve out a door at the far end and play tennis at the other end without any deflation during his game. I guess they think people only use doors to get in and out of places, Henry thought, but the locked door of a winter tennis bubble is a hilarious fact daring you to be creative. As he stepped back to make sure the bubble was fully inflated he realized this tent type was the kind they used in Afghanistan. He had come around in a bubble like this after the jeep blew up, and he shuddered at the memory which ambushed him.

36

He worked hard for Wilson Noel for a couple of weeks and appreciated the coastline when he took a break and, instead of eating his lunch in the truck, drove into the Goulds to have a meal cooked in that restaurant with the painting of Venice as a window. He met Martha here and they both laughed that they were going on dates. Thanks for taking me to Italy, she said. I don't mind splashing out, he said.

Then she drove back into town to deal with a patient recovering from injury to her pelvic floor. Henry picked up supplies and hand tools and materials and food and ice and beer and bandaids and fresh water. He knew little of this shore. Driving back from the Goulds you passed through some pretty towns along the road and, unfortunately, the first thing you saw when you hit Renews was a memorial centre with no windows for a young bright hockey player who died early and the funeral home with gaudy brick pillars and chainlink fencing, the home that Tender had been laid out in.

Then, one day, Martha's car pulled up. Unexpected.

She opened the trunk and took out a box of garbage bags and

a jug of detergent and a squeeze mop and a red ten-gallon plastic bucket.

Another car arrived and parked behind her, a two-door Fiesta. There was an electrical mast hanging out of the open passenger window. It was the Poole brothers from the Goulds.

I called a few people, she said, and bumped us up on the electrical list.

You could have told me and saved me from volunteering.

Both Pooles climbed out of the car on the driver's side, unbuckling their knees that were cramped in the pushed-forward front seats. They had a reciprocating saw on the back seat and coils of wire. When they got out of the car they brushed themselves off, they might have had sawdust on them.

Have you got power, Mark said.

You mean electricity?

Just a little bit to run the saw.

You make it sound like a little bit of electricity can exist where large amounts do not.

There's an existing service.

Henry told them the power was cut off eight years ago.

Well now we're up to speed, aren't we.

We may be slow but eventually we catch up.

They were careful pulling the mast arm over arm out of the car window, then they lugged it to the corner of the house and propped it up in the crook of the front porch where the old service was. They were both looking around to see what they had there. It looked like they were still half hoping there'd be hydro stored somehow in the non-conforming wire. Have you got an extension cord?

Boys I got nothing electrical, Henry said. Nothing in that line of business whatsoever.

He's got no power, Mark.

He's waiting for the power, Wayne. Before he moves into the investment of electrical wares.

That's why he haven't been by the shop.

He might be better off staying—what do you call it.

Off the grid, Wayne said.

We shouldn't bother him on a commitment to electricity.

Tempt him you mean.

He might get used to it.

Run up a bill.

Who's next on our list?

Martha stepped in. Guys, we really appreciate you being here.

They were into it now. He and Martha were pursuing Tender's ambition. It astonished him and made him feel guilty. That he was enjoying her. He was supposed to be bearing a cross but this was an ambush of joy. Seeing her, realizing she had drive and could lead manoeuvres better than himself. One of the Pooles was staring at the roof of Baxter Penney's house across the road and the other pointed with his forehead over at John and Silvia's. Their porch light was still on from the last time John was out. The yellow bulb shone in the daylight, betraying a house packed with electrical potential.

Go over and ask if they have an extension cord. And string it over the field.

That's a good two hundred feet, Henry said.

He's got a point there, a very good point in fact. It's going to take a couple of extension cords, Wayne.

The two brothers discussed feeding it across the road from Baxter's.

Same distance and then you've got a wire on the road and I don't want to deal with old Baxter Penney, do you want to deal with Baxter Penney?

The other Poole, Mark, was sizing up the front of the house. Then he looked straight up at the eaves. Have you got a ladder? he said.

Christ.

Wayne Poole and Mark Poole. Goalie and zamboni driver. They walked inside to study the panel.

All this has to be stripped out, Mark said.

This is the good white wire I just stapled in.

You can't have wire running over the ceiling, it has to be enclosed and you need ten-two wiring in the outlets. Look at that fuse box, Wayne said.

I'm expecting you to replace the panel.

They sized things up in a disapproving way, as if this was the first time they'd ever seen a house in as shabby a condition, and it irritated Henry that they were posturing, these men with no tools or a gasoline generator.

We'll have to run back to the shop for a panel, Wayne said.

Mark said in the meantime Wayne could open up the wall with the reciprocating saw.

You have any plans for that old fuse box?

Henry could tell, in the tone of the question, that Wayne had his eye on it.

You're saying that panel's no good.

It might be fit for a camp. For instance, I've got a little camp down in Horsechops. If I ever put a service in there.

Are you saying you could use it?

I have a camp, he said again.

He did not want to ask for it.

You can have it, Martha said.

This seemed to turn Wayne a little bit. He glanced over at Mark.

If you're only using the house for a summer place.

It's true we could just put in a few outlets and such, Mark said.

The wiring upstairs, like he says, it's good wire.

We could let that go.

As long as they know it's not standard.

Martha said she was fine with that, they weren't living in a standard way, were they, she said to Henry.

MARK AND WAYNE BORROWED an aluminum ladder from Colleen Grandy—avoiding Baxter Penney entirely—and strung the extension cords across the field from John and Silvia's. They installed the new panel and removed the old mast. They actually worked hard. They stopped work at ten for a coke and a chocolate bar and then at noon when the church bell rang out they sat outside with their sandwiches in plastic wrap and more cokes. They were done by four o'clock. Henry pulled a few beers out of the cooler and they all sat down outside and stared at the back hills where the cows were grazing. A patch of sunlight drifted across the green and burgundy gorse.

If we'd known you were doing up Nellie's old house, Mark said. He lit a cigarette and held it out of the wind. We got confused with that American down the road—Rick's got an embargo on that house. Who knows why. Can't do no work on it, is that right Wayne?

Wayne said he didn't know he just got his instructions from Wilson Noel.

Mark turned his attention to the history of Tender's house. Old Careen his wife was after dying was it, Wayne? Then he married Nellie Morris.

Again, Wayne didn't know and it didn't matter in Wayne's mind. The past was beyond figuring out.

They drank their beer and Mark finished his cigarette. They were giving a thought up to Aubrey Morris who had built this house a hundred years ago with about as much tools as they had and now they were finally putting good electrical wiring into it.

Nothing's changed in fifty years, Wayne said. I remember my father talking about this house. He said the Morrises had money. Well I'll tell you, if they had it, they must have buried it in the yard someplace because they didn't put it in the house.

I wonder where she's buried, Martha said.

Where who's buried.

Nellie Morris. We'd like to visit her. She's not in the cemetery where Tender is.

She's in the home in Aquaforte, Wayne said.

Henry and Martha thought about those words. Those words did not mean she was dead.

Are you saying she's alive?

She was two weeks ago. My grandmother's in there. Talks to Nellie every day.

But we have her last will and testament.

Mark: You don't have to be dead for a will and testament. More than likely she just signed over authority.

37

When the brothers left, the handles of some grocery bags lifted up and fluttered. John and Silvia drove by. They had the kids. I had no idea she was still alive, Martha said. Tender never visited her. Not that I knew. He just always talked about her house.

She was opening a physiotherapy book and, as she flexed the binding, it bucked free. It sort of flitted like a small animal.

Henry: What does this mean, this fact that she's alive?

It means we have to visit her.

Does it mean we own this house.

We have to make sure she doesn't, at the last minute, change her mind about anything.

She may not be in any state to change her mind.

Someone could change it for her.

Let's think of other things.

Let's get the kids.

John was standing on the grass barefoot with washed hair in a white bathrobe, a towel over his shoulders under his robe. Silvia was in the porch brushing the dog. Clem and Sadie were making bracelets from willow branches with a boy from down the road who was recovering from having all his teeth pulled. Wolf bolted out and Henry fell to his knees and wrestled with the dog. Martha explained they'd come to borrow the kids.

Let there be light, John said. He held an aluminum tray with four large raw steaks and he shoved the steaks on the roof of his shed and opened the shed door and wheeled out the propane barbecue which you lifted like a wheelbarrow. Stop making love to Wolf, he said.

Henry: I'm so horny for your dog.

You with a woman over there and you're after our dog.

He has so much love to give, Martha said.

As though there was a relationship between them. Silvia asked where did you put the steaks and John had forgotten where the steaks were and when they all saw them on the roof of the shed John acted perplexed on how they had gotten up there. Blame the dog, Henry said. John had to stand on tiptoes to get the steaks and then he laid them on top of his car and donned an oven mitt to lift the lid on the barbecue and turned the nozzle on the propane clockwise, it was threaded so you had to consciously want the propane on. John and Henry had spent five hours one afternoon putting this barbecue together. Men trained in precise technical instruments were on their knees howling with tears of rage at the barbecue installation instructions.

They told them what they had learned from the brothers Poole.

Live in the house, occupy the house, do not give up one inch of territory to the enemy, John said.

You heard the propane coursing through the rubber pipe and belting out the burners full bore and John struck the match with the oven mitt on and threw the match towards the grate of the barbecue and a blue curtain of flame shot up with a terrific whump of force, a sound you almost felt on your legs and eyelashes as you sat in your Adirondack chairs with an open beer, then the flames behaved themselves and knelt under the grate and conspired patiently, waiting their chance to kill the meat except John was once again looking for where he'd put the goddamned steaks.

They had to be careful with their swearing and with talk of horny dogs and usurping house ownership for this road out to the lighthouse was a Catholic road with many gravestones dating back to the 1700s, graves that were groomed and clipped out and lilac bushes trimmed back once a year by relatives who now lived in other parts of the world, but the old-timers who still lived on the road did not like curse words and they eschewed vulgarity and what was considered vulgar was very mild indeed. Their friend Tender Morris was living in the graveyard now so they had some licence to be themselves. They had paid the price and the older generation like Baxter Penney heard their silly ways, the inane almost pathetic ways of the young and the wayward—for they were all wayward, this generation, even if they knew how walls were wired and cement mixed and a rotting sill replaced.

Henry drank his beer and Martha sat on the arm of the Adirondack chair and they watched with great pleasure as John Hynes scraped the barbecue then sprayed a non-stick product onto the grill. There was a whiff of the spray. The steaks were now, inconceivably, in a plastic bag tied in a half hitch and hanging from the clothesline.

Sadie was too deep into the bracelets so Henry took Clem's small, warm hand and they walked him over the path in the field between the two houses, a path that families had been using as a shortcut for a hundred years. A little bone in Clem's wrist clicked and suddenly Henry felt grown-up. He had a responsibility that was not of his own choosing. Baxter Penney was across the road and what would he think of him and Martha with this little boy in tow. Baxter, recovering from the neglect of his cows. A hot power was pushing through Clem's wrist into Henry's arm like an electrical pulse and it was all he could do to let go of the hand when they'd cleared the tall grass and reached the back of the house. His best friend's son. It is impossible for any of us to understand everything these days and the way these days are marching it will become even harder for one of us to even specialize in a field, for fields are being divided into narrow drills and it is difficult for a person to raise their chin from the crop they are sowing to see what is being broadcast from afar.

Martha showed Clem the light switch and asked him to do the honour.

Ta-da!

The old days are over, Henry said. And Clem ran from room to room, flicking on lights. Henry turned on the new radio and the first electrical song was opera.

Clem: Is that a hockey game singer?

Let's go outside, Henry said.

They stood in the backyard and looked. Each window neatly lit against the side of the house. A house with the hum of electrical components.

38

Come on, coat, he said.

They drove up the shore to Aquaforte. It was right on the road and had a little verandah with three chairs and the chairs were occupied with women watching the traffic go by. He carried the garbage bag in and Martha asked at the little window for a Nellie Morris. She's after having her lunch, the woman said. She'll be in her room.

They walked down to number 17 and knocked. A man in a white outfit in the hall said he'd help. The man opened the door and called in, Nellie? You have company.

She was sitting in a chair beside her bed.

We're living in your house, Henry said.

She said, Of course you are.

We brought you your coat, Martha said.

And Henry removed the coat from the bag.

That'll be good for the winter, she said. Just hang it in the closet over there. Behind the door.

They sat with her and remembered she was ninety-eight years

old. There had been newspapers on the walls from when the *Titanic* sank, and she was alive for that.

We came to ask about the well, he said. If there's a well that works.

A well, she said.

A well to go with the house.

I recall that voice, she said. You were at the funeral. Patrick's funeral.

Yes, Henry said. We were both there.

You left early. I was on my own with Gertrude Poole. I had to go to the bar to get a shot of screech. Did you see those boys up there sitting by the casket?

Martha: They were his nephews.

They wanted it open to see if uncle was in there. But he was all broken up. Did you get married?

We're not married. But we're together.

My daughter was married. She had two weddings. Just like my own. I had one in St John's and one in Renews. We brought our own liquor—there was an open bar at both. It was the wintertime and they pulled us there in a sled. My father had a banner put over the road with our names on it. But now my daughter's wedding they had this mountain of lobster, scallops, crab—more than what Dermot Ivany will land this year. The salad had something tasty thrown on it.

Did she know who they were? Was she just talking to talk? She had worked at McMurdo's pharmacy in town. Then married Melvin Careen. She had a daughter but the daughter died young.

Melvin Careen was my husband, she said. He was a Newfoundlander born in Brooklyn. His father was high steel—

the building going on up there. Have you been upalong? The money. All the doodads.

We came about a doodad.

A well, Martha clarified.

Oh yes the well. You knows as well as I do Pat we always meant to get around to digging a well.

That stopped them.

What did you do for water, Martha said.

I must have woken up a married woman, all told, twenty thousand times thinking we'd have a well at the end of the day. We went to the brook.

You drank water from the brook?

You know better than that, Pat. We went down to the cove for fresh water. There's a little spring in the rocks.

In Kingmans Cove.

That's where we're all from. You're from there too.

They sat there and talked with her about the seniors complex. They knew Rick Tobin who built it. Well tell him we need more windows. And where are the boats? He promised tours. You can't see anything from these rooms.

How are the bathrooms.

Who cares about those things.

39

Martha drove back into town—she was overseeing the production of photographs of a lumbar region to supply a website image bank. The body, she explained, is no longer thought of as segments, but as a dynamic chain.

I thought it was thought of as the servant of the mind.

Henry cleaned up things and used the last of the water from the blue container. He drove down the shore to Bay Bulls. He watched the shrimp boats come in and the men gently nudge heavy tubs of shrimp in the hoist up to the wharf apron where there was a conveyor belt to transport the shrimp directly into the side of the plant. Seagulls sat along the lip of the conveyor belt. He drove into the Goulds and up to Bill Wiseman's office. He explained things to Bill Wiseman.

If you work things out with this Martha Groves, Bill Wiseman said, all you'll be getting is a quick claim deed. If no one says boo to you for fifteen years, possessory title. I can't stress this enough, buying this house is putting money into a penny stock. No one can grant you good title. All you can use is a legal term: This is the title Henry Hayward has with an understanding.

HE DROVE SLOWLY BACK TOWARDS Renews and stopped in to Wilson Noel's and bought a set of identical padlocks and a keyed entry deadbolt. He drove down the shore road and pulled into the grass of the house he may or may not own a half of and tore the padlocks out of their packaging and slapped a lock on the front porch storm door and one on the door to the shed. He installed the deadbolt to the rear door. He left a set of keys behind a frying pan hooked on the pantry wall in John Hynes's house and crossed the street and gave a rear door key to Baxter Penney. In case Martha ever needs to get in there, he said.

PART TWO

1

Renews was an old place, a town built on the mouth of a river with wharves and fishing stages that allowed quick access to the sea—the locals speak of the *Mayflower* coming into port in 1620 to take on fresh water and slaughter animals before continuing on to Plymouth. This was their first landing in the new world, but of course the *Mayflower* hauled up its kegs filled in the river and butchered pig purchased from a Mr Morris and moved on. The pirate Peter Easton operated from here and buried his treasure beneath oak planks under several hills and peculiar rocks. After breaching Fort San Felipe del Morro in Puerto Rico—something not even Francis Drake could do—Easton settled with his two thousand tons of gold in Savoy. The French and the English marched overland in the dead of winter and blew up each other's fortifications and voluntarily burned themselves to the ground on occasion, to prevent resources from falling into enemy hands. The native Beothuk were driven inland early on, terrified of the European destruction. The masterless men followed, living illegally along the riverbanks deep into the ponds of Butterpot, refusing the authority of the British crown who hunted them down and strung them up on the yardarm. William Jackman, a man from Renews, saved an entire crew of a Labrador shipwreck by swimming twenty-seven times out to their ship in the freezing Atlantic. He probably had a rope in his teeth. William Harding, having suffered trenchfoot, influenza, scabies and syphilis, had his intestines slung across the faces of his comrades during the third battle of Ypres.

Renews was allowed to build up several centuries of secure English access to cod, thanks to the Treaty of Utrecht, but the invention of refrigeration and the majority vote for confederation with Canada tore away any sustainable fishing practice that made sense to a small community. The only independent country in the history of the world to voluntarily give up self-rule—damn you England and to hell with you Canadian wolf.

Renews was a place to gather yourself before heading off to what your new life was. Renews. You could say the warm marine layer from New England drifted up to shake hands with the cold Labrador current and form a bank of sirens that dissolved souls, but the ones who survived into modern times worked for the Department of Highways and the fish plant in Bay Bulls and the university in St John's. After running through the cod and salmon and herring and mackerel and tuna and turbot and shark and redfish and periwinkle and shrimp and lobster and halibut and scallops and haddock and flounder and squid and three types of crab and caplin and eel and lumpfish roe and pollock and sea cucumber and whelk and sea urchins—after all that they managed to clear land deep in the woods for rudimentary failed aquaculture and then marched to the sea again to stake out cultivated mussels in the sheltered ice-free saltwater coves and they converted front rooms of tidy bungalows into hair salons with pun names and worked for forestry and dairy and they laboured intensively with poultry and they hung signs off mailboxes selling fresh eggs and they operated convenience stores with tanning beds and bed-and-breakfasts with backyard nine-hole mini-golf courses and mink farms and retrained under federal package settlement programs for displaced inshore fishers. They worked nights at the seniors complex in Aquaforte and nursed mornings in the cottage hospital in Bay Bulls. They spread road salt in winter and replaced culverts in summer and many of them flew to Alberta temporarily and others concocted schemes to siphon funds from tourism by applying for grants to build pressure-treated walkways to ancient cannon and reshingle old churches (and burn one down if necessary when not all of them got their stamps). There were many ways for a family to stitch together a living in Renews and a subsistence living included moose-hunting and turre-shooting and rabbit-snaring and berry-picking and trouting and the planting of root vegetables and the cutting of firewood and the selling of rails and posts for fences by way of a handpainted sign in your driveway. Chest freezers were full of game and pork and turre. Backyards stacked with seasoned teepees of wood. They say cities are the engines of the new economy, not rural places, but we know deep down this is untrue and that the engine is in Asia and neither the cities nor the rural places of America amount to much economic clout. But people in various rural places have more in common than they have with their racial counterparts in the cities. They might be alarmed at the aging structure of the population but the way things are going most people will live with a bit of city and a bit of the rural in them, such is the force for movement that has forever dominated the cycle of trade, love and prospects.

2

Baxter Penney was to take Henry out lobster fishing before supper. Remember to be home—he tapped the steering wheel. A truck was passing, driven by Emerson Grandy, his hooks resting on the steering wheel. Henry looked and there was a horse, high and heavy and close. His bright orange hide rippling fast. He had a big head and chest pushing against the top of the wooden trailer, a yellow mane of furious hair brilliant in the sun and the mane lashing out in parts at the wind and the wet alive eyes of the horse, delighted and wide open, urging the pickup to just once dammit go berserk on me. But Emerson Grandy was doing a steady hundred kilometres as he merged gently ahead of Henry and slipped further on as he slowed for what they call the featherbed—a dip in the road that told you Fermeuse was next. The truck drove the horse down that side road, never a moment on the brake, a mad but consistent gallop past the scrapyard and up through the newly dynamited pass of slate, taking that thrill horse out for its weekly ride. The truck might be powered by that horse and so too are my exertions powered by myself, Henry thought. I have no army telling me what to do except for the army of compulsion that is inside each and every one of us.

Henry pulled off to the old road to Kingmans Cove. He eased the car over the potholes that splashed up yesterday's rain, the entire land dry and bright except for these potholes. He drove down to the land that was untouched except for large rusted barrels and torsos of machines that had either helped build the road or been dumped here since the cove was abandoned.

Kingmans Cove was what they had left behind. Footings and foundations suggested by the borders of damson plums and crabapples and double-petalled roses. When building a wall, Henry remembered, lay the rocks in their natural beds. When pruning a tree leave gaps so small birds can fly through.

He walked out to his cellar, his spiritual centre, and felt with his feet the old potato drills that belonged to a King or a Grandy or a Morris and a Noel. They all lived in Renews now but three hundred years ago this was their home. The reason they left? A paved road and a power line. A bus for schooling. Easier access to a hospital. No one chooses to be isolated. There are no eccentrics. Everyone wants to be modern, and here in this cove they were deprived. If a ship foundered here they tore into the bounty, they did not save souls. During a court trial a woman said, Why did they come up on those rocks and tempt us so? No one can refuse the temptation of the modern world.

Henry lifted up a branch of leaf formation. With a trowel he dug roots out of the gravel and laid the plants entire in a green garbage bag on a flat cardboard box from a tray of soft drinks. These were the children of the children of the bushes and plants that used to service the families of Kingmans Cove. Across the way he saw that orange horse being delivered to a field in Fermeuse.

He did not understand, truly, why he did this. Why didn't he just spend a hundred dollars at the gardening centre in the Goulds and get an instant backyard in easily transferable potted shrubs and perennials. Something, he knew, was happening to him.

Irises by the brook. A bank of rock offered up wild strawberries and he unstrung the runners and pulled yards of puckered tendrils the colour of pigeon feet from the stone and bundled these up in the bag. He walked to where the trees started and carefully dug out a young white pine. These were Wilson Noel's trees. He walked back to the trunk of the car and laid the trowel and the bag in the box and slammed shut the lid. Then he sat in the cellar and stared at the orange horse in Fermeuse and thought his druidic thoughts.

When he got back to the house Martha Groves had arrived and she was laid out in the sun with a hat covering her face, a pickaxe and a crosscut saw beside her. The shadow of the corner of the house was passing over her knees. She had been busy cutting sod away from the house and collapsed here.

I saw this horse, she said.

THEY MADE LOVE in the bed upstairs, the new mattress and duvet and sheets still with their creases from the packaging. He pushed her around the bed and sort of turned her over and licked her and they were careful. It's okay, Martha said. The house rocked with the weight of the bed and their movement on the bed. Somehow the horse had made them decide on the bed. This agreement on seeing an unusual horse. They had been waiting for an image or a conversation and the horse comment had made Henry take her hand and she agreed when she heard that the horse had passed him. She agreed to climb the stairs. Even then, when the bed appeared in the doorway and the floor joists deflected with their combined weight, the house knowing they were together upstairs and the house moving with them, even so they were nervous and Martha closed her eyes and absorbed him and then there was a panic in her eyes, like she was falling off a cliff. They played around and learned a little bit of each other and then they got serious and energetic and Martha came and that made him come and they both knew the baby was in there and for the first time they felt perhaps this was love and not something to be ashamed about. People seventy years ago had made a child in this room and it felt like Tender was in the room encouraging this behaviour.

Henry lay back in the sheets and held Martha, the sun shining through a white cotton curtain he'd brought back from Afghanistan. He was alive with this result and he felt something profound had occurred but he distrusted the look on Martha's face. She must be pretending. She must be of two minds and resigned to this complication. But then he saw she was lining up her columns of commitment and sending them forward to deal with any querulous rebellion. He helped Martha with a box of tissues.

You don't skimp on anything, she said.

That's not true, he said.

You either have it in good supply or not at all.

I have no oven, he said.

That's good, Martha said, like he'd told a joke. A joke with some exercise.

We need a cookstove in here.

And a chimney liner.

I'm glad you came over, he said.

I don't know what I'm doing.

It's okay, we're all mature and we're all lunatics.

This is not our first time around.

There's no romance. It's only love we're talking about here.

What does that mean.

It means a bigger thing.

You mean I can't expect any romance?

We're taking care of each other.

You're talking about kindness.

We're going to be kind. And funny.

You have a nice cock. If that matters.

Likewise. In your own department.

Great I have a department.

I find it profoundly meaningful to be doing this with the situation. That presents itself.

And yet you enjoy yourself so well.

They knew it was dirty but the only way to make it clean was to admit it was dirty. If you were honest about it it was clean.

Outside a motor revved high and then sputtered, like a two-stroke engine, near the corner of the house, the house upstairs still uninsulated so you could pick out everything almost the heartbeat of a man approaching the back door. Come on Henry, a voice said. It was a holler from the door.

That's Baxter, Martha said.

He lurched out of bed and pulled on his pants and down the stairs, reaching into his shirt with his arms and bending his torso so as not to strike his head on the landing. All he could see of Baxter Penney was his rubbers as he'd given up and just the back boot of his stride left in the doorframe then his figure in the kitchen window walking up to the road where his bog bike was rammed into the wild roses. On the dirt shoulder, idling. Henry ran after him and jumped on the back of the quad. Baxter could see Martha's car was there and yet he had not seen her.

They drove past Colleen's and then the American house and out towards the automated signal in Kingmans Cove. It was getting near dusk now but it was still warm. Baxter with a yellow bucket bungee-corded onto the back carrier behind them, the metal handle swung a little screech as they bounced down over the gulley to Kingmans Cove and zipped over the cow fence then parked by the pen for the sheep and unhooked the bucket.

They walked down over the grass bank and the loose scree to a steep rock face that had been lifted up out of the ocean and twisted vertical by glaciers ten thousand years before. Split into shelves of rock that were like two hands praying where the preacher doesn't close the hands together but speaks the sermon into the hands and the words are funnelled up to God. In these hands, along the fingertips of God as it were, is where Baxter walked out, and in the low tide you could see a long stick, the bark peeled off it, jutting out of the water. Baxter looked into the water below and carefully nudged up the stick and gave it a quick jerk and thrust it down again and said, over his shoulder, Get the bucket.

Baxter lifted the stick out of the water and on the end were the vicious tines of a rusting pitchfork and then up and out came a green arching flick of seawater full of black lobster fixed on the middle prong of that pitchfork. Baxter dropped the face of the pitchfork into the bucket and the lobster's claws and tail flexed in agony against Henry's bent thumbs and Baxter shook off the lobster and twisted the timber around again to the sea surface where the pitchfork had been anchored, baited with the head of a herring. He thrust the fork down again on another lobster that must have been feeding and puzzled and waiting unfortunately for something to return. Up it came, this smaller lobster, one you'd throw back if it was in your pot, and Baxter did this three more times for five lobsters total that stood on their heads or flexed their tails staring up out of the bucket, antennae and claws scratching slowly on the flush plastic and the tails batting down on one another, settling further into the bucket. That's two for me, Baxter said, and the three small ones you can share with your missus. You're going to have to cook them right away—they don't last.

3

They boiled the pronged lobsters and ate all of them with a bottle of white wine and a pot of butter with garlic in the butter. Henry told her about Baxter's comment. He said, Your missus.

That's part of coming clean, she said.

But that night it rained and the wind slammed the rain against the windows, the sheers on the windows moved and they felt the wind through the walls. They had torn off the pink rose wallpaper and used scrapers on the sheets of newsprint that had been glued with flour paste onto the walls a hundred years ago. He'd read the news while he flaked it off. They did not wear masks, but tied T-shirts around their faces. He read of business collapse and troubles in the Balkans and teachers on the Labrador attempting to illuminate St John's on the social conditions of the local population. With the newspaper scrubbed off there were gaps between the wooden planks and you could feel the air running in under the clapboard. This news had kept people warm.

They were in bed in the dark now staring at the chipped ceiling, making pictures out of the random shapes, listening to the sea and the rain hitting the house. The house did not sound like it was going to make it. The roof was solid and holding its own and they felt proud that something they owned was protecting them from the elements, but then they heard a splat and it was a leak somewhere. He got out of bed with the flashlight and shone the light on the floor into the second bedroom. He turned on the light. The house shuddered again. This was where the worst damage to the house was, where that man Careen and Nellie Morris had slept. The bed was there and the little box of ammunition full of letters and photographs. He did not like entering this room but he pushed through his reluctance until he discovered a wetness. It was near the chimney and it was where he had torn out a portion of the ceiling. He went downstairs and fished around for a bucket and brought it up and put the bucket under the leak. It plunked hard, an annoying loud plunk, so he took a pillow off the bed and stripped the pillowcase off and threw the pillowcase into the bucket. He got back in bed and grabbed for Martha because his hands were cold and she yelped but he kept his hands on her and pulled himself to her and you heard the rain dimpling on the roof and it spattered down, bouncing and leaking in between the slats of the old white ceiling, running along a course of the slats to the area above the bucket. The bed moved with one gust and then there was a new drip and he walked back down to the kitchen and found a pot and brought it up and did the same with the other pillowcase. It was disenchanting to have leaks. It deflated you. They lay in bed under a brand-new duvet and listened to this rain and felt the house strain on its foundations, the eaves pulling up against the roof trusses. It was windy but not excessively so, and when they felt this tremor in the bed they both worried that the house would have to fall down.

It's not much wind, Martha said, for the house to be doing this. I mean, it gets windier, doesn't it?

The wind can blow the milk out of your tea.

They were unsafe in the house, was Henry's feeling. The house would not last another winter and they would have to abandon any thought of living here. Martha rolled over and held him tight and he realized he was inside her, she had made him hard and pushed him in and he hadn't done a thing.

He felt the baby move.

He pulled out.

What's wrong.

He said it felt like Tender was in the bed with them.

But Tender *is* in the bed with us. We've said that. He will always be there. Is that something we can live with?

This wasn't something that made him happy. Not this time. But he understood. Henry had simply misjudged how complicated being with her was. He thought he was throwing himself, like a martyr, into a situation. And then when duty presented itself he realized he was in fact enjoying himself. Martha was full of independent life and he loved that life. He enjoyed seeing her active in the world. And so, when Tender made an appearance, it caused a conflict in him, that he wasn't sacrificing himself at all, but astounded at his luck.

You have to remember, Martha said, that Tender is happy with this. He's happy to know this.

I will try to adopt that way of looking at it, he said.

There will always be the three of us, Martha said.

4

Wilson Noel said did you feel that last night?

Henry paused to think if he'd heard correctly.

I've lived here fifty-four years and that's happened once before, you must have felt it. The sea pounding the bedrock.

He couldn't wait to get back to Martha with the news. As he drove past the shore road the sea had a run of high surf and the curtains of water were being pushed in by some distant force. These were not young waves. After hundreds of miles of movement they had reared up to plunge into the headlands, waves that had been born in another hemisphere entirely. The sky was bright blue.

It wasn't the wind, he said. It's the sea. And it happens twice in a lifetime.

But Martha was preoccupied or she was upset. It's nothing, she said. But he knew it was something he'd done. Just say it, he said. It's ridiculous, she said. Then she turned her shoulders and faced him. Okay, it's the pillowcases. I found your buckets with the pillowcases in them.

He wasn't expecting that. We're not going to save the pillowcases, he said. Or anything off that bed. I didn't ruin anything.

I know it's foolish of me to feel this way I just—you put your hands on them, on that dead bed and then you handled me, she said. You should have washed your hands, she said.

This made him exhausted. She was right, of course, but the work was getting to him. The labour was mixing in with their pleasure. I'm sorry, he said.

I'm sorry too, she said. I'm sorry for feeling it. I wish I didn't feel it, it's just creepy sometimes to be living in a house that's—

I know, he said. It's alive this house.

It's not though. It's a lovely warm house but it's Tender's house and Tender's relatives' and he's dead and they're dead.

Nellie's not dead and this is not Tender's house. This was a part of Tender he didn't know existed. We're building a brand-new extension of Tender. I wasn't thinking last night, he said. I was tired and solving a problem and I wasn't thinking.

I know you were, and you're good at that you're really good just think a little more, okay? I know it's hard but we've got to think about everything, okay?

MARTHA COULD NOT STAY. She had clients. What can I say, she said. I'm good at what I do. They kissed and he felt the baby in her. This time it delighted him. She looked up at him and fixed her hair in a buckle behind her head. She phoned someone and said she was on her way and they kissed again and she pushed him towards the hallway and then did a violent gesture and said no I have to go and she was angry with herself for having given in to this roughhousing but was also possessed with the notion that she deserved this type of passion.

It was the height of summer now and it was pleasant to be outdoors in just a shirt. The sun ripped the mood out of you. Martha shut her car door too hard and jerked the car out of the drive and up onto the road. She was a fast, erratic driver who did not look in all directions but she managed to not have accidents and he listened to her car accelerate down to the main highway and then slow up fast to the stop sign. He could not believe it. Almost as soon as the sound of her car had gone, so too was the truth of what had occurred. Had anything occurred? He smelled the air and she had been there. He walked back upstairs and studied the bed and yes something had happened. There was a green elastic hairband by the flashlight and in the double bed were a few strands of hair. Her hair. She had on a pretty bra. She took care to wear good underthings. Or had that been an expectation, that something might happen when she came out here. Yes. He knew now that she had thought of something before it had even occurred to him.

It is complicated to love someone, he said to the house. As he loved Martha he also felt he was losing his love, for the person he loved was staining her own dignity by loving him. What did Gandhi do in the face of British acts which stripped Indian dignity? He did not belittle them, he marched for salt.

He set about beating apart a Canadian-made solid wood coffee table but he couldn't stop thinking about her. Of the little white pearl buttons on her shirt, it was a turquoise prairie shirt with pockets that buttoned down. Of how she felt against him as she was tying up her hair. He thought less of them in bed than in the moment when she realized she had to leave. The force of leaving him made more of an impression than her giving in to him, or was it she that took him. Martha had been on top of him. She had really enjoyed herself, but it was almost as if it had nothing to do with him. She had been selfish but he had committed. He was glad he could allow her that enjoyment. Perhaps it was the house that had allowed it.

The arrangement was it was all up to her. He was here for her. But he realized this was not fair to himself. Also, to her. No matter how much he implored her to be in control, she would take his feelings into account. Or the possibility that he might realize he's a fraud and run.

He carried the top of the table to the burn barrel. He shoved it in and stepped away from the flames. This was what they did in Afghanistan. The truth about war is there is a lot of garbage. Since his return to civilian life he was moved at the efforts of recyclers. The care that went into separating plastics from metals, and the idea of a compost heap. I wonder if it's possible for an army to manage a compost heap. They burned plastic by the ton, we dump waste by the tandem load. They'd once cooked a meal pouring gasoline over a mound of sand and lighting it. More damage has been done with waste than with bullets. The open burning of everything, the raw exhaust of modern components buffeting into the air. Hardly any effort to even position these heaps downwind. What did we inhale.

A truck honked—John was here! And ten minutes later he came over. He had a piece of the lawn mower pullstart with him. He needed duct tape.

You weren't in there with the widow were you?

She's not married, John. They weren't married. She doesn't like that term.

John was winding the coil tightly in his fingers. I mean it's impressive, he said. Henry handed him the strip of duct tape.

We're thinking of going public.

Trust me buddy, you're public.

5

An old place should have drawers filled with precious ampoules in balsa tubes plugged with cotton, but Henry had been shitting in a big yellow plastic bucket lined with white garbage bags. That's how crude it was here. The extension smelled of wild roses and there were plenty of large, overgrown rosebushes with stems as thick as bamboo. The smell of roses found its way into the room. There was a rotting sill and a gap between the wall and that was how the scent got in. It made the decrepit nature of the room and the squalid situation of having to shit in a bucket pleasurable. He laughed at the luxury of a good bath, and he knew how Nellie Morris must have felt when she'd left the house and moved into a seniors home that had running water.

He was tying off a garbage bag and replacing it with a new one when he realized he was wrong about where the scent was coming from. It was in the bags. The bags were scented. It was the scent of garbage bags he was smelling, a cheap scent of flowers. He was crouching over a bucket that had been there when he bought the house. He hadn't even bought a new bucket and now all he had was the knowledge of how much his shit weighed. This was worse than how he'd taken a shit in Afghanistan.

He went to Wilson Noel's and bought a sheet of plywood and two pounds of wood screws, a quart of white interior paint and a nylon paintbrush. He drew a plan and cut the board with a hand saw and screwed the boards together and recessed the front panel so that it angled in as it fell to the floor. That way, he explained to Baxter Penney, you can tuck your heels in.

Baxter looked at his sawdust toilet without taking his hands from his pockets. He sort of dipped one knee to get an angle on it. Fancy, he said. But you got the electrical in here. Code one means a bathroom into her. You could hook into next door's septic system (he meant John and Silvia's). What you should be concentrating on is a roof.

Henry painted the box white and drove into the Goulds to find a toilet seat.

He found one with cartoon tropical fish swimming in a clear gel layer. It was a toilet seat for kids, and he thought about Clem and Sadie visiting and what they'd think of this seat. But he needed a seat for everyday use. He had to think, too, of adults. He settled for a lid that slowed on a hydraulic piston. It seemed to be arguing with itself, and trying to calm down gracefully.

He bought four identical buckets at a marine supply store. He was making a composting toilet, he said with enthusiasm.

John and Silvia were unsure about the sawdust toilet.

What do you do when it's full, John asked.

You carry it to the compost and dump it and then use two buckets of water from the rain barrel to rinse it out with a teaspoon of pine-sol.

That's the compost nearest us.

You're upwind.

We have a dog.

They walked over to John and Silvia's and it was a relief to sit in one of their wide chairs. I don't think, John Hynes said, you even have a chair over there. Does he have a chair?

He was sitting on an overturned kerosene bucket when I saw him yesterday, Silvia said.

That's the thing he used to shit in.

The wetsuits hanging on the clothesline. The wind had blown all the clothes pegs together. John and Silvia had taken the kids down to a stretch of good beach. Henry had planned to do this when he bought the house, sort of live in the house as it fell down around him, sleep in the old bed upstairs until the floor gave way then sleep downstairs in the parlour and keep up a relationship with the beach until he was forced to buy a tent and live outside. That's what Colleen Grandy had suggested. A spiritual life. But the house possessed him and, unwittingly, the thought that Martha Groves owned half of it and was keeping an eye on him made him appreciate the good timbers it was constructed from and the private history of a family that was contained in letters and photographs in that ammunition box and it made him fall in love with the idea of preserving something of Tender Morris's house and his family. We are living in a time where it is easier to know more about a stranger's family by researching online than it is to know one's own. History is the constant upheaval of peregrination. Henry's family hadn't stayed put for more than a generation. The truth is neither did these families, but the houses stayed in the families and the families were so large that there was always one member who kept up the house and passed it on down to a ninth son who did not see the need to move. It had more to do with the size of families than their predilection for staying in one place. Tender Morris, look where he died.

6

Baxter was right. He had to concentrate on the roof. The sunlight drove him to climb a ladder Melvin Careen had built out of scrap lumber. He measured the roof and wrote the dimensions on an envelope. He could borrow a wand and he had propane, he just needed the material. Down the road Keith Noyce was spraying garden seed on Colleen Grandy's new front yard. He hadn't seen much of Keith or Colleen. The spray was like the green paint Henry had seen some richer Afghans use to paint their rocks to look like grass. Perhaps the boy was embarrassed to have seen him cry. He picked him up when he was hitchhiking with his gas can, but they didn't talk much. Keith listened to music with earphones. He had that stoned way of being surprised. His finger full of nicotine.

Nice to see him getting work, though.

But what of Colleen? Had she been walking?

A dumptruck pulled into the side of the house. It was Leonard King. I was searching for rock for your well and I come upon this.

Leonard patted the side of the dumptruck as if it was obvious what he had inside. Henry, from the roof, saw the yard of soil.

It's an old potato garden, Leonard explained.

Henry asked him to elaborate.

There was a garden by a cellar so I thought I'd lay it down in behind your house.

Leonard was an enthusiastic person, but he also appreciated someone listening to him as he told these stories. He enjoyed finding out what struck someone as interesting. Leonard wasn't quite sure what part of himself, or the way of being himself, was the bit that engaged the curiosity of an open mind like Henry's. He spread his hand out and then waved his arm slowly about. You got no soil here, Leonard said. The garden that goes with this house is across the road. In fact, this house belongs across the road. They used to have their vegetables right up by Baxter's. My father told me that. That's the Morris garden in behind those alders. By rights you should be over on that.

But no one owns it and the house is here.

Someone owns it. I think this land you're on is someone else's. Now that's only what I heard. I don't know who would make a claim on you, but if they ever do, you got land over there that must be yours. Anyway I can put this potato field right in back where the sun shines.

Nothing, in Leonard's mind, could be solved if it couldn't be solved with a backhoe and a dumptruck. He raised the truck bed and out slid the yard of topsoil. Then he sized up the work Henry had done. He caught the eyesore. Let's haul that garbage Henry, take it right now while the dump is open. I'm on my way to Aquaforte, Leonard said. Leonard hated carrying an empty tandem. How much. Leonard said don't bother with that— twenty dollars would be too much. How about forty, Henry said. No I couldn't do it for forty. He handed Leonard a fifty and

Leonard hated taking it. Henry found a pair of cotton gloves and Leonard said he preferred to work bare-handed. They spent an hour loading the truck. Henry told him the house had no well. I can dig you a well. And by the time Leonard was pulled out, they'd arranged a time to excavate. Amazing to think an afternoon could break a hundred years of no water. He watched Leonard drive off and then saw Keith Noyce pushing the lawn mower up the road, intensely listening to music, looking for more work.

Go no further, Henry said. What's your rate.

7

Henry went inside and collapsed on the bed and listened to Keith Noyce mow his lawn. His father was coming, Keith had said. It'll be nice to meet him.

It was a comforting, uniform sound, the lawn mower. The drizzle of a motor exercising and I don't have to lift a finger. He thought the boy must be liking it here now. Keith had told him he'd always felt a little lonely on these visits to Newfoundland. In New York they'd had a dog, he said, and the dog was run over. She was badly wounded, his father explained to him. They couldn't save her, his mother said. It would be wrong to save her, or to prolong the life for the son to see her. There was too much pain and so they put the dog down. Keith had cried in bed and in the morning panicked. He was twelve years old. He went to the vet's to see the dog. Henry understood this is what compulsion is and compulsion is what makes a person fall in love and generate hate. A woman in a green environment apron hesitated while feeding a rabbit with a beaker, she was sorting in her mouth the proper words and then came up with it. I'm sorry, she said, but your dog has passed away. I know that, Keith said. I'm here to see her one last time. They walked down a yelping corridor. The sounds of animals dampened as the woman opened a door on a spring and lifted up a sheet of heavy freezer plastic. In a cooler vault in the rear, she unfastened a hatch on a grey fridge. Your dog is in there. It shocked him. The dog was fine. She looked completely unhurt except her fur was shirred in places where it looked like she'd been pushed along surfaces. She looks good, he said aloud.

Keith was comfortable saying that because this was his dog. You could get away with saying inappropriate things if you loved and if you possessed and made it obvious your clutch was from commitment. But I love you. The woman said the dog felt nothing. She had a tone of pride in her work in not causing pain. We inject in the hind leg, she'd said, right here. She put a fingertip on the joint. But I don't see any damage, Keith said. Is the damage on her other side? The woman was puzzled. It's a needle, she said. There's nothing more to it. My dog was hit and run over by a car, he explained. You're mistaken. The woman was delighted to be able to tell him this. Your dog arrived in perfect health, she had no injury at all, she left this world very peacefully. And as she said this something clicked in her. She had gotten through all the verbal obstacles of breaking bad news but now another level of awareness had struck, one that no teacher had ever briefed her on. Keith had the facts now though not arranged properly and for a second he thought perhaps it's possible they have dogs that are not the dog in question, but made-up dogs that are not his dog after all, and he had exposed this truth, but he looked again at the angle of the dog's face, how the spots were on the nose and this was his dog. The dog looked stuffed and that was what rigor mortis did to you. This dog walked in here, the woman had said. She was a fine dog and we hate having to put down fine dogs. We had a family lined up but then they changed their minds and we waited three days and, as you can see, we are above capacity.

Then he saw the truth pass out of her face. Sometimes truth is like a physical liquid that can leak out, or when it turns into liquid there is no container for it. His dog had been fine. His parents had argued. His parents were splitting up, he knew that, but what he did not know until this moment was that no one had a practical answer for the dog. The pure truth of the event leapt off the orb of her eyeball, it was a visual story that bounced off his eyes.

That was when he was twelve and that summer his mother moved to New York and shared an apartment with an old school friend. Keith continued his schooling near Lake Placid and lived with his father. His father brought home styrofoam bowls of soup from the cafeteria in the basement of the building where he had his healing practice and they ate their lunch together before both went back to school and work. They continued this even though it may have been more convenient for the boy to stay at school all day. They had not missed a meal together, and the boy would have to be a lot older, much older than his father was now, before he appreciated that, Henry thought.

Keith visited his mother and knew he was more like her than his father. He was, in fact, most like his grandfather—his mother's father. He did not sleep as he lay on their couch. And at three in the morning he left her and her female lover a note to say goodbye. The garbage trucks hurled down Fifth Avenue. A man dropped off the back of the truck and whipped out the white bag of garbage sponsored by the Doe Fund then ran across a crosswalk and jumped back aboard the rear lip of the truck. The garbage bin empty. Someone else must put in a new bin liner later in the morning.

The silver tower on the Empire State Building like a picture tube in a TV, or the filament in a lightbulb. The lightbulb broken off. Some silver in the Chrysler Building too. In Madison Square, park staff cleaned up sidewalks, green coats with a white maple leaf on the back. One was wearing homemade cardboard shoes over his personal shoes.

His mother kept grudges, but limited them, so she got over much grief by drying out the grievances on a clothesline then stacking them in a little drawer behind her ear. She lived carefree and immediately. A grievance her son kept in his own little box behind the ear was this very method, a method kept to manage the mortal life. I want to be an actor, he said to his mother's lover, Althea. She was brushing her teeth and Keith had walked in on her and Althea had not asked him to leave. But there was no money for theatre school and his parents were preoccupied with work and transitions and hauling the infrastructure of two professional lives around the world.

His father had set up a pattern and Keith appreciated the routine. He found himself lured into his father's work. His father's trips to Peru. Summers in Newfoundland. How much is decided not by the intentions of a people but by how close the sun revolves around the soil layer of a particular geography. It would take Keith years to understand that it was not the content of his father's work that interested him, but a person's dedication to a set of limitations. Conviction and commitment. But he was only eighteen now and so he followed, with animosity, his father's spiritual path to Peru and then to Newfoundland—a good solution to anger but one that did not provide a heavy bag in front of him to lash out at, only miles of open air that infuriated him. This hinterland or frontier—this place of the close-knit family—did his father acknowledge his neighbours in Renews? Colleen Grandy, the woman whose husband was away in Alberta, she cooked them both a boiled dinner and carried it over, two plates covered in tinfoil, and his father had her in and set her down and talked about what he was doing while revolving the chunky amber beads on his necklace. This lonely woman who someone should be cooking for, is what Keith thought, lonely and starved enough that she was engaging with the Americans. When she was gone they tore off the tinfoil and devoured the hot plates of food.

After thirty minutes the sound died and Henry Hayward woke up and thought Keith might be out of gas. But he was finished. He came in to get paid. Henry ran downstairs and acted overly awake. He saw the fifty-dollar bill on the table. Leonard.

Tell me, Henry said. Why do you hang out with Justin King?

He's my friend.

He's got lots of friends.

Yeah well I don't.

Henry picked up the bill and gave it to him.

That's too much, Keith said.

Be lavish to someone. Make their day.

I've got a real one for that.

Keith pocketed the fifty dollars and stepped outside to collect his jacket and the lawn mower and push it up the road. It was getting close to suppertime now. It takes time to make money this way. Henry had been through it, summer jobs, manual labour. It was what had bonded him to John for life. Friends with no end.

Henry watched the boy push the mower back to John's shed and then walk briskly down to the lightkeeper's house. Past Colleen Grandy's house and he saw Keith look over. Did Keith know about the rumour. Henry recalled the times he'd picked him up. How Keith stuffed taxi vouchers into his denim jacket pocket— vouchers that he traded for pharmaceutical drugs. There was a house in the Goulds, Keith said, that was a grow operation and part of the boy's occupation was as a mule along the shore. The money was a lot easier than manual labour. He's a good person, Henry thought, yet he's unaware that it doesn't matter if he's good if others see him breaking the law. Self-confidence. Did his father or his mother give him that.

8

Henry stopped in to the Goulds for groceries—Martha was coming that weekend. The thought of her there for any duration made him nervous. He didn't know what to cook. He drove to work and was entertained at the store by Wilson Noel walking out into the street with the end of a roll of white electrical wire. Cars slowed to a stop as Wilson paced off a hundred feet. In other stores you weigh the coil of wire and subtract the weight and you know how many feet you have, but here they don't mind walking across the road with a tape measure and making traffic stop.

He drove the dumptruck and Leonard King told him stories. You know Colleen Grandy, he said. Not that I know anything. And Leonard made a gesture with his shoulder that suggested something.

She's going to Peru, Henry said. She's having a spiritual awakening.

He did not mind saying it like this. It cost him nothing. He was not mocking Colleen, merely providing a defence.

It's not Peru people are talking about, Leonard said.

At the end of the workday there was still a lineup of customers at Wilson Noel's. Henry needed roofing, so he got in line. Justin King was at the counter but he wasn't doing anything. There was Emerson Grandy, helping himself to four-inch nails. The man could do anything with those hooks. Henry looked outside to see if his horse was with him. Emerson was throwing the nails into the scale. Then he spilled the bucket of nails and Justin stooped over to help him and Emerson said, sternly, No I'll do it. He spent the next half hour while Henry waited to be served picking up every nail with excruciating patience. He placed three pounds of them on the scale. Then Justin slipped the nails into a paper bag. You wouldn't think a paper bag could hold that many sharp nails but someone early on created a weave for pulp, that withstood four-inch nails.

Wilson Noel came in and wrote up an order. Got your nails, Emerson, he said. Then, Justin take this, and handed the young man a slip of paper. Justin darted out the door. Wilson had to leave that counter and walk around to the other counter where the calculator was. The dark paint on the sheet of plywood counter had worn away here and the meat of his hand sat on the knots and grain of the wood. He tallied the list of items and then punched this number into a cash register and then spoke to the customers about their mothers while opening up an alphabetized ledger—there were about sixteen of these well-thumbed ledgers on the counter—and writing down the customer's name and itemizing, once again, the things he was trying to buy. Wilson stopped writing to think about what was the best diameter pipe to be used for a surface well, they had agreed on three-inch but some people prefer the two-inch and he stopped again when a customer in the back corner of the store was asking if he had to use the all-weather plywood or could he get away with the D grade. Wilson asked him many questions to diagnose the severity of the construction and came to the conclusion that the work on the inside could conceivably be done with D grade but the exposed outer shell must be all-weather.

It came to Henry finally and his order for six rolls of torch-on roofing was handed to Justin King who had arrived back with many lengths of vinyl eavestrough. Go get Henry some torch-on, Wilson said and Justin ran out the door and hopped in the passenger side of Henry's car.

Drive around the back, Justin said, and he did that and backed up to a garage door and Justin jumped out and ran in and was gone for a minute. Then he returned. He was trying his best to lift a roll of torch-on but he was lifting it end over end in the gravel, destroying the clean edge of the butt end, the end you wanted to hang over the eaves by an inch very neatly.

Henry said, I wouldn't be buying that roll what with the butt end all dented and small pebbles driven into the bitumen finish.

Justin looked shocked. They weigh seventy pounds each and Henry helped him carry it back into the dark warehouse. Together they found six good undisturbed rolls and lifted them one by one to the car and put one in the well of the passenger seat as they were heavy. Then Justin tore up the hill on his own steam. Henry drove back up to the parking lot. He had to stop for Wilson who, for some reason, was in the gravel parking lot operating a forklift to delicately raise a dozen lengths of one-by-eight tongue-and-groove from a pallet on the back of a fourteen-wheel flatbed that had just pulled up and was still idling, dust settling from the shoulder of the road, the driver unclasping the nylon stays on his load. Henry parked beside the load. They all waited for this manoeuvre and Justin jogged out into the road to halt traffic while Wilson Noel changed gears and made the forklift beep and lurch. The yellow machine twisted around, the two hundred pounds of lumber almost slipping off the forks onto Henry's car. But then all was balanced and Wilson proceeded to delicately place the lumber in the back of an open hatchback, angling the forklift sideways to push the lengths of tongue-and-groove, still wet from the sawmill, through the back seats and over the stick shift, just shy of touching the pebbled veneer on the glove compartment. Wilson was leaning over the side of the forklift to peer into the hatchback and size up his progress. He thought he could do a little better so he withdrew the lumber entirely and began the procedure again. The customers inside the shop had the same lean in their torsos, all staying where they were but tilting their hips to get a good look out the open door, their hands still half in their pockets, to appreciate Wilson's manoeuvre. Henry stepped inside and joined them. Wilson climbed out of the forklift and had a talk with the flatbed driver about the area he'd drawn for his moose licence. He had an either-sex licence and Wilson wanted to know what pool he'd been in to get so lucky. There was no orderly lineup but the men inside knew who was next. Finally Wilson Noel returned and Henry paid for the roofing while Wilson answered the phone with four other men waiting in queue. Now how's your mother doing, he said into the phone.

9

The grass seed had taken root and it was a uniform blade that sprouted. No clover. Keith brushed the fence with creosote and helped with the roofing on her new greenhouse. If he had enough of this work perhaps the mule delivery could vanish. Henry asked Wilson Noel if there was work for Keith Noyce. He's a friend of Justin King's.

I got enough on my hands with one of those guys, Wilson said.

He glanced over at Justin King, trying his best to carry a sheet of plywood over his shoulders and bent head. The thing is, Wilson said, I'm not supposed to help him. I'm supposed to lay off giving service to that American and anything connected to him. Leonard King says he knows why. I don't want to know why. I just listen to Rick and try to keep Rick happy. I don't be needing to get him mad at me.

Well that was interesting. The long arm of Rick Tobin, causing injustice. Surely, Henry said, the son of a man shouldn't suffer.

Look at Justin, Wilson said. That's Leonard's nephew. Leonard used up ten years of favours to have him on board. You know why he rides a bike to work—he lost his licence for drinking and driving. The young fellow is a ticket. When he drinks he has to find a set of car keys.

I've seen him, Henry said, standing up on the pedals of a ten-speed, taking the hill into Fermeuse.

That's how he gets to work.

Well if there's anything around Renews for the kid. Rick doesn't have to know everything.

Wilson stretched up tall, as if reaching over his own prejudice. There's that land in Kingmans Cove, he said. I suppose he could help Justin clear it. That's only cash work. Rick don't need to hear about it.

I can ask him for you.

I'll do the asking. But you can come along and give a hand. Help resurrect the family garden, Wilson said.

Nice, Henry said. The past is making a comeback.

WHEN HE GOT HOME he put the groceries away and wondered what on earth he could make for supper. When Martha arrived he had two steaks cooking and he was peeling carrots in a bowl of water. She was exhausted from clapping a child's back. Percussion, she said, to get mucus off the chest. She lay on his daybed while he cooked. He was self-conscious about cutting up vegetables, that it had been a while since he'd cooked for two. He pretended to a proficiency for the sake of her attraction. He was, in fact, nervous slicing an onion. He was careful about it. But she took, correctly, his deliberateness as a sign of love. Cooking can be as intimate as the other thing. And he was not himself for the sake of attracting her love.

Next time, she said, cook the carrots first.

They went to bed early and were happy to have found each other. They were dealing with the guilt of that though, of being too delighted in the face of Tender's death. Martha pulled her face away to see him. I'll tell you what Tender said, the last time I saw him. He said if anything happened to him, I was to find somebody. A good man. Well Henry Hayward I've found him.

I guess though, Henry said, people can feel like you found him a little early.

It's never too early, she said.

THEY WOKE UP and it was bright daylight. Henry said he was afraid to get up. It means working on the house.

You need more fun, she said.

They made love under Martha's direction. She gave the orders to this lovemaking and Henry followed the commands. Then Martha jumped up immediately. Let's take a swim, she said. He rinsed his hands in a bucket of dirty water. He found the car keys and filled the trunk with empty water containers. She was sitting in the car, the doors open. Sometimes, when she was bent like this, you saw the pregnancy and it shocked him. She had packed the wetsuits from John and Silvia's, they were on the line and she'd run through the empty field between the houses and tiptoed up and snagged them. John Hynes had said, many a time, help yourself.

I thought you meant a dip at the overfalls.

The sea, she said. I haven't been in the sea yet this year.

They drove down the shore on the longest day of the year and counted the old houses and tried to extrapolate that number and decided there were fewer than a thousand houses left on the entire island. We have one of a thousand things, Martha said. Built of wood a hundred years ago. And we hardly paid anything for it, he said. Before he could think of what he was saying. Martha had paid a lot for him to be involved. His statement was swept into the big reserve Martha kept. She was, he kept forgetting, mourning. She might only be with him while she mourned. Who knew how the emotions would turn and they had confessed that they were both open to a change of mind.

But then she turned to him and said, Thank you for doing it that way.

She meant in bed. The way she liked it. The way that allowed her to think, a little, of Tender Morris. She had said it to him, inasmuch as she allowed them to make love in the first place. It was a bizarre agreement, but he took it. When you are in the land of the perverse, only bizarre things made sense.

The beach was a private beach and it cost a dollar and this was the start of something new, of not really minding these things. Henry had grown up frugal but now there was enough money to get by because the life was modest and he realized he didn't have to let paying for things bother him. They ducked under the rough yellow rope and walked past the wooden dory shaded under a copse of fir and juniper and decided to wait at the top of a set of stairs with one banister, the stair treads covered in sand, while a group of boys not yet teenagers tore up the steps, chilled and stuck with sand, their calves and shoulders made of sand, knees pulling at their long wet swim trunks.

They carried the wetsuits, trying not to trespass on a game of beach volleyball, unfolded the suits and pushed their feet into the hot neoprene rubber. A wedding party was on the beach, the bride dipping her foot in the sea. The men skipped rocks.

They were out of the way of the volleyball players, but as he zippered his legs into the suit Henry knew something was wrong.

There was a gathering near the bright sea, strange vocalizations, alarm you would say, and a wide swell was pushing new water deep up onto the dry sand. The volleyball players stopped and turned. The wedding party retreated. The sea sounded different, it had gone moseying in a new direction. The volleyball had been in midair when the commotion started, and it landed in the sand without anyone diving for it and now a sheet of water slipped in and touched the ball before arresting its progress and letting it sink into the sand.

Get out of there, a mother was screeching. Or it was a grandmother, in her fifties, with no intention of going in the water that afternoon, happy in her folding chair, but now up to her breasts, her black cotton dress floating up to the side of her, a sunhat blown off, her short hair and wire-rimmed glasses, up to her armpits, the dark stains of water high up on her, reaching out a tense white arm for her grandson who was too far out and laughing.

Then the wild running water drew back fast and clicked at the pebbles deeper in the sand. You saw the speed of the water now. The woman lost her footing and toppled over. She was helped out. Her grandson was helping her. Drenched.

People all over were running out of the waist-high water that was pulling back out of the bay, charging out with their knees held high. The wedding party escaped injury.

And then the big wave hit, a rogue wave and it crested and frothed high up past the volleyball net and almost to the very solid ground where the steps and stones began.

Out in the surf, a lone man, a chunky dog-paddler, was staring back at them. He was patient. He was beyond the new breakers and it was obvious he could not return. Heads were counted and it was all right now on the beach except for this man who no one seemed to own. Who was he and who does he belong to. His head low in the water, just his nose and eyes and his wet, short hair. It looked like he was perched on a submerged rock. He was not panicking.

A riptide, Henry said. He had the wetsuit on now and he turned to help Martha into hers. Immediately, adults ran up to them. They mistook the professionalism of wetsuits for authority. There's a boat, a woman said, pointing up into the trees. And three women and two men were up on the high ground in the trees turning that dory around and dragging it through the long low branches of the big fir, minding their feet, before anyone noticed it was a decorative boat that had rotted out and been retired and hadn't touched salt water in ten years. But the physical exertion of pulling it this far made them tug it to the water. Perhaps it had one last ride in her. The waves were high now, surging in, and the nose of the boat rose and wrenched to the side, it looked like the boat might overturn, but then it righted itself. Henry got in. Martha was about to take the side of the boat like you'd hurdle a fence.

You can't get in the boat, Henry said. I can't have you out in this.

A girl was near them. Make room, the girl said. The owner of the beach was now walking fast down the stairs.

How old are you, Henry said.

Sixteen, she said. I have my red cross.

Get in.

This surprised Martha. But he was right. She was too pregnant to be chancing it. The floor of the dory was wet. There was no plug in the hole in the back, the girl said, the drain plug, she clarified. The girl was realizing she was with a person who knew nothing of the sea or boats. This dory was not seaworthy at all and the owner of the beach, who had ahold of the stern, was shouting this out to Henry. There was only one oar and no oarlocks. What was he thinking. Another wave surged over them and the boat lurched side-on and it stayed upright but was thrown back onto the beach, the water retreating and they were stuck on dry land, Henry hurt his knee and they had almost crushed children.

Martha pointed at the motorboat, the glare of sunlight off its chrome gunwale. Coming from Aquaforte. A little white open boat. The man submerged gave up concentrating on the beach and turned his shoulders to the white boat. He was quick to understand the odds. They admired the slow experienced loop the white boat made around the man in trouble. The boat threw him an orange life jacket and then continued to circle him. The patience felt threatening, like they were about to gaff a seal. They cut the motor and two men—you could see their expandable watchbands flashing—bent over the side and tugged him aboard by the shoulders while the boat was still coasting. Up and over. It was very clear, the bright sun offered a high contrast to the boat and men and their background of white sky. It wasn't that rough out there. The man they saved was on the middle seat now, gathering himself, facing the back of the boat, his neck down looking at his bare feet. The man at the motor handed him something. It was a plastic flask of alcohol, it didn't have the glint of glass. The man lifted his neck and drank it. They did not bring him in to shore, they did not even acknowledge the commotion on the beach, the rotted dory that was beating sideways into the surf, but opened wide the throttle and the bow reared up and hammered over the whitecaps, back from where they came.

Henry helped drag the boat back up under the trees and they were too exhausted now to swim and they peeled off their wetsuits and got back in the car and drove home. They pulled into their garden and saw John Hynes walking happily over the field that separated their summer houses, he wanted to hear of their nice swim. They told him what occurred. It was later that they found out who the man was they'd tried to help and it was that afternoon when they'd first laid eyes on the American from down the road, Larry Noyce.

10

Henry didn't realize it until Baxter Penney told him. Baxter was walking backwards out of his barn with two sticks of lumber he'd cut himself and was drying in the sun. It was like he'd cut down one tree, limbed it, seasoned it, run it through a sawmill, burned the slabs for kindling and was left with these two dressed timbers.

Henry: They don't make them like they used to.

Baxter: Well they might, but I haven't run into any.

Baxter said the yellow house is opened up and the man from the States who owns it, he was up. Picked out of the water today, he said. Heard about it from Aquaforte.

Henry brightened. We were there, he said. I can tell you all about it.

Baxter was very interested to hear how it all looked from the shore. Between them, all angles were pored over.

The American is up for the summer, Baxter said. To join his son. What I heard is there was trouble with the man's wife at home and that's what brought the son here.

The boy's been here since the winter.

Yes that's right. You know him.

Henry realized, as they talked about Keith Noyce, that Baxter must have a story about him and Martha. Baxter must visit Aquaforte and lean on a fence someplace and tell a man at a convenience store about the fellow who bought the house across the road. What does he say about me to people? Took over a house belonging to his buddy who died in Afghanistan and he shits in a sawdust toilet and washes in the river. He sleeps with the widow when she visits. Henry knew that people lived with lots of complications. As long as you don't smear it in their faces.

He filled the kettle with water from the blue container. Martha was outside talking to Leonard King who was sitting in his idling flatbed truck, one bundle of clapboard aboard. Baxter could tell they were enjoying these days without running water, for he knew they would soon be over and another form of living would occur here. The second-hand fridge had waited patiently for electricity to arrive. Henry swung the door open and appreciated the cheery interior. It's a stint you've signed on for, Baxter said, this time without water.

When Baxter left, it turned cold. The wind from the north, from off the bay. The light receded over a hill. Martha was pulling on a sweater. Henry zipped on a windbreaker. They took the dirt road out to the lighthouse.

What did Leonard want?

He can get us some rock for the bottom of the well.

The little yellow house had its lights on, a figure inside at a table having supper. This is Larry Noyce. A car parked outside, a rental. The silhouette of the American stood up from the table and waved. Then the dark shape came to the door and opened it and said hello.

11

They stepped over the rope gate that was on the driveway and took the steps and the dark outline receded. Colour arrived to the face and shirt and they shook the American's hand. Larry Noyce. He had beads around his neck and a loose silver watch on his wrist. There was the smell of sage burning.

We've slept in the same bed, Henry said.

That puzzled the American.

Henry explained his room at John and Silvia's in town—the room Larry had used all those years ago when he was stranded in Newfoundland. That's a strange way of putting it, the American said.

You're a spiritual man, Martha said. These are spiritual connections.

Henry said they'd seen him in the water, and Larry Noyce was rubbing the back of his neck, making the beads jump and the watch slip down his hairy forearm. I didn't know I'd caused such a commotion. It takes a while to get any depth, you have to go in a long ways. I was in the brook and that's a lot warmer. I was paddling out there and didn't even notice the tide at all it was so calm but I felt okay I just couldn't get back in to shore.

Keith his son was out at the Copper Kettle with Justin King. They removed their shoes and Henry stared at a large poster of a magnificent hilly region of South America. The name at the bottom was Machu Picchu.

I met your son, Henry said.

You're the man who picks him up.

Did he tell you about his gas can?

It's right here in the porch.

They saw how neat it was in the house. There was not much of anything but clean and simple. A light wooden vase. A small fire going. Sage was burning in an abalone shell. Books open on the kitchen table.

It's cozy in here, Martha said.

That's my love for humanity, Martha: electricity and steam. Chekhov wrote that. He was reacting against Tolstoy and you, Henry, are looking a little Tolstoyan. Have either of you read Spinoza?

I don't read, Henry said.

He doesn't read philosophy or fiction, Martha said.

My son Keith, Larry said, I had him on a bet. I bet against God. I bet against pessimism. I pushed all my chips in on him. And now I'm just praying he gets to twenty. He doesn't ever have to like me, he just has to live while I'm buried in paperwork and nostalgia.

The way he spoke so aggressively about his son, it was the same manner in which he left his kitchen table, opened the front door and beckoned them in. Enthusiasm and truth. Larry Noyce looked at Henry and asked him if he ever thought of having children. All the time, Henry said. I've been avoiding having one my entire adult life.

Women, Larry Noyce said.

He said this with affection, with Martha obviously pregnant. There was no malice meant by this trouble with women.

Colleen has mentioned you, Martha said.

Colleen Grandy.

She's a friend of mine.

I work with her husband, Henry said.

Henry decided there could be something in what Leonard King was alluding to. Or, at least, he wanted to put the matter to rest.

Colleen is terrific. She loves Peru. Have you ever been to Peru?

Henry: I've just been. Through your poster here. I hear you're taking Colleen.

I wish I could go, Larry said. It's a package she's arranged with another outfit. But I'm having a ceremony here at the end of summer and a weekly meditation too.

I like the idea of bringing Peru here.

Larry: There is a character in a Kazantzakis book who knows the world without ever leaving Crete.

They toasted his arrival—and survival—with sparkling water, and to the men from Aquaforte who picked him up. I don't drink, Larry said, excusing the water.

Martha: I don't either.

One of the men in the boat, Larry said, he had hooks for hands.

Henry had to change his mind about what he'd seen. It wasn't expandable wristbands but hooks. I know him, Henry said. He's not from Aquaforte. He has a horse in Fermeuse. Emerson Grandy is his name.

They turned to the dark windows and Henry said, You can see his horse from Kingmans Cove. I feel like that horse is my animal twin living a mirrored life over there.

That's a very Peruvian thought, Larry said.

We all have had a spiritual crisis or two, Martha said. You don't need to go to South America to resolve one.

They put on their shoes and Larry Noyce said it was a pleasure to meet them both. They walked out into the twilight and at the rope gate Henry turned to catch Larry in the light of his own kitchen. He was cleaning up the dishes in his sink.

He's reeling out his own true behaviour, that one. He forgets how his bearing affects those around him.

Martha: He has no training in covering his spiritual condition.

What had happened to Larry's wife? The story Keith had told him in the car, of the dog and lover. Larry Noyce, studying the spirit, had not seen that his wife's anger stemmed from hurt and isolation. Why couldn't he have indulged her a little more. Henry shook his head—he was transferring his own feelings of Nora to the divorce of this man of spirit.

They walked, with no flashlight, out to the cellar in Kingmans Cove. They talked out many words in sentences that formed themselves without intention: Larry Noyce is of the opinion that others should not be affected by him—it is their responsibility, not his. No, his spirit is of goodness and who should mind being affected by it? Though it's daunting. That comment about women. He knows, everyone knows, something is going on with Colleen Grandy.

12

They found the dark hump of the cellar and looked out to sea. There was a flapping in the wind. A garbage bag. Someone had dumped garbage out here. Henry walked over to it. A dumptruck load strewn into the valley where a house once stood. The garbage looked familiar. The way the bags were knotted and panels of green wallboard and acoustic tiles. It was his garbage. Leonard King had taken it to Aquaforte.

No of course he didn't, Martha said. He'd have to pay a dumpage fee.

I'll tell Wilson in the morning.

Don't say anything.

Leonard has to clean this up. You can't dump garbage here, not my garbage.

Wilson Noel would settle it. Wilson has a good heart—he'd told Henry that he'd found a small job for Keith Noyce—out here in fact. He forgot to tell Larry that.

Well, that's not the father's business, Martha said.

True. Let the boy surprise his father. It'll be nice to see this hill with the old gardens again.

It's a south-facing hill.

Potatoes, turnip, cabbage. And look at this desecration. Wilson will be livid.

They stared at the sea and Henry said his prayers silently and the wind pushed tears from his eyes. Just because an experience is an old one—being affected by nature—doesn't mean it shouldn't affect the heart. He put his arm around Martha and she kissed him on the neck. Planting kisses. We live individual lives with the consciousness of death and awareness of the past. But the most important part of that sentence is the individual part. Let yourself be humbled by the experiences people have been having for thousands of years. And speak of it.

Look over there, Martha said.

It was Colleen Grandy steaming down the trail, her arms up by her chest, determined, as though pulling a thousand-pound trailer. Colleen's great pace was impressive, on her way out to the lighthouse and back. Henry had seen soldiers in the army with the same fixed concentration and they were good at killing many enemy and recovering too from killing the innocent that were only driving suspiciously. They were supervising a convoy when a US helicopter opened up on a crowd of men in a square. Tender said they have a rocket-propelled grenade but they could be Afghan Army. The Americans said they weren't A & A so it looked like they may have to entertain battle. In twelve minutes all the men were flattened and the Americans moved in and asked the Canadians to stand back. It was several days later Tender heard at the camp that the Afghan men did not have an RPG, but a camera with a telephoto lens.

Colleen was thin, in a sleek track suit and her hair pulled up in a ponytail. Sole-minded. Henry told Martha that, during the day, she'd pass by and catch his eye and they both called out cheery greetings. He was delighted to be a neighbour.

Before she reached them Martha made their presence known so as not to alarm her. She crawled out of the cellar and waved and said hello. Colleen Grandy jiggled her hand just by her shoulder.

Rick says he has a dory for you, Colleen said, and he'll bring it over next time he's home.

She has a nervous quality in her jawbone, a caffeinated jerkiness, but combined with the exercise it makes her alive and open. They spoke briefly but Colleen had to keep her pace, she spoke to them while moving side to side. They watched her walk back and disappear into the hills and then they too began their return into Renews, slightly affected by her gait. The lights on Larry Noyce's yellow cottage were off now except for a porch light to help the son home when he had bicycled back from the Copper Kettle.

Henry: Do you think she's in there?

She wouldn't be that stupid. Or more like it, Larry Noyce has discretion.

What does he have to lose? What they knew of Larry Noyce Henry had picked up from Leonard King and Colleen Grandy. Involved with a medicinal plant from South America. Returning to the western world a manner and a magic that allowed one insight into the origins of life. And here was Colleen, proof of that communication. Silvia too, probably, the way John talks. Not that Silvia was sleeping with Larry Noyce. Just the spiritual element: women were drawn to this more than men. Are you drawn?

Martha: Yes I think it's fascinating.

What I'm saying is not a negative judgment, Henry said.

She laughed, Perhaps a negative judgment on men.

The sheep were making their way down the hill to shelter in the trees for the night, their white smudges. The cows were sitting under the trees—the cow and calf John had saved. Clem and Sadie had taken to calling them Big John and Little John.

As they walked home they noticed the light from their own house. John and Silvia were up and Clem had turned on all the lights. The bedroom window. Could you see into that window, a figure slipping on her bra? The window with a child's handprint on it. Don't lean on the glass. Let's move over here. The dead are with us and the neighbours are watching. He rubbed his hands together and they sounded like sandpaper. They had made love and viewed the world from that window.

The truth is, Henry knew, any time you try to nail down a truth about somebody, you come up on one side of them, left or right, that makes them worse than what they are, never better.

13

He pulled Martha's juicer out of its cardboard box from the trunk of her car and clicked in the assembled parts. There was a lot of laughter on the radio, content not deserving the laughter. This would be the first time in a hundred years this house had ever heard a juicer. My god the laughter was ongoing.

Do you always have to be cheerful, Henry said, to be a Newfoundlander?

John Hynes is not cheerful, she said.

John Hynes is the exception.

That's why you like him.

Yes I collect exceptions.

Do you have a shelf for them?

I nail them to the outsides of sheds.

Larry Noyce is cheerful and he's not a Newfoundlander, she said.

There is some logic you're nearly getting. There's a word for it.

Tautological.

I didn't want to show you up.

Don't worry, she said, your eyes are condescending enough.

You mean I betray my feelings through the lining of my eyes?

My god you're so easy to read.

That's why no one likes me.

Everyone loves you, Henry.

Listen, widow.

Okay let's not be mean.

I'm sorry. I was playing.

That was pushy.

You know how I feel about it.

I know. I just want you to be nice to me, but there's a big guilt.

He wanted to question Martha on the guilt. Was it guilt, or mixed feelings. But this would be a cold inquiry. He did not want to turn on the juicer as it made a lot of noise and the admissions they were getting to were sacred, old admissions that required ambient sound. He looked out the window and saw Keith Noyce bicycling down the road.

The American, he said, is offering a spiritual path.

It used to be a financial path and a path to good dental care.

He thought about what she said.

Newfoundland women marrying American servicemen. Isn't that witty?

Henry laughed. It was fast, not witty.

I'd love to see your rankings. And your shelves full of exceptions.

Henry: I nail them to posts and let the crows clean them out.

The American is divorced.

He wanted to say something about a divorcé and a widow. Martha noticed his delay.

You can be pushy. I'm prepared for it.

No, I limit my pushy moments.

So it requires restraint.

Shit she's all over me. A little shield fell over his eyes and prepared him. He turned on the juicer and fed it the vegetables. Noise. He stretched the back of his neck. She was seeing all of this and knew all of what it meant. She thought it best to pause and, when he turned off the juicer and they could hear the radio again, she reached out and held his wrist and said, Do you want to go upstairs?

14

We were a couple for a long time, Henry said. I packed a bag with the last of my things and slept for long stretches. I was lonely and my heart felt empty, he said, and I did not like being alone. My chest was thin and I had no desire to eat. He watched the shipyard cranes unload containers and stack them on the wharf apron and John Hynes did his best to tell every available woman that Henry was single and he slept with some women and felt the raw morning light walking home from narrow apartments.

Oh great, Martha said.

It made me laugh at my own plight but deep down I was even more alone.

Poor poor you.

Do you want to hear this.

Go on I'm sorry. We always talk about Tender and never about Nora.

Your sympathy is coated with pleasure.

You can take it.

My heart was broken, he said, and John Hynes had phoned him then from Alberta to say, quietly, it's over now Henry it's all changed, the old way of life is gone entirely. John was shaking on the phone. John is like that. He cares for his friends. I felt like that character in *Alas, Babylon* who gets the phone call from a friend in the loop and the codeword hits his ear and he realizes armageddon is waking up on his doorstep.

So you do read.

We read that book in high school. That's the last novel I've ever read.

Rick Tobin had been talking to John and John was passing on the info. Something primitive rose up in Henry, a red crest of broken feathers that we all feel resides, like a diaphragm, underneath the heart. So that was how he got to be over there with Tender, and how he ended up in the jeep that morning.

It was the most words he'd said about the past. Martha wasn't looking at him but then she was. She's always looking at me, he realized. Well what else would she pay attention to, we're indoors, we're in bed.

He took her hand and held it up in the air, a foot from the ceiling.

Martha said I suppose we should eventually get up in case someone comes over.

15

He was on the roof now, finally, with a flat shovel. Tearing off the old felt. Bent over in the afternoon sun he rammed the shovel under the head of a nail, then pried it up. He was happy to have work gloves on and old jeans and a shirt he must have bought ten years ago. It still had some life in it. Martha tossed him up a bottle of beer.

Hot dipped, she said.

Come here and I'll galvanize you.

He stood tall and crowed over the land and a cool northerly was blowing in off the ocean. He waved at Silvia next door who had loaned him John's truck for the drive to the dump. Then he got dizzy because of the drop in blood pressure. The tingle in the back of the knees. He leaned against the old chimney wrapped in blue tarpaulin. When you're on your roof you own the view. You become kingly. My land, you say.

But bad weather was hauling in around Aquaforte. A leaky roof is miserable. He shovelled until there were bare planks and then ran down the ladder and collected the strips of shingle that had blown away and made a neat layering stack of the strips in the back of John's truck. He weighed down the shingles in the truck bed with the old fridge and roped it all down.

He said he'd be an hour.

He drove the truck with the oldies radio on and his elbow out the open window. He lifted one finger perceptibly from the top of the steering wheel when a vehicle passed, and saw a finger go up too. He was part of it all. They were living a rural life.

He drove down to the Aquaforte dump.

He idled at the little cinder-block gatehouse to show his garbage receipt. No one there. So he drove in a little more.

You're in a hurry, the man said.

Henry shifted into reverse and stuck John's receipt out the window.

Mr Burden asked what was aboard. The fridge it goes down there—he pointed to a peninsula of old appliances. And the rest up the ramp. That was Henry's first look at the incinerator, a cast-iron teepee three storeys tall belching out raw green fumes, the flames licking out of the open shaft at the top of the ramp.

He drove slowly to avoid puncturing a tire. There was a full-size pickup parked down by the fridges and stoves. He knew the truck, it was the one that carried the orange horse. Henry idled and jumped out and untied the fridge and slid it out the back. It caught a corner and tipped and the fridge door opened for a last embrace. It felt good to harm large appliances. The two men were watching him and he saw that it was Baxter Penney. That surprised him. His sense was Emerson Grandy drove him around the bend. But there he was with the man with hooks. Why on earth they'd park here to have a conversation he could not fathom.

He drove back up and reversed onto the ramp. It felt high up there. Keep the wheels straight, Henry.

There was a chute and, as he peered in, he saw the furnace of flame down there sounding wet with fire. It was licking its chops. He walked back to the tailgate and tossed a piece of felt in. It wafted down heavily but then paused and blew into bright flame, mid-air. He threw in some more pieces. You could only get so close to the opening because of the heat, so he fired the shingles in one by one. Slow going, and the smoke began billowing up. He hadn't brought a mask. Particulate from any number of really bad things down there. Car batteries and vats of clotted cooking oil and the general debris of flammable waste. It was cooking good and compounding and the heat was lifting the small bits of felt back up now, little magic carpets, and they were aloft, landing back in John's truck. Little fires sitting there.

I'm going to catch the truck on fire, is what he thought. There was a long heavy piece of felt on the floor of the truck. I'll slide it all in at once and jump in the truck and gun it. He hauled on the length of shingle, he put his hips into it. He needed momentum but there was no transference of that pull into a sliding motion. The sheet of felt split apart and he fell backwards. He moved his feet apart for purchase, but there was no floor under him. The floor was slanted. He tumbled into a silver dented slant of a chute. His knees spread out and his elbows, the edges of his body sought something to snag upon, just twist around and grab out with a hand, but it was all sheer. They make these chutes so dumptrucks can empty without a hitch.

He turned completely around and realized he was falling feet first and a terror blew over him and he knew his life was over. It was bright as he fell though he did not feel heat, just an absence of colour and shape and the intense panic of death. Life turned white and he knew he would land in a vat of burning oil, or hoses spraying flammable propellant, his feet in contact with rotating blades to churn him into a hurried fire. It was over now, the finish, my god I'm done.

His feet stopped and his knees buckled, and something in him flexed his legs so he sprang off the peak of fire and fell further, to the side of a heap of burning, he was below the fire now on soft ash. He crouched instinctively in a bed of cinders and he was alive. Above him the pyre of mad flame and whiteness, a sound of hungry rushing. He was dry and unhurt. Those high fast flames, preoccupied and unaware of him. The fire did not have horse's eyes, but the eyes of an alligator, on the front of the head. They were staring up and did not know he was there. He felt no heat. He did not feel a thing but the sound of rushing air beside him. It was hilarious that he was alive and exactly the same except he was inside a church, it felt, that was burning down. But that wasn't it. That wasn't the unusual event. This was ordinary, this church here was going about its everyday business. It always contains an assembly of fire. Fire is its congregation. *He* was the unusual event. He laughed to himself about this, quietly, crouching there: he had survived. I have a good story to tell. Where's the way out.

He gave the wall a kick but it was cast iron two inches thick. There was no door but there were ventilation slits around the base of the incinerator. Ash drifted over his face. Earlier he had been on his roof, and now he was under his roof. The roof was piled above him, burning. He looked up at the hatch again where he had fallen through and the shape of a helicopter whipped past in the small parcel of sky. He waved. It couldn't possibly be looking for him. It was not a military aircraft but something he knew marine biologists travelled in to study bird islands. A fluke to see it.

He felt his ear. His ear was hot. He knelt again and turned back to the ventilation slits. He crawled over to breathe in the fresh air. He could see outside. But there was no door.

The only way out was the way in. They were going to have to hose in a ton of fire retardant and lower a ladder. He was happy with this answer until he sensed the heat in the kiln of the walls. It would take a long time for this fire to cool enough to allow him to climb out. His shoulder felt hot and his elbow, the hinges of his body. He heard a heart beat. Had he ever noticed the shape of his lungs or the air in them. His lungs felt warm. A new shock. He wasn't going to burn to death: he was cooking.

He yelled out for help.

His own voice surprised him, the word "help" had blurted out without him thinking to do it. It was polite. He didn't want to cause trouble. You're going to boil to death, Henry. He yelled and kicked at the ventilation slits and saw the tongues of his shoes fall out. What the hell. His laces had vanished and the soles of his shoes were soft and covered in gummy ash. He cupped his hands to his mouth and bellowed with all his might. His arm was cooking now, the elbow painful where he bent it to cup his mouth. He turned around to give the other side of his body a turn. A sheet of his own shingles fell down on top of the fire. Roofing felt. What the fuck was going on. Was someone up there emptying the truck? He yelled again and repetitively, he yelled long and loud with his hands to his mouth and when he bent his elbow he felt pain. Help. His only hope was those two men.

16

Emerson Grandy passed over the bottle and Baxter drank from it. They watched a truck amble into the dump. Undecided. Then it pointed down near them and stopped. A man unroped a fridge and dropped that and then turned the truck around to back up towards the incinerator. It reversed, slowly, up the ramp.

Emerson: That's John Hynes.

No it's his truck.

Emerson Grandy watched Henry unload the truck. Emerson was not happy with how he was going about it. He was apprehensive. He drank the rum. As he lifted the bottle and dropped it again he lost sight of the young man.

He must be bent down for something, he said.

But there was no return of him. And he knew something wrong had happened. The entire approach to unloading was not done the proper way from the get-go. The truck parked a foot from the chute of the incinerator. Smoke partly covering the truck.

It looks like he might have fallen in.

What do you mean.

I don't see him no more.

The men pulled open the doors and ran up to the ramp. The truck was alone. But they heard him shouting.

Baxter Penney ran to the front gate and got old Mr Burden. That fellow just fell in. Mr Burden had a grey cell phone eighteen inches long. There was no signal. Come on, Baxter said.

They ran down to the incinerator where Emerson Grandy was peering into the chute. Baxter threw in a bunch of felt. Just to see what would happen to it—the way you might throw a coin if you dropped one accidentally and were wondering where it might roll. To see if they could see him, I guess. Emerson put his hooks to his mouth and yelled down, Get to the back! Then they all climbed down the embankment. The incinerator was built into a hill. Two large iron doors were held together with three lengths of rebar cleated at the top, the doors eight feet tall and they were opened once a year to scrape out the lead and metals that had not burned.

They found a boulder and together the three of them knocked out two of the hinges. The third was over their heads and they had to angle the rock carefully to push it up and out of the hinge. Then they swung wide the doors and peered in. A figure in motion. A shape running around the perimeter, low to the ground, and out past them, a burnt shoulder, running. The man who fell in. He ran out over the dozered fill and kept running until the shoes fell off him and he hit the edge of the trees and then he staggered into the trees as if hiding there in his sock feet. He stopped beside two big juniper and looked to talk to them before turning around. Then he saw the men and resumed being a cared-for citizen. He came back to them, frightened.

You're all right, Baxter said. It was one of the men from the truck. He was shaking his head. We thought we were going to have to go in there and get you.

They came towards him like he was an animal. They picked up his shoes and helped him out of the marsh. They sat him on the old fridge he had just dumped and they went at closing up the doors he'd escaped from. Henry let the fridge embrace him.

17

They walked back up to John's truck. The truck still needed to be unloaded, and Henry was in shock. But they helped him. They fired in bits of felt. He was standing pretty much in the same spot he'd been before, but this time with Emerson Grandy and Baxter Penny and Mr Burden from the gate. They heard the licking and Henry shied away. Mr Burden peered into the bed of the truck with his hands in new work gloves, watching them work. Mr Burden was upset. He was going to have to fill in a report. Usually I'm up here with them when they unload, Mr Burden said. I been here ten years now, and you're the first to fall in.

You're never up here, Baxter said.

I heard one of you shout, Get to the back. But inside, Henry said, I couldn't tell where the back was. The voice had sounded like it came from within his own body, the way they say a ptarmigan sounds when it takes to flight.

Emerson Grandy said, You need a drink of rum.

Where's the bar? Henry said.

They walked down to their truck. They had been sitting in the truck drinking Lamb's out of two styrofoam cups. They handed him the flask. If they hadn't been there. Drinking at the dump.

I know this truck, Henry said. You drive a horse around in it.

He downed their rum and, in the lee of the open truck door, he felt heat on his arm. The wind had kept him from noticing. I should get to the hospital, he said.

They shook hands and Henry thanked them. He half hugged Baxter Penney. Baxter understood the need.

There's a cottage hospital four minutes from the incinerator—Henry has often passed it and wondered what a hospital was doing this far from humanity. Now he was grateful for it. He strolled in, cinders head to foot. Nurses in blue flannel pyjamas. What happened to you, my love. They wrapped wet towels on his arm and face. Then a young doctor, from Syria, checked his lungs.

I've looked across the Syrian border, Henry said.

Oh yes, what did you see?

A lot of communication towers.

And heavy industry, I hope. Afghanistan, the doctor said, is downwind.

He was prescribed a pill for infection and a topical cream. A nurse gave him a cup of milk and a pill. When they were done, Henry drove to Gas Land in Aquaforte. He bought a twenty-six-ouncer of rum and two cans of Pepsi. Then he stopped at the pharmacy and filled the prescription. What happened to you?

He drove home with both Pepsi cans open. He found the oldies station and cranked it, opened the window and allowed the wind to massage his face and arm. He was delirious with life. He had decided not to call Martha—how can you hear what had happened without imagining the worst? It was a gorgeous, sunny day.

He arrived in the driveway and Martha came around the corner and stopped.

You look different, she said. An evil twin. Your hair is shiny.

She noted the bottle of rum in one hand and the prescription bag in the other. Then he told her what had happened.

She took him over to John and Silvia's. She was trembling. He had a bath and turned the bathwater black. He kept drinking and Martha made him a fast dinner and he ate that and kept drinking and shouting who the fuck falls into an incinerator?

That night, in bed, he kept repeating the fall. He added the mulching equipment or a spray of oil to keep things burning. Sometimes he landed on a long spike and the spike drove up through his leg and chest. There was a bucket of boiling tar he landed into and it splashed over his face. Mr Burden had said he was lucky. Half an hour earlier, a dumptruck had come with a huge load of carpet ends and stove oil. She was going pretty good then, Mr Burden said.

He dreamed he was in the jeep, rolling into the incinerator. All of them aboard, Martha too, and Tender was dressed in his goalie equipment. His big pads and wire-mesh hockey helmet, looking back at them with great hilarity. The handbrake jammed, a gun in the way. Tender could not stop the vehicle from falling in.

18

I can't do this if you're going to be so careless.

It was an accident.

I'd rather be alone. I'd rather be alone than go through what I've already gone through again.

I wasn't thinking.

You have to be more careful. Make a special case of it.

I'll try.

It's important!

How much danger made a dangerous life unacceptable? Why did a life have to be dangerous. Should it be? What was that all about. He wanted to feel safe, especially now, when what remained to him felt precious.

She had to drive back into town to work. She only had one month left. They were not living together. Henry realized they wouldn't move in together until the baby was born. The baby was the wedding ring. He was the last one to hold the ring finger of Tender Morris. That tattoo of the house of gold. Tender wasn't a religious man. But spiritual. That's what Larry Noyce would say of Tender if he'd met him. House of gold—Henry shook his head. He'd been inside the house of gold. Commitment is the danger.

That night he turned off the lights and walked up the stairs to the bedroom. There was no hall light at the bottom of the stairs— he had not wired one in and the Pooles had not insisted. He was in the dark on the stairs and felt the presence of something. He understood that he was being watched. Clem, he said. It was not a boy or a real person but there was something standing on the stairs above him. There was no material but an overlapping. A girl in a white dress but it was not Sadie, he did not even think of Sadie. She was standing on the stairs or hovering within the stairs. It was not visual but something residing in his chest, an understanding that ran into his knees and up to his heart. He bolted. He ran through her and reached the light switch at the top of the stairs. He flicked it on and the lightbulb flared and blew out with a pop. He kept moving to the bedroom and stretched up for the pullchain, but the chain was not there. His hand made a wider arc to find the chain but there was nothing at the end of his hand. He understood his sense of the world was drifting away. He was not in a house now but some larger place, some fathomless atmosphere that was not of any time or location. He hardly felt the floor. He panicked and was losing even his sense of self and then he felt a tickle brush his wrist and he pulled and the light arrived all around him—the room.

19

He phoned Martha and told her about the girl in the stairs. It felt like a reaction to the incinerator. Somehow this small ghost in the stairs in the dark was a retreating wave from the high tide of the incinerator. Martha absorbed this. She did not like the idea of a ghost. She walked around with the thought for a few hours and then called him back, cheerfully, you need to have a party. You need to invite people. Invoke a residency. Establish your identity. Make noise. Keep all the lights burning!

He phoned Emerson Grandy and a man answered. Henry asked if it was him.

Who wants to know.

It's the fellow you pulled out of the incinerator.

Oh, Henry, he said. We thought you were a goner.

He explained about the party.

No, Emerson said, that's all right. And if it's all the same to you don't call here again.

Which astounded him.

When Martha arrived he told her Emerson's reaction.

He's shy, she said.

Trust me, that man is okay in the spotlight.

But they had the party anyway. They invited John and Silvia and Larry Noyce and Colleen and Leonard King and the Poole brothers and the people of Renews. Henry mixed three jugs of watermelon rum. The wiring in the house was well used and the corners of the rooms were inhabited with life and something about the mix of ages reminded Henry of the parties they'd had at the base in Kandahar. John Hynes was telling them of a man down the road selling firewood but it was just old boards for sale.

Board is no good, John said. You can't stack it to get air through it. Do you need board?

Jesus no, Henry said. I got boards coming out of my ass.

They drank the watermelon rum.

Colleen: I shy away from Pepsi.

I got to keep my pants on, John said, or that rum will go right through me.

Silvia: It's the caffeine gives you the hangover.

Henry: That's why I drink with juices.

John: I'm after putting on some weight with the White Russians.

Henry felt the warmth of his friends. He was grateful that the one closed paragraph of his life—pouring out of a jeep in the morning, Henry holding Tender Morris's Sig Sauer when the shit hit the fan—was beginning to slacken. The heat had melted the wax seal on that and now he was back in the fresh air of the world with the scar of the event he had never really told Martha about. How could he, when John was saying aloud right now that he was putting on the song that he'd lost his virginity to. He's asking Martha now what was her song.

Song? Martha says. You mean album.

Great laughter.

The truth is I don't have the guts to say it, Henry thought. Have I ever had the guts to say anything that was awkward and makes me guilty? When they were teenagers they stole things from a hardware store and John's father questioned them and they could have lied, Henry was prepared to lie, but instead John told his father the truth. He told him, Henry realized, because I was watching.

John: Quit mocking me, inwardly.

They drank and danced and ate a paella of crab and shellfish that Colleen Grandy had made. There's three pounds of crab in it, Colleen said. And lobster. And shrimp. But it's the crab. It's loaded with crab. There must be I'm not lying there's three pounds of crab meat.

Henry asked Colleen about her father. Why he didn't come. He hauled me out of that incinerator and he asked me not to call again.

Dad's an alcoholic, Colleen said. If mother hears he was there with a bottle of Lamb's she'll leave him.

This stunned Henry. A man's heroism not to be celebrated because of a weakness.

Larry Noyce came over and commended Henry on all the renovations. It's hard to get a skilled man to do any work for you, Larry said. They're all working their tails off in Alberta pulling seventy-hour weeks.

Henry: And when they do come home they do not look for work.

No, Larry said. They jump on their quads and hunt or pull

two kitchen chairs into the sheds with the barn doors open, staring down a hundred feet of straight paved driveway to the main road.

He doesn't know, Henry thought, there's been an embargo placed on him.

Wilson Noel came in and Henry remembered the garbage in Kingmans Cove. He hated to rat on Leonard but Henry could be blamed, it was his garbage. He explained to Wilson what happened and Wilson was puzzled. I told him to fill in the old gulleys, Wilson said. He'll cover the garbage with good fill, don't worry about it. Did he charge you?

So it was on purpose, everyone knows that garbage is fill. Only Henry feels it's an outrage. He said to Wilson that Leonard wouldn't take a dime.

Finally Baxter Penney arrived. This party is for you, Henry said, quietly. I didn't know about Emerson. Colleen just told me.

Baxter: I've been a lot of places with that man. He gets up in the morning and sits in the woods waiting for it to get light out. He wants to get further away from Fermeuse, out into the ponds of Butterpot. Someone told me he has land out there. But Emerson doesn't let you know everything. He keeps some things to himself.

He allowed Henry to pour him a rum and said I guess you heard what happened to Nellie Morris.

20

Henry found Martha. Let's go outside, he said. Just for a minute. People can look after themselves here.

They left the house and walked down the road and turned to look back at the party as if they were rowing away from the house and they heard the music and laughter and the light in all the rooms shining out these bright crisp rectangles. Then he told her what he'd just heard about Nellie Morris.

Not to be cruel or anything, Henry said, but at least that settles the house and who owns it.

We've made this house come alive, Martha said.

It's come alive on the day Nellie Morris passed away. Here's to you, Nellie. And thank you for your house.

They walked back into their own celebration which felt now like the passing of a torch.

John was remembering to drink sparkling water and elderberry juice. He was not happy to be leaving his family again for work in Alberta. But he was also eager to do it. Embrace the suck, is what they say in the army, and the truth is both compulsions exist in us: to stay and to leave. It's for the family, John said, which makes leaving some kind of commitment to stay. It's not easy, we all know, to keep things going. To make a living.

21

They buried her in Renews, right next to Tender Morris, on that road into Kingmans Cove. The most surprising part was to see Baxter Penney in a suit—and to finally meet his wife. All this time and Henry had never met her. Hello Mrs Penney, he said.

Call me Sarah.

After the funeral Henry dug the garden where Leonard had dumped the potato soil. He was moved by what had happened. He had been forcing himself to adopt this life, much like this garden had been transplanted here. That's what I am, a transplant. Though I've been baptized by fire, he thought. And I've delivered electricity to this place. A baby is coming don't forget and I've passed the ashes of my own life. Those ashes were a girl on the stairs and I stand here now with a rusted spade once used by Melvin Careen and perhaps Aubrey Morris. To plant potatoes late in the season. To watch a new thing grow. To eat it.

The Poole brothers came by. Wayne said their grandmother told him about Nellie Morris. The last thing Nellie said was Mrs Poole, call an ambulance. Put the milk in the fridge, get my pills, I'll see you later, Mrs Poole.

Nellie left on a stretcher. She knew Mrs Poole would get an ambulance and the nursing staff may not. Her brain was ticking over.

He built a cold frame from wood and plastic and dug out the grass. Rocks, shards of glass and heels of slippers. John came over with his curiosity. He was scratching his armpit with a car key. I feel like I'm living next to a civil war arrangement, he said. Man returns to marry dead brother's wife.

If I was to make a period movie, a civil war movie, of what people did in the past? I'd have them washing their bodies with no running water, walk in slippers just to discard them, break bottles in the corners of their gardens. I'd fling coils of ancient wiring around and empty vienna sausage tins. You're growing a beard?

They went inside and Henry made them stiff, cold drinks and John shook the paper cup into his mouth, rattling the ice cubes against his teeth.

When you're young you should meet old people, he said.

I woke up to a knocking, Henry said. It was a woodpecker. Big round hole in the clapboard.

That's your northern flicker.

It was Nellie Morris, knocking on my head.

Don't let her build a nest in here or she'll never leave.

John couldn't stop himself from stroking his chin. When you have a beard, he said, you have to eat more carefully.

A beard makes you fussy.

Letting yourself go means you become, in time, more prim.

John looked exhausted. Are you sure you know what you're getting into, John said, with this relationship business?

If you know more than me let me know.

We just fought for three days, John said. Thank god we made up. We were sick of each other. Silvia took that healing workshop with buddy down the road. She and Colleen took it. At the community centre, the one for the dead hockey player. Her laptop was in the back seat in the sun. I must have lost my mind. I opened the door and flung the laptop down the hill. Why I couldn't tell you but I was furious. That'll teach her something, is all I said. I was supposed to get Clem's plastic suitcase that has a deck of cards in it for playing coddoddo.

I've played coddoddo with Clem.

He invented it.

He's going to become something.

I had the kids on the road on their knees pushing pieces of wood. The sun was over the cove and two kayakers were paddling out to sit in the sea and listen to an Ojibway elder at an outdoor microphone discuss abuse, abandonment, federal treaties, sexuality. Anyway we've been miserable for three days. She's been doing yoga and reading a book Colleen loaned her by Halfass Ramadan or something but it's pushing her further away from being cheerful is all I can say. And here I am prancing around telling jokes and cooking meals and taking care of the kids. She hauls herself out of this mood and she's met with what.

With cold resentment, Henry said.

I saw it, John said. Saw my own liquid iron sink into her.

There's a medicine for that, John.

I once had a prescription and it was the same medicine my father overdosed on. Fuck medicine is what I say. I'll take my chances with cancer and depression. But look this is what I know deep in my heart: if Silvia had kept up being sad for a fourth day I would have rolled up my socks and worked on all fronts to keep the family rolling. Such is the chemistry of my temperament.

You're not worried about Larry Noyce, are you.

You mean am I worried the way Rick should be worried? I think not.

Rick should come home more often.

John took, from his wallet, a photo of his dead father. He keeps his wallet in his left back pocket, because his father was left-handed and kept it there.

The sun, John said, was shining on those kayakers, still hopeful for a cosmic change in their lives. You could see them silently slipping their paddles into the sea. Cars on the hill with their magnificent braking systems slowing dramatically as they noticed my children on all fours playing on the road.

And when Silvia got home she said where is my computer. You must have left it in the car, I said. The car doors were open. Someone stole my computer. In this town, someone took it. Jesus what am I going to do.

And she got lost in this passion, Henry. I tell you I could have nailed her to a wall and fucked the bejesus out of her. Then Clem shows up walking briskly, in that manner he has. Carrying Silvia's laptop. Clem found two kids with it. They said they found it in a field.

Silvia: It was stolen from the car.

I believe they found it in the field, I said.

It doesn't work. It looks like it was thrown.

You can get your work off the hard drive.

John opened a beer and looked at Henry. I'm such a bastard.

22

Rick Tobin arrived with a fourteen-foot dory roped expertly into his blue Toyota pickup. He jumped out of the truck and marched directly to Henry and hugged him. He was upset and he was hurting Henry the way he held him. It was the incinerator, of course. Henry kept forgetting that other people were living his event for the first time.

You can have this dory, he said. It was built in a shed with one electric light by my father. He built it for Tender Morris, Rick said. At least Tender ordered it and paid for it, so I guess she's yours now.

Baxter Penney was on his way into the Goulds but stopped his truck and came over immediately to look the boat over and said, You can tell she wasn't built around here. The lift in the bow. When Rick told him it was from Conception Bay he understood and was satisfied. Rick doesn't belong here, Baxter said, so why should his boat.

It was brand new but built traditional, the type of boat that had prosecuted the cod fishery: a banking schooner dory. Baxter was delighted to have his hands on it.

We'll leave it in the truck and find a place to launch it, Rick said.

Kingmans Cove is your best bet, Baxter said.

Of course it is, everything's better in fucking Kingmans Cove. Why don't we all still live there?

What pissed Rick off was the comment that he didn't belong here.

Baxter drove off then, and would be happy to tell someone in the Goulds about this Conception Bay dory. Henry went in to get a couple of beers while Rick stared at the house without saying anything. He had passed it many a time, he finally said, but had he ever considered it? It was more a thing from the past than a dwelling to be inhabited now. He strode inside and drank his beer. He passed the chimney and pushed his finger into the soft lime mortar between the bricks.

Martha should send someone out here to help you, he said. A representative to oversee her side of the investment.

I might have overpaid by a hundred dollars, Henry said.

If you got it for a song, Henry, then that song's a dirge. It's a song unfinished. A song that needs so much help you have to rewrite it. You are so outside of music on this here songsheet there is the possibility that you are deaf. Rick laughed and finished his beer and slapped the chimney. You can't even get insurance, a shale foundation. And you own half of it!

They walked to the back of the property where there was a brook. No well, Rick said. You could run a pump off that brook and bury the oil tank and use it for a septic system. There are cheap ways to have running water.

Rick knew a guy in Alberta who had a pump that worked off no power, it had a flap to it and the brook, it has to run more than one mile an hour, pushes the flap and that flap pumps the water up the hose. A ram pump.

THEY DROVE THE DORY, slowly, over the dirt road past little coves that looked too steep, out to Kingmans Cove. How did they get down to the water? Rick wasn't from this place, Colleen was, so he did not know how people launched boats. Years ago they fished here in Kingmans Cove. They had wharves and ladders and slipways and stores all over the treacherous rock. But there was not a stick of that left here now.

We could snake around this bank, Henry said.

They reversed the truck and Henry wondered what they must look like from a distance. What would Baxter Penney think. They used an area where, in old photos, there had been a slipway and they carried and rolled the dory to the water and threw the oars in. There was a tongue of pebbled beach that fed up to a dry brook and Henry could pull it up there for shelter.

Look at this, Rick said.

An iron loop that had been hydraulically punched into the rock.

You're not the first one to leave a boat here.

They left the dory and drove back. Rick had a red cooler full of T-bones from Alberta. John Hynes came over—he had shaved—and they barbecued the steaks and ate them with a stack of boiled corn and a pound of butter and three dozen beer. There were no women around—they were all over at Larry Noyce's, meditating.

You have to give that dory a name, Rick said.

John: How about the *Happy Adventure*.

At five in the morning Henry awoke to the sound of a truck

honking and it was Rick driving past the house with four hours to spare to catch the ferry back to the mainland and the long drive west over Canada. Henry did not, for one minute, see Colleen and Rick together.

23

All day he considered Colleen and Larry Noyce. Perhaps because he was staring in their direction as he worked. Was this part of my hundred people? After supper he carried the oars down the road, walking in the middle of the pavement. He had a jigger and reel and his rubber boots went up to his knee. He wore work gloves and an oiled cotton jacket and a trucker's cap. That's where he met Baxter Penney who was dumping garbage over the bank. What could you say to Baxter, please don't dump garbage? Your people have lived here for four hundred years but now I've waltzed in and would prefer you to get involved in a costly recycling program.

He asked Baxter where he might find fish.

You don't have to go out far, he said. You can catch them in there past the mouseholes.

The mouseholes.

You don't know the mouseholes. Baxter shifted his feet to turn his body. When you see that white rock in the cliff.

I've never noticed a white rock. In the cliff.

It's a rock it looks like a fish, Baxter said.

He said it as though God had made the rock appear like a fish for these are the ways we give sign.

How about Emerson Grandy's horse.

You want to take your bearings off a horse? Baxter thought about that and the type of man before him. Let's consider the church, he said. You line up the cross over your shoulder and when you eyeball the lighthouse, that's all you need to catch fish.

Henry walked down into Kingmans Cove with the oars and the yellow dory was hauled up against the low tide. What a happy, ageless prospect. He knew Baxter didn't like to speak of temporary things. A horse can move and then where would you be. When they'd bought the house and were drawing up a plan to submit to the registry, it was Baxter Penney who told them to refer to the cemetery for their base measurements of location. Fences move, he said. Dead people don't.

Sure enough, Tender hadn't moved an inch. Hello Tender. Hello Nellie.

He lifted up the bow and pushed the dory down to the water and then picked up a few of the log rollers and walked to the shore edge and threw them under the dory and rolled the *Happy Adventure* into the surf. As he did this he heard a sound that felt a long way off, some roar occurring in the ocean. He stood up and looked at the water. Three specks in the sky just above the horizon but they were moving fast. They were pummelling forward towards him and they screamed directly overhead, it made him duck. Overland now and gone, but they were towing a massive turbulence that filled the little cove with the bellow of a distant massacre. A little wave of wind passed through his body like the ghost on the stairs and he realized he hadn't heard the sound since Afghanistan.

He tossed the four rollers up onto the high beach and realized he'd forgotten the plug and water was coming in. He jumped aboard and pushed the plug in the floor and shoved off with an oar and quickly settled the oars into the oarlocks. His heels got purchase against the knees of the dory and he spun the boat around and headed out to sea.

A strange feeling came over him. He was rowing away from the land and he saw where he lived. It wasn't just Kingmans Cove or Renews, it was the land of earth. This is how astronauts feel, he thought, to look back from space. He delighted in how cheap an experience this was, to understand space travel.

He rowed along the shore and studied the banks for what could be considered mouseholes. Then he remembered the white fish in the cliff face. He passed many things, nothing decisive.

He coasted and then decided he liked the look of the water just off the lighthouse. There were motorboats out further but he tried the jigger here. A whale breached out by the larger boats. The whales were after the caplin, which the cod were feeding on. He let out the heavy green filament until he struck bottom and then brought in a yard of the line. He jigged. The *Happy Adventure* rode high in the water. As he fished he got a little seasick. That was the swell. Some people lay flat rocks in the bottom so the boat doesn't ride so high.

He pulled up the line and rowed out a little further into the head of the current. He was in two hundred feet of water now—he could measure it in yards of line. He felt like he was floating in the branches of a very tall tree, dangling a line two hundred feet below to the ground, trying to bring to the surface something from the deep past.

He fished so long without a bite that he was forgetting what it felt like to have a fish on.

Sometimes he had to pull up his line because he wasn't sure, the weight could be a cod. But the jigger clunked against the side of the boat and there was no fish.

It was a beautiful evening. He decided to row out to the motorboats. One or two of the boats had sounders and the other boats kept an eye on this technology and the sounders found the caplin which the cod were feeding on. The men were gutting the fish over the side and seagulls left their high-tide perches and wheeled in to grab the clots of stomach and intestine. All day long, from the shore, you saw this glint of fibreglass hulls and the whales spouting and the seagulls turning with one black wing high in the air, all circling around, deep below, the carpets of caplin.

The sun was still high and the sky was clear and it took him fifteen minutes of heavy rowing to get amongst them. They were drifting and then starting up their motors to realign themselves. There was one on a Sea-Doo. Starting and stopping and dropping line and pulling it up frenetically like he was riding a rocking horse. One boat came over close and an old-timer asked if he could take a picture of the boat. No one did this now, rowing out in a dory.

You rowed out of Kingmans Cove, the man said. And turned his head a little, like the past was making a comeback.

The sun was bright but it was getting a little foggy now down by the water. At first he could still see the other side of the bay so it wasn't bad. But then that disappeared and he only had the lighthouse. Then that vanished. I can still pick out the rocks and cliffs below the automated signal.

There were no fish. The motorboats had caught their limit, even the Sea-Doo had bombed off for Aquaforte, for they said weather was on the way. Henry was alone, having to row further out. Several humpbacks arrived and snorted around the dory, just fifty feet away, playing with him, definitely diving under the boat—their long white flukes like blue arms—and coming up the other side to blow. He tried to stay calm. The shore had vanished now but he could hear the birds on the cliffs. He fished. Birds were out on the water too—the sound of birds was all around him. He listened further to the sea. It crashed up against the rocks below the lighthouse and he twirled the dory around fast and closed his eyes and listened, guessing where the cliffs were.

He caught five fish one after another. Big fish.

The sun tried to burn through the mist. It turned the fog a brilliant opaque yellow. It was very bright out there on the open water and yet no direct sun or any concentration of sun, the entire sky and sea turning a bright but dull particulate of golden light and it hurt his eyes, the brim of his cap was no good against it. He'd never seen anything like this before.

He gutted the fish. He pulled a sharp filleting knife up from the vent through the belly to the gills. He grabbed a string of blue intestines and pink heart and orange britches from the spine and slung them over the gunwale. The guts floated on the water and he could see now how much he was drifting. Gulls careened in to pull the guts out of the water. On the last fish, he rinsed the gutted body and a tremor pulsed through the fish and he lost his grip. The fish righted itself and slowly swam away, its head pointing into the depths with deliberation, and descended into the dark. It had gone home. It had no idea it was gutless.

The fog lifted and it was clear now, but a large cloudbank was coming down over Fermeuse. The cloud was charcoal black and it towered up and leaned towards the sun. It was marvellous how dense and high the cloud was and then it passed over the sun and devoured it. A lightness left the sea. The wind twisted around to the north. He looked at the horizon, and the long line of the flat sea seemed to rise. He picked up his oars and turned the dory around. The wind whipped in and the sky darkened. He had to row against the wind and a swell pushed the boat south. Please, he said, let me get back into the cove. He rowed, the oars erratic in the choppy waves, but he got himself back into the shelter of Kingmans Cove. The boat sideways on the waves but he made it, the hills of Fermeuse protecting him from the wind. The horse of Fermeuse was over there, coughing and licking its chops and staring right at him. He beached the dory and hauled it up though the weather felt gentle now. He carried his bucket of fish into Renews. As he walked past the lightkeeper's house, he saw Larry Noyce at the open door of his car. He was busy with a hose and a bucket of sudsy water. He was spraying the hose inside his car.

What on earth are you doing.

Then he saw the fish guts on the seats. The head of a cod sitting on the dashboard.

Someone threw a bucket of fish into the car, Larry said. Too bad it's been a hot day.

Henry put down his own bucket of fish and went to lend a hand.

It's okay, Henry. You don't want to get involved in this.

HE WALKED HOME, shocked at the violence of the act. Who would do that. Of course, he knew who would do that, but Rick Tobin was in Alberta.

He told Martha the story.

Yes, she said. Rick is away but who runs things around here.

She admired his fish. Let's have one before bed.

He skinned and filleted two fish and dipped them in flour and fried them in butter on the hotplate.

I was talking to Colleen, she said. Her parents are selling a cookstove. It's a good stove, she grew up with it.

What's wrong with it.

They're just tired of wood, Martha said. It's Emerson Grandy. I'm okay with him.

They sat down and ate the fish with salt and lemon. Then he remembered to tell her what had happened to the fish that swam away. Gutless. He realized, in telling her, that it was shocking. And Martha was perturbed by it. That's you, she said.

I'm gutless?

That you'll get away, no matter what. Then she added, This is the best fish I've ever eaten in my life.

24

They drove slowly north to Fermeuse. It was a dirt road here. A tow truck was winching Emerson Grandy's vehicle onto the flatbed. Hughie Decker. Two kids and the orange horse were watching him.

Henry: Are the Grandys home?

The kids ran inside. A woman looked at them through the storm door and then disappeared. Colleen's mother. Then she came out and admired Martha's figure. I'm Emerson's wife, she said. You know Colleen.

Then she turned her attention to Hughie Decker and asked about the truck. If it's not computer-related you can fix it?

It might be the fuel pump, he said.

She peered in and pointed to a flap of the timing belt. Hughie, you didn't see that?

It must have jarred loose when I towed her up.

Hughie drove off and the woman, watching him go, said, He had it made. Had the business handed to him by his father. Hughie couldn't keep it going. They handle all the rentals out here, contracts for that. Now he's working for Andy Baird in

Aquaforte, who bought him out. The stove, she said, is in the corner of the kitchen.

It was old-fashioned and nothing ornate about it. A workhorse. Then Emerson Grandy came in with his hooks. He'd been in the shed, parting out some ATVs to sell in the classifieds. Leaning up against the wall of the shed was a stack of interior doors. Doors look upside down when they're off their hinges because the doorknob is the eye and the eye is supposed to be high up on the face—Clem had told him that.

You'd like a beer?

They remembered the alcoholism. Too early for us, Martha said.

You like the stove, Martha?

She did and they settled on three hundred. Cash. The trouble with this stove, Emerson Grandy said, is getting it out the door.

There was a woman on a couch that must have been Colleen's aunt, for she looked ill. Martha sat down with her to let the men drag the stove out. Perhaps the kids were related to the woman. No one acknowledged her but Henry understood Martha was offering her some quiet advice. The only old thing left in the house now was the couch she was sitting on. As soon as she gets up, Henry thought, they'll switch it on her.

They were selling the stove because Emerson found he couldn't be junking up bits of wood any more.

So you found a limit to your hooks.

It's not the hooks, he said. Arthritis.

They took off the warmer and door handle. Shifted the kitchen table. Removed the cast-iron top and stove liners and tray. The men lifted it out. God it's heavy. It slid out, taking a layer of paint off the trim. Out to the truck. They got it all packed in and took a breather. A small terrier came for a pat. The horse too. They were living at the edge of the world, Henry said. Whales sleep under the clift, Emerson said. You hear them at night.

Henry unfolded a tarp to drape and tie over the stove.

Better, Emerson said, if you let the wind blow her clean.

THE TRUCK LURCHED OVER a bump and Martha said, Easy orange horse. Henry checked the rear view mirror—a dry spray of ash funnelling from the stove. The bump and Martha's reaction, he felt the ambush of emotion. The moment of Tender gunning it over that disturbance in the road, then turning to laugh at them. Tender knew it was not an IED, but what he did not realize was the mound in the road was a decoy, to halt a convoy.

Henry gripped the wheel and tried to think like an official, that death was a tail-risk outlier event. Martha asked if he was okay.

You're a hard worker, he said.

And good at it.

Wheelbarrow, rake, pick and shovel. The way she used the rake reminded him of how boys in Afghanistan fished plastic bottles out of a sewer hole.

They arrived home and left the stove in the truck. In the morning he'd get John to help him in with it. The firebox was blasted clean from the wind, as though a junk of wood had never been burned in it.

25

They took the car to the overfalls. The descent is so steep your toes dig into your flipflops and your free hand is grabbing at the bushes. The gorge is deep and the sun figures out a way to get down in there in the mornings and late afternoons. Henry and Martha climbed down this hill with their bathing products and feet barely staying in their flipflops. They have been, for the first time in their relationship, arguing. It's a very young argument, both of them are shy to raise their voices, but the work has made them tired and Martha had an appointment at the hospital for an ultrasound. They had gone in together and heard the baby's heart. The monitor with its ecstatic graph that reminded Henry of the seismic tests he's done on concrete and in mines. And now she was due in less than three weeks.

Perhaps it was the hospital—the event at the incinerator ambushed him—or maybe seeing the terrifically alive heartbeat in Martha that made him uncomfortable, but he realized his entire life was changing. They were growing familiar and this made Henry realize he wasn't going to avoid conflict with a woman.

They walked down the river to a manmade section, there used to be a swimming pool here, or a cordoned area bordered in short cement walls and at a gap there's a chute of water and they sat on this ledge with the bottle of shampoo and washed their hair and their armpits. They were furious with the washing and sick of each other until they heard voices and, up on the trail, some teenagers were falling down the trail, sort of skidding in their big sneakers and the teenagers had seen them and were pretending to not see them. Keith Noyce and Justin King. The boys were encouraging the girls to keep coming down anyway, even though there is a man and a woman here washing their bodies. The teenagers look shocked that people are using the water for a practical function.

The boys are wilder than the girls. Justin and Keith running directly into the water and falling in fully clothed, their sneakers still on, baseball caps floating towards the falls. The girls undressed and were wearing bathing suits underneath and they stepped into the shallows barefoot.

On the way home.

Martha: When you were a child you didn't get a chance to speak. To feel close to anyone. You didn't have any control.

Henry: Yes this is true.

Martha: See I like talking like this. This is real.

Henry: I like it too, thinking about the little me.

Martha: We should remember to do this. Think about the little people inside us. Let's not ever get complacent.

Henry was trying to turn a corner on arguing. He thought perhaps arguing was something you did with specific people, but the truth is you argue with the one you're with. With Nora his face would grow stiff while he heard that he was the problem and caused her grief and he'd shout back it's your generalizations and how you tell me I'm wrong rather than how you're hurt. And Nora would say you're being hurtful now and there's no need for it. That whole side of his relationship with Nora returned to him from behind a bone in his skull.

It took him a few minutes but he turned the corner on this old anger and apologized. Martha was not responsible for this anger. He was still in the routine of Nora and this was not fair. It was not fair to Nora, either, he realized. These are selfish ruts. Ruts and chemistry and the ways of the individual. Those kids at the falls. Would Keith Noyce ever turn the corner on the anger he has for his parents.

He said this to Martha in the car.

You're mentioning this because you think Keith can't talk to his father?

His father is too hard to please, Henry said. The boy is sick of it. Of trying to get his praise.

26

There was something different about the light and it was Martha who spotted the moths. The trees out front decimated by satin moth. The caterpillars just now turning into white wings and fuzzy bodies. A robin with a satin moth in his mouth, like he's delivering a small piece of mail.

They heard a rumble, the sound tanks make on roads in Afghanistan. It was Leonard with the front-end loader tottering over the road. It slowed out in front of Baxter's and jerked into Henry's driveway under the ruined trees, Leonard King snapping at the gearsticks to make the turn and raise its bucket to avoid the stove still in the back of John's truck.

Told Wilson I was dumping garbage, hey?

I'm sorry Leonard, I was confused.

Never mind, he said. But some day I might ask for a favour.

The loader lurched through the gap between the truck and the house. Leonard King, with his big white beard, twisted the machine around the corner of the house and then to the bottom of the garden and settled the back anchor. He lifted his rear wheels as the diesel burned loudly out of the pipe exhaust. He sank the loader into the garden. The bucket fell through the bush and curled in on itself and suddenly lifted forty gallons of earth and rock and bush and grass and garbage too, broken bottles and a vinyl shoe and strips of shower curtain and the purple sleeve of an acrylic sweater. Leonard swung the arm of the bucket over and dropped the earth and returned to the hole. The bucket felt around for a soft area and dug in and lifted another load of earth, this one of clay and water, a denser material that had not been disturbed since the glaciers left this plateau ten thousand years ago. The waste and toil of civilization accounted for the first eighteen inches. Now we are back to prehistoric times. The bucket chewing without sentiment through soil and rock. Leonard leaned the hydraulics into solid bedrock and pushed until the rear wheels nudged against the anchor brake and the smell of gear plates drifted onto Martha and Henry as they stood in the open doorway to watch. Leonard released the torque and lifted the nose of the machine and then returned the bucket to the rock with a thud—a tremor they felt in the soles of their feet. Leonard scooped out a rock the size of a hippopotamus, this grey wet rock slick with an oily gushing water. It looked for a few seconds as though grey ice was melting in the tucked crook of the front-end loader's arm. Leonard lifted this rock clear of the hole and gently landed it at the far end of the garden where it rolled and found its natural bed. That's when Emerson Grandy arrived and stopped everything.

First it was friendly enough: You going to keep my stove in your truck?

Henry: I might build a camper around it.

He thought Emerson had come from natural curiosity, to witness Leonard in action.

That'll be the hottest camper on the island, Emerson said. But then he waved up to Leonard and it was a wave that said halt what you're doing.

Can I come into the house, he said. I've got to show you something. Emerson checked the kitchen table to see if it was dry and then, with his hooks, he pulled a pair of drugstore reading glasses from his shirt pocket.

On the paper a very sophisticated drawing of land and houses and property lines. Henry recognized, immediately, the contour of the coast and the houses and the surnames of the owners of the properties. The flourish of a compass arrow pointing north. A deed.

This land here was given up for a parcel in that field next to John Hynes.

Emerson tapped the paper with a hook and straightened up. He took off his glasses and closed the temples with his chin.

My wife didn't know who you were when you come for the stove. She said she wasn't going to matter about it as long as Nellie Morris was involved. But since there's been a change on that score.

You mean she passed away.

He agreed that was the change. So I'm having to tell you that my wife owns the land.

The land we bought from the Careen brothers.

Yes sir that's correct.

We've been fixing the place up, Henry said. You've seen us here.

I don't get over this way very often.

Martha: You don't spend any time in Baxter's barn.

I don't have occasion to look over this way is what I'm saying.

We've been working like dogs. There's money gone into it.

My wife is not claiming to own the house. The house is yours to keep, she wouldn't want anyone to say I ever said that.

It's not her house.

Aubrey Morris built this house and he sold his lot to Melvin Careen. That was the Careen house what you bought from the sons. But Aubrey had a sister you see. Aubrey built this house for his sister. Then their father remarried and had kids and moved into it. And the sister had to stay in the old house. But she was given the land—

Emerson Grandy, realizing they were standing in the house in question: This house over us now. But what's underfoot isn't Aubrey's. They swapped gardens you can see it here.

You've been seeing me and didn't say a word.

To be honest I didn't know my wife had any fingers over on this side of the cove. I married into it. And it's not her, it's more her sisters and brothers. You saw one of them on the chesterfield. It was her really that made a commotion. You see, Aubrey's sister she had nine children. And all of them have children. She says herself she don't want to interfere. We don't know if you're acting on Nellie's behalf or whatnot.

Martha: What you're saying is I'm allowed in the house but not on the land.

Carol has no trouble with that. You could probably make an arrangement with her. The way it was with the house you see we all figured Leonard King would tear it down one day case closed. The other way is more difficult I can see what you're thinking in terms of going further and buying the land.

We weren't thinking that. I was thinking I've already bought this land twice over what with Martha here involved.

And my wife appreciates you have a situation over here with a child on the way. But you see there's a lot of her family and they're scattered and not all of them would agree I can guarantee you that to sell off this parcel.

Let me say again we weren't thinking of buying anything.

Carol now she'd be up for it but I know there's other brothers and sisters too and I'm afraid you'd be best off concentrating on the land you own—

I like the idea of concentrating.

Which is over that fence there on that little rise. It's a good piece of land if I say so myself. There's a garden there.

That's the land where they buried the well with chimney bricks.

That's what I'm after saying.

And you thought it best to come over, seeing as you have no part in the land.

My wife's family can get upset, son. She's not upset on her own behalf but the family expect her to keep an eye on things. I saw the bucket of Leonard's machine going to work and I thought it best to intervene. It was the wife who got in a twist over that. A well that means a septic system and a lot of permanent things in the ground. I said I'd speak it out.

Something in Emerson realized the story was unfair to Henry, especially with Martha in the condition she was in. But they knew Martha had a house in town, it wasn't like they were telling a pregnant woman to go homeless just a few weeks before she was due. And it compelled him to come up with another thing. I was after having a heart attack, Emerson said. I felt it in both arms, right up to the elbow. This was ten years ago. I thought I was going to be sick, that I had a bug. I was telling this to Rick Tobin as we were laying down this cement well in Aquaforte. I was to guide a length of pipe to join up with the one I had my hands on. But I had my head turned to talk to Rick and my hands were resting on the lip of the pipe. Down it come right on my hands. Rick drove me to the hospital. And I came home wearing these.

27

He had two weeks to make things right. When the baby came he would have to retract and take care of the centre. The chaos before him made him wild. They went upstairs and checked the ammunition box that was full of the letters he'd rescued from the garbage. Martha found the legal letters. The threats from the Careen family. She read out the letterhead and the lawyers involved: Gardner Coombs. And there, on the bottom of the page, the associate attorney: William Wiseman.

Bill Wiseman removed his mouth from the straw and swivelled in his chair to open a folder in a cabinet behind his desk. Melvin Careen, he said. He died before the matrimonial property act.

There was an open hamburger on his desk. No plate.

Henry: You're saying they have a point.

They don't have a point. They have the entire law on their side. Every sentence, the whole dimension is theirs, Henry. A deed! They have a very old piece of paper signed by a magistrate that says the land is theirs.

Martha found a letter. From you. Thirty years ago. Trying to get Nellie Morris out of that house.

Thirty years ago I was not much more than a typist.

You could have come clean with me on this.

You remember my words?

I'll never forget them: this deal is not going to fly.

Some would say that's more than clean.

BAXTER STOOD IN THE SPACE where there used to be a piano by the wall when he was a boy. Nellie didn't have a right to pass the land down to Patrick Morris. The Careens is just going along with it to get the house off their hands. Nellie had a child who died—that was out of wedlock.

I met Nellie. She told me her daughter married.

Her daughter never got old enough to marry. Nellie worked in McMurdo's in St John's. That's where Melvin Careen met her. He'd been married, his first wife died. Melvin Careen showed me a deck of cards once—he found them in his dead wife's sewing machine table. They had three boys.

The Careens. I think they were playing cards with that very deck.

You met them. It's good you bought them out. House was built by Aubrey, but wasn't finished when Aubrey went away. Maybe there was a trade of gardens. If Emerson Grandy says his wife's family has a deed then that must be what happened.

I saw the paper.

You seen the paper. An agreement until the aunt passes away.

No—that was only verbal.

Last time I met Nellie, Baxter said, she was standing in the

pantry right where you are, combing her long hair into a paper
bag.

All this, in speech, was impossible to follow. It had to be
written down. That's why people wrote things down. Or they
didn't.

28

Leonard King said move the house.

Can you elaborate on that.

Up on skids and push it over.

Henry had seen old photographs of houses moving. Some were floated across bays, towed across ice, moved on flatbed into different bays entirely. But then to Leonard everything could be solved with a backhoe.

Martha is going to have a baby very soon.

It'll take a morning, Leonard said. He made it sound like he did this every day before eating porridge.

What about the chimney.

Knock it down, he said. You can't fit a liner in it anyway.

And the well?

We'll dig a well over there. I'll have it done when the baby comes.

What about the well filled with chimney bricks?

Is that the land you own?

Apparently.

Leonard thought about it. He had never dug out an old well. Henry you don't know what you're getting into with an old well.

You're saying move the house but you hesitate on reopening a well.

Might be poisoned, or dry. There could be another reason for filling it. Could be car batteries down there. More than likely they used it for a while as an outhouse.

So before you abandon a home you shit in the well for a couple of years and then stuff it with chimney bricks.

You're best off with a new well.

29

Henry drove the truck for Wilson Noel, completely discouraged.
What he had liked about working for Wilson was keeping an eye
on the community. He wanted to oversee anything happening
here. But the ground was shifting beneath him. At noon he sat
in the truck and ate his sandwiches. He would move into town
with Martha. It was the only way to manage things. Wilson Noel
tried to cheer him up. I've hired on Justin and that fellow you
mentioned, Keith. To do that clearing down in Kingmans Cove.
We don't have to tell Rick. Wilson remembered what it was like
to be a young man. And also a child should not be blamed for the
actions of a parent. He recalled last winter, when he'd come across
the three of them shooting into the King camp. At least they're
industrious. And where there's trouble, try to buy the trouble and
own it on your side.

Yes, Henry said. That's what you've done with me.

That Saturday morning they drove into Kingmans Cove
together and Henry helped him chop out some trees and burn
the tops. The boys were there, Keith and Justin. They rode in
on a trike. Henry and Wilson demonstrated the operation of his

chainsaw and how to douse the bonfire. Wilson dragged his toe through the dirt around the blaze. Keep the fire within this circle, he said.

When the men drove off the dust rose up on the dirt road out of Kingmans Cove and the sky was blue and white and the trees here had been unmolested since resettlement. Keith and Justin turned to look at the work ahead of them. It hadn't rained much and Keith had to walk down to the brook to fill two five-gallon buckets which they used as a fire caution. There were some teenagers like them swimming in the pond the brook fed into. They were Noels— Wilson's kids. Morgan Noel, he didn't want to work with his father. Keith could hear Justin start the chainsaw by dropping it below his shins and pulling the cord, the dangerous way.

When Keith got back with the buckets he picked up the axe to limb the trees Justin had sawed down, just as Wilson Noel had showed him. He fed the fire the wide green branches. Justin's chainsaw bit through the wood and sawdust sprayed up and the noise of it ran through Keith's ear and buzzed the brain and he hated his job and wished he had the saw.

The flames crackled through the shiny needles. Sometimes they got ahead of themselves and had to wait for the fire to dampen before adding more brush. They sat around in their cut-off jeans and T-shirts. It was a hot day and they took off their shirts. They were thirsty.

Keith, Justin said, go get us some water.

There's water there, he said. He tapped the white emergency bucket with his foot.

I'm not drinking water from the brook.

Keith took the sheep trail down to the brook and heard the Noels in the pond horsing around, it sounded like they were swimming and jumping off a big rock and through the trees you could see the pond and the orange rectangle of an inflatable raft with a woman sunbathing on it in a pale blue swimsuit. It was Colleen. Keith stared at her and the Noel boys that were in the water, their hair plastered back. They had boats they'd built out of old lumber, boats that sat low in the water, military boats with nails for turrets in housing that swivelled. The oldest Noel was Keith's age, and he'd told his old man no I don't want to cut brush for minimum wage. That's why Keith got the work.

Colleen Grandy on the orange inflatable raft. It was hard for him to believe what they had done together. She lay there with her long hair completely dry, the wind just pushing her inflatable raft out a little and she had on brown sunglasses and a paperback novel was open over her leg and the corner of the book touched her where the bottom of her pale blue swimsuit covered a little mound below her navel. This very nice shape and the corners of the pages pushing a little into that mound under the pale blue and white fabric as she floated in water that must have been six feet deep.

It was dark at the brook in the shade of the tall trees and he found the gallon container full of tapwater that Wilson had said was for drinking. He drank off a glass and knew Justin would want more than one glass of water.

He took the trail back and could not see him, but he heard the chainsaw and he walked deep into the trees and found him. Justin had made another fire here and was loading brush onto it. It makes sense, Justin said, to have a couple of fires going. We can burn more and we don't have to lug it all the way to the road.

Keith handed him the container and Justin drank it down while the chainsaw was still running and he pulled the butt ends of the trees away from the fire and told Keith to run back for the axe with the orange handle and put some more brush on the old fire.

They sawed some more trees and limbed them and then the saw ran out of gas and Justin walked back to the road and refilled the chamber with the gas/oil mixture.

Are the Noels up?

Yeah.

Are they swimming?

Keith said he'd heard them through the trees.

Look, he said. And Keith peered into the open chamber where the fuel goes. The fuel was boiling.

There was a wind picking up now, it was the same wind that was slowly pushing Colleen Grandy out into the middle of the pond. Several times now the new fire, in the trees, leapt out and singed the moss and Keith stamped out the singe and added more branches. He heard Justin working in the woods. Wilson Noel had not told them to do this. But he knew Justin wanted to impress him. Justin had ideas of how to thin the woods that might not align with the way others did things. Justin was always complaining about the methods of adults. Justin's uncle Leonard King drove the car in a low gear, not letting the engine rev.

As he limbed the trees he would come upon a rock and these he threw towards the fire to make a partial ring on the lee side. He did this without Justin telling him to. It was what Wilson Noel would do.

They threw a last heap of boughs on the fires and then walked down to the brook to eat their sandwiches in the shade. Keith opened a bottle of warm Sprite he'd left in the brook and they shared a chocolate bar and they heard the splashing through the trees. They walked towards this screen of brush and looked through and the Noel brothers were still enjoying themselves. The Noels had cans of coke and Colleen Grandy was on her stomach now, slowly paddling the inflatable raft in to get her own soft drink. She looked like she didn't want to get even her feet wet. Colleen Grandy, Justin said. She's pretty good for her age.

They walked the sandwiches back up to supervise the burn. They were only gone maybe ten minutes but the woods were different. It was the way the smoke was coming up, not in a localized punch but sort of runnelling up thinly over a long line of land. The fire had caught and was in the ground. Justin laid his sandwich on the gas can and ran into the field. Keith followed him and they both started stamping at these little fires that had hopped around before brightly changing their minds. Keith found a fire under a big tree and had to push branches aside to get a foot in. There was a breeze. The wind was blowing life into all of this.

Something audible happened. The ear picked out another, windier, sound that was now the dominant aural cue that trouble was upon them. A roar blew up as boughs on a sawed-down tree caught and the whole length of tree, sitting on the ground, blew into a fence of flame. Long orange hairs of fire bent over in a flurry and pointed straight into the ground then returned to stand up on end thirty feet deeper into the woods.

We need water, Justin said. Where's your cell.

We need a landline.

Maybe someone at the pond.

Colleen Grandy will have a phone.

He watched Justin run. He ran through the woods on a path they used that would take him straight to the pond. Even if someone had a cell phone it wouldn't work in these woods. You'd have to climb a hill and even then you couldn't be sure. He'll have to take the trike out to the main road. He imagined Justin tearing through the woods. Colleen Grandy lifting her head and shielding her eyes to see what the panic is.

30

Henry Hayward had seen the smoke. It was too much smoke for the work the boys were doing. He climbed Aubrey's ladder to his eaves and witnessed the fire. He could smell it.

He drove down into Kingmans Cove to see if he could help. The fire had chewed a black carpet through the valley over the old cellar and punched a charred line deep into the hill of trees, smoke coming up off the more mature trees. That was a lot of trouble. The boy Keith was down there watching the fire eat into the woods. Colleen Grandy was with him. Henry felt responsible for the fire, that somehow he had taken a spark from the incinerator with him, nursed it and let it loose in this field.

Run!

Henry turned and it was Justin King standing tall on his trike, shouting into the valley.

Then a plane. A slow yellow plane with fat pontoons on the wingtips and four propellers. This plane was all belly. It came in straight over the fire and then banked out onto the sea taking the sound of its propellers that sort of chopped at the air. It did one complete arc above the smoking valley just to point a wing at the fire. It drove itself inland searching for a pond big enough to land on, then turned again, sharply, on a wing and doubled back and sank below the trees. Henry heard it through the woods. It would be on Butterpot Pond now, its vast cargo hold gathering water and those young Noels would have a great view of it. The yellow plane returned to the sky and Colleen Grandy took Keith's hand for they must have been nervous and they stared up as the plane flew low and the gates beneath the plane opened suddenly and it looked like paper flew out, a confetti drop that turned immediately into a curled fabric that straightened in the air and Justin bellowed out to them again, RUN.

It was as if a message was being floated down and the air inflated the message as it descended. Colleen and Keith stood there, too late to move. The water hit them both and flattened them to the ground and the water drilled the ground as if it had gone through their bodies and broke into pieces that flashed up against Keith's chest and the sound of it trickled off and he looked at Colleen Grandy as the water continued to fall on him like something tall that had fallen and the water drenched six acres of land and the silver trees beside them, the tree limbs sheared off and branches split wide open, taking sleeves of black bark from the trees and the wide plane was almost down in the trees now, dipping into the hollow of the marsh. It continued on and never came back. Colleen Grandy holding Keith close and Justin King turned them both over and said are you okay is anything broken can you talk to me, talk to me.

Henry Hayward drove down into the valley just as Justin King reached them. It was Justin's voice and shape in front of the sun and Keith Noyce who said he could not get up and Colleen Grandy could not or would not let go of him.

Jesus, she finally said, when Henry got there. That was fucking amazing.

He understood, at that moment, everything of the relationship between Colleen Grandy and Keith Noyce.

31

Keith got out of the idling car outside Wilson Noel's house in Aquaforte. Wilson Noel once had a bonfire on the family land in Kingmans Cove that went into the night and, as they roasted hotdogs, Wilson Noel took a spinning rod and flung a red and white lure deep into the dark night. You heard the lure hit the water and he waited a few seconds for it to sink then he reeled it in and the rod bent over and he fought hard and caught a herring. The herring flapping in the firelight as he thrust his thumb and finger into its eyes.

Wilson Noel opened the screen door and listened to Keith's apology. It was the first time Keith had ever seen Wilson Noel serious. Even when he'd found them shooting into the snow of the King cabin he had a sense of humour in his face. But here he was listening to Keith without any pretense of collusion. We're going to replant, Mr Noel, Keith was saying. Every tree you lost we'll—

I didn't lose a tree. You crazy sons of bitches burnt them down.

Keith's father, sitting in the car, heard the outburst. The screen door was creaking as Wilson Noel held it open. He did not invite the boy in and he did not use the little sliding lever to keep the piston on the door ajar.

I'm sorry for that, Mr Noel, Keith said. Here's a map of the area that my father drew up and you can see where the fir are going to go around the family garden you had planned.

I want pine, he said. White pine, and birch, and I don't want them in rows.

He took out a pen and held Keith's map in his hand. He scratched out some of the markings and made others, here and here and here. He was deliberate in dirtying up the map.

Mr Noel was without humour because of his sons who had come home from being hit with seven tons of water while swimming in the brook that ran into Butterpot Pond. They could have been drowned and then burnt as the entire brook and all the cabins deep into the wilderness area were vulnerable and who knows where that fire would have eventually gone if the wind wasn't a prevailing wind and had blown it to the marsh.

32

Henry knocked down the chimney in one day and carried it out in buckets. Martha painted a dresser in the back garden.

You shouldn't be doing that, he said.

I'm wearing a mask. I'm outdoors. I'm being careful.

It's not Larry Noyce she's seeing, he said.

Martha: How do you know anything is going on.

It's going on.

What did you see.

The way they held each other. That wasn't the first time they've been together.

The bricks were not good enough to build a new chimney with. They sort of fell away as he worked first on the roof and then down through the roofline and the bricks were hardly cemented together but merely standing like children's blocks one upon another. He could not open the windows otherwise he would have thrown them out that way or used a rope to lower the buckets down. He'd done that before in the early days of working with John Hynes and Rick Tobin. These windows were painted shut.

When he was through he shovelled the mortar into a wheelbarrow and filled the barrow seven times with heavy green powder which was what remained of the lime mortar. The work allowed him to think. And what he thought was conspiracy. Baxter and Emerson were at the dump conspiring. Baxter and Emerson have a history with Rick Tobin.

The chimney foundation was ten big flat boulders stacked into a mound. He lifted these out of the hole in the centre of the floor as the house and crib would need to slide over this ground.

Larry Noyce stopped by and asked if he was going to rebuild the chimney. Henry told him about moving the house.

I have bricks, Larry said. In my cellar. From when they tore down the old lighthouse.

You salvaged them?

The house we have is the lightkeeper's house. His family lived there. I feel some responsibility for the old lighthouse—I kept the best of the bricks.

They opened the cellar and shone a flashlight and the bricks sat in a quiet heavy stack. It looked like they were hibernating. They were a warm colour, like ruddy bullion. There was a two-litre plastic juice bottle sitting on the bricks.

My god they are beautiful.

I only kept the good ones, Larry said again.

It can be an interior chimney. The weather won't get at it.

Henry asked him about the juice.

It's the root, Larry said. The medicine for the ceremony. It needs a cool dry place.

Your fridge not working?

It's a little illegal to have possession of it, Larry said.

How did you get it here?

Federal Express.

As he closed up the cellar Henry told him about the mine in Fort McMurray, the event with Jamie Kirby. It's like you have the jewellery box of Kingmans Cove, Henry said.

33

A transport truck arrived with four wooden utility poles that had been standing along a railway spur near Witless Bay for twenty-five years. Leonard King was renting the poles from the Used Lumber yard up on the main road. Six men arrived in the back of a pickup truck and they jumped over the tailgate and helped guide the winch that lifted the poles onto the ground. They used pulp mill hooks to drag the poles along to each corner of the house.

Henry picked his way through the new land and moved an old piece of fencing and used a lever bar to roll several rocks away from the path that Leonard was to take. As he did this the men used two hydraulic jacks from Hughie Decker's garage and began lifting up a corner of the house. They rolled the creosoted end of a pole under the corner of the house and then jacked up the other corner. They did this methodically around the house until the poles were under and then they jacked up the house again corner by corner and proceeded to bind the poles together with strapping and chains and long poles that went under the floor beams and tied and nailed these to the poles. This elevation was done slowly and the creaks of the house guided them to how fast they should go. Leonard did not want them to break a pane of glass.

By the time Leonard arrived with his front-end loader the men had stopped for a break and drank thermoses of tea and plastic bottles of cola and sandwiches and cellophane-wrapped confections. They threw their garbage in the grass. Leonard must have been thinking about the project in his sleep for he did not hesitate and rammed the loader into the small alders and rotated his machine until he was on the east side of the house and ready to pull the house with the bucket of the loader. The men had heavy ropes slung around the house and tied with a pulley and connected the ropes to the bucket and Henry joined the men on the house corners as Leonard pulled with the bucket. Heave, heave came the call and the house cracked itself out of the shale footing and smeared the flat slate out in front of the utility poles and dug into the grass and then found the surface of the earth and then, very neatly, slipped greasily over the garden. Leonard had a spotter behind him who agreed with the direction and who told Leonard how to back up as he pulled the house along.

The house made progress across the old field. The roof of the house broke the horizon and it looked confident on this new land. Could you turn the house a little, Henry said, so it faces the sea. Just nudge a corner about three feet.

Leonard opened the door to the loader and stepped out and looked around. You've got a good view from up here as it is, he said. Climb up and you'll see what you have from upstairs.

Just turn the house a little.

He had moved into Tender's house and now he was moving that house away from the cemetery. The dead don't move but houses do.

A couple of men shouted out that they'd found rock in front of the house. They were picking up flat plates of slate to show Leonard. There's a foundation here, they said. Underneath the matted yellow grass was the distinct border of a house. Leonard quickly paced it off. Well, he said, lucky you.

By the early evening, the house sat on the old foundation.

You said a morning, Henry said. They were drinking beers now in behind the new house placement. Staring at the hill that jutted up and levelled off that reminded Henry of the widow's hill in Kabul. He'd forgotten its real name.

It could have been done by one o'clock but you'd have had to move the kettle off the stove.

Leonard looked around the land and pointed with his beard to the bottom of the garden. I'll come by next week, he said, and dig you another well.

34

You could see the whole cove now in this new position that was, in fact, where the old house used to stand. Henry was being a slave to origins. The past was forcing him to live the way it wanted him to live. But he was open to it. Soon, Martha said, you'll be refusing booster shots and brushing your teeth with a twig.

The chimney took a week to build, for you had to let the cement cure in stages. John Hynes showed him how to pin four plumb lines to the corners of the chimney to keep it straight and Henry mixed cement in a wheelbarrow and slathered the mortar on a course of bricks.

Martha: Are you going to put a light on top?

When he was tired and dirty they walked out to Kingmans Cove and fished in the dory. It was on the water he enjoyed himself. They put on their boots and coats and he carried a bucket with the jigger and they walked down the road. They fished with the tide to make the rowing easier and he did not go out so far that they were vulnerable to the weather or a change in sea. He hid the oars up in the long grass of the hill so he did not have to carry them home.

On the last weekend of the fishery they got to the cove and there was no dory. Henry ran down the hill and checked the grass. The oars were not there. Someone had found the oars and taken the *Happy Adventure* out.

We were in it yesterday.

So they're in it now.

They checked the sea. They walked back home and Henry said he'd search the marina down in Bay Bulls. Hughie Decker was there winching up a trap skiff. He hadn't seen a dory come or go. Henry drove home and stopped in to Baxter's. Martha was already talking to him and Baxter was excited.

I heard someone say Justin King was at the Copper Kettle, Baxter said, talking about forty fish he caught last night and I thought to myself what boat has Justin got to go fishing.

Justin King took my boat?

Now where would Justin put that boat is the question.

Henry said he checked the marina.

Everyone knows your little dory. Rick Tobin's father built that. What he's done is he's tucked it away. You go around to the point in Fermeuse with a pair of binoculars and check the coves between here and the lighthouse—you'll find your dory.

You mean it's beached someplace along here?

Take my moose binoculars. Go around the point.

Henry drove to Fermeuse. What Baxter meant is you can check the cove pretty easily from the north side looking back over the water. He took the lane into Emerson Grandy's. He was out of the car before the engine stopped. Emerson was feeding the horse at a rail. He could tell something was on the go.

Henry trained the binoculars on the far shore and the first thing he saw was the stern of the *Happy Adventure* glinting in the evening sun.

She was beached on a cove halfway to the lighthouse. Just sitting there five hundred feet from his house, the first thing those binoculars picked out, like it was a cartoon show and the dory was painted on the lenses of the binoculars. He told Emerson what had happened.

You lie in wait tonight, Emerson said, they'll come back out on a quad.

You mean they're still using the boat?

They'll use it till it sinks.

But why wouldn't they hide it further along the shore or somewhere out of sight?

Thieves, Emerson Grandy said, don't like to work.

35

Martha begged him not to go but he said he'd be careful. He wouldn't get into a physical altercation—he just wanted to know who was using his boat.

Baxter said he wanted to help, in case of trouble. But Henry said he could handle it alone. He walked on out to the lighthouse and then veered off the trail in the long grass where you could see someone had climbed through to get down to a small cove. The grass went both ways as they had come back and gone down at least once. Evidence. He saw the dory. They would come back again tonight on a quad and then jump down here and use his dory and get their fish then beach her like they've done, just tied up to an old log of driftwood, look at the side of her and she's got her sternpost all beat up and the transom is cracked and one oar is fucking missing.

But what is the use of waiting now. Justin King will know as half the cove will have heard now that Emerson Grandy knows. They wouldn't be coming out now.

He heard voices.

Laughter.

It was, impossibly, a woman's voice. The feet leaving the trail, silent in the long grass. Now over the slope and roll of stone as they found their way to the beach.

He got his flashlight handy. He stepped out from the wall of rock and shone the light upon the dory, and to the hands balancing it. The faces. It was Keith Noyce and Colleen Grandy. Colleen's face was at the height of exhilaration—as the flashlight hit her, the features fell into the shock of knowing she was doing something wrong.

It's me, he said, Henry Hayward.

Oh my god, Henry, she said. I'm so sorry I'm so sorry.

There was damage here and Colleen knew it. She tried to explain but then they all heard the quad.

Colleen and Keith scrabbled over the rocks to hide. Baxter was looking over the embankment and Henry shook his head so only Emerson came over and down the hill to the boat. Colleen and Keith were hiding around the cove of rock.

You going to wait it out?

Henry told him his thinking.

Well let's get her around back to the cove.

There's only one oar.

No matter we can get her around on that.

Emerson jumped aboard and Henry put one foot in and pushed them off and Emerson took the oar and guided them around a sunker and, gripping the oar with both hooks, paddled them along into Kingmans Cove. Henry shone the flashlight on the rocks. Emerson was in the front of the dory but he used the oar the way a gondola oarsman would handle it, high and long. The strength came from Emerson's wrists and forearms, strength that poured in from his feet. Baxter was waiting for them at the beach on his idling quad. Its headlight shining right on them.

36

Leonard King was down there with a sump pump all morning arranging the footing out of flat rocks so that a twelve-foot length of thirty-six-inch polyethylene tube could sit on it. Okay, Leonard said, time for a favour. My nephew is a good boy. You can leave your shed door open and he'll borrow a tool and it will come back. He wouldn't take no one's boat in the middle of the night.

He'd like Henry to stop whatever rumour was going around that Justin King had stolen a boat. Justin has a job with Wilson Noel and he's already after burning down his land so he don't need to hear he's a thief too.

I'll go over and apologize to him.

Although he knew now, from Keith, that it had been him and Justin who had taken the dory the night before. They'd gone to try fishing at ten at night and got greedy and the weather turned on them and they had to ditch the boat early. Anywhere they could find shore. They did their best to tie the boat on and then they hauled their fish home on the trike. Keith had wanted to bring the dory back to the cove and then he thought it would be fun to do it with Colleen. She had no idea what he had in mind. Until they hit the shore.

What are you going to do about it all, Henry said to her.

About Rick, you mean.

About any repercussions that are being set up.

My god don't tell Rick is all I'm asking, Colleen said.

You think he doesn't know?

It's one thing to suspect something, she said. He can live with that.

You're wrong, Henry said.

LEONARD DISAPPEARED DOWN the hole and Henry fired up the wand and rolled out the torch-on on his roof. He worked for an hour then ran out of propane and climbed down the ladder with the empty bottle. He looked down the hole. Leonard was leaning awkwardly against the metal ladder, his head against a rung of the ladder staring down at his feet.

Are you okay?

Leonard made a gurgling sound but it was not comprehensible. Was he concentrating on something down there. Leonard was unable to raise his head. Henry unplugged the orange extension cord and the sump pump stopped and Leonard rose himself off the ladder, his neck and head and shoulders all came to life and his head was like a flower to the sun. His eyes wide open. He shook his shoulders and climbed up the ladder. He was laughing and twisting his neck. I was electrocuted, he said. I couldn't get my head off the ladder.

Leonard stood at the top of the ladder very bright now and alive again and whipped his head back and forth like a swimmer and laughed and wiped his eyes clear. I was stuck on the ladder.

Had one hand on the sump pump and it was running up my arm and shoulder and out my head.

Henry got him a glass of water and he drank it off and tossed the cup onto the grass and banged his chest solid and said, They say it's good for the heart.

Then he went back down the hole.

Leonard you can't go back at it.

Work to do.

Henry tried to coax him out but he said fire up that pump. I know what not to touch now.

THAT NIGHT THEY WALKED into Kingmans Cove, the abandoned community that they both liked to imagine still existed. It would be one of the last times before the baby came. The *Happy Adventure*. The foundations of old houses. The cellar. As they walked Martha said that Colleen had asked her to be a helper during the ceremony Larry was planning. To be there for her, she said.

What kind of ceremony.

A drinking of a herb. A vine or root.

That chanting thing he does.

They will be intoxicated.

Henry wasn't sure she should witness that.

I should be there. It'll be safe and it might be something wonderful. It could be a ceremony for the birth. I guess what I was thinking is you might want to do it.

Do what.

The herb.

That juice in his cellar.

I think so.

There was a load of fill now over the Morris garbage. The hillside burnt to cinders. But there was something else different. It was Martha who noticed it: the profile of the cellar was caving in—rocks had been disturbed. Someone had removed rock. There was a heavy quad track. Some idiot with no sense of the sacred.

Jesus there's rock everywhere on this coast.

They could harvest rock from the new highway.

No Martha, they have to come all the way out here with a quad and rip rock out of a hundred-year-old cellar.

They both were astonished at the effort.

They followed the track and the quad joined up to the side road and must have gone right past Tender's house.

Baxter, Martha said, would have seen who came by with a quad and trailer.

Yes, Baxter would know.

He sees everything.

Though I'm half afraid Baxter might be involved.

Ask him in a neutral tone, Martha said.

When they got to Baxter's he knocked on the storm door. He explained the situation and Baxter waited to hear more. The side of the cellar, it's been carved right off. You never saw a quad come along here with rock, did you.

Baxter was puzzled. You mean besides Leonard King, Baxter said. He took what you wanted for your well. That rock is in the bottom of your well now.

They crossed the road and Martha said aloud, So Kingmans Cove is full of modern garbage, it's burnt over and the cellar's torn out and thrown into the bottom of a well. She put her hand on her stomach. The past will never be resurrected.

37

Silvia and Clem and Sadie were out picking the tiny strawberries and the kids were bored with the work. I'll meet you at the beach, he said to Martha. Come on kids. We're going to give your parents the afternoon off.

Henry walked down to the dory with this truth. He was in charge of things now. It was all up to him, finally. He loaded up the *Happy Adventure* with a picnic and when Martha came down he got the two kids aboard with life jackets and he pushed the boat out and jumped into the bow and Martha gently rowed across the bay to a beach they'd only ever seen but never stepped on. A dory full of kids, Henry said. And you, eight and a half months pregnant, rowing a boat. Now this is my way of a ceremony for the youngster.

It feels good, this, Martha said. I should have been rowing all summer.

They got close to the far shore and Martha shipped the oars and Henry jumped over the gunwale and steered the nose in to the calm beach.

Henry pumped the Coleman stove and boiled the flat-arsed

kettle. Pull out the whiskey, he said, and Clem got out the tube that a bottle of scotch goes in and inside the tube Henry had a roll of paper and markers. On a quilt they all drew pictures of the coastline they had just come from, out to the lighthouse, clear pictures that even included John's truck as they saw him arrive.

When's the baby coming, Sadie asked.

In about ten days, Martha said. Not this Sunday but next Sunday.

Henry was having that feeling he'd had in the dory: that it was good to look back on the land you lived on. It gives you perspective, Martha said.

You realize you can easily leave it, the way we all at some point have or will. That something will be waiting for you once you leave, something you had never imagined but, once possessed, would not ever be rescinded.

He told Martha how wounded he felt about the cellar.

You're as spiritual as Larry Noyce, she said.

I don't need his ceremony.

I'm still going to do it.

As long as there's nothing in the air. There's no smoke is there.

I'll take care of myself.

The kids had finished their pictures and rolled them back into the whiskey tube. They boiled the kettle and ate their sandwiches and decided to head back. A bit of mist is coming into the bay, Martha said. It'll be okay, Henry said. Clem and Sadie were nervous that the boat was going to float away on them. Get in, they said, get in.

We have to have a discussion about the fog, Martha said.

It's a direct row across the bay. I timed it. It'll take fifteen minutes.

They got in and pushed off and Henry told the kids they had to stay in the stern and not move around. He laid into the rowing. He was facing the back of the boat and Martha was in the bow looking into the fog. I don't like this, she said. I can't see any land.

But Henry could see the land they had left. He kept this land to the back of the boat so he knew he was rowing straight across. He checked his watch. After ten minutes the kids announced that they couldn't see any land now, anywhere.

Henry stopped rowing to listen. His ears widened. Just the sounds they were making in the boat. No sea against the coast. A small faucet of water pouring off the oars. The wind picked up a little and there was a swell and they were buffeted by a dense fog that had texture and you couldn't see anything now. Henry dipped his oars in. Martha, sternly: You have to turn more, Henry, you have to paddle into the cove more. But he felt he was turning the dory and turning so much they were just carving a big circle. You don't want to miss the cape and lighthouse entirely, she said. That meant rowing out to sea. She wasn't happy with the situation. Henry, very quietly: You have to stay calm, Martha, and not say those things.

We're scared, Sadie said.

It's okay kids. You just have to not move too much and we'll be okay.

He rowed without a word. Nothing but fog and the waves and feeling like it could be possible they were out at sea now rowing to Ireland. There was a different wave pattern under them, a wave perhaps that doesn't live in waters close to shore. The kids stayed quiet, stunned by their predicament, waiting for Martha or Henry to say something they could believe in.

A little wave breaking behind them. Henry rowed towards it.

Martha: I saw something tall above us.

Henry peered up and it was a cliff. It looked just like the drawing Sadie had made.

I can't recognize it, Martha said.

Henry rowed closer and the waves were crashing onto a shelf of rock so they had to look out for shoals. The tall stem of the automated signal floated there. They were at the end of the boardwalk. They had drifted that far out but had hit the cape. He gave one oar a few flicks and turned them with the high coast above them and rowed back along this wall of rock. There, in the rock, he saw Baxter's white fish.

The kids were okay now but Martha was quiet and he couldn't see her. Dry land. They got up into Kingmans Cove and back to Martha's car. Support our troops. The sun had come out again, down in the bottom of the bay. At John and Silvia's the kids were busy telling their father what had happened and they were very precise about missing the cape and drifting out into open water and sharks finishing them off. They had no compass or flare or phone.

So you've learned a lesson, John said.

Silvia was looking at Henry with disgust.

Don't be too hard on me now, Henry said.

Silvia finally spoke: She could have gone into labour out there.

38

There were two cars in the driveway. Larry Noyce had cleaned out the living room and placed camping foam on the floor around the woodstove to hold ceremony. There will be eight of you, Larry said. There were three men from town Henry had never met before. A woman from South Africa. Silvia and Colleen were beside him, preparing their sleeping bags in the corner. Martha was asking Larry when exactly he wanted the lights turned off. Martha was not taking the ayahuasca, but wanted to help Larry and look after Henry and Colleen and Silvia if things went badly. You could sense that a child was almost in the room.

One man touched the leather case of his phone. It was enough to put Henry off. I like to leave the room sometimes, the man said to Larry.

Well don't leave the space.

You mean the house?

Yes. Don't leave the space.

The South African woman, next to Henry, said you have to be humble, and be grateful. Be vulnerable. Open yourself up rather than curling into yourself.

She had travelled the world and done ayahuasca many times. Her name was Zola. This country, she said, is fabulous. Water, crown land, health care, and people aren't afraid.

Henry: I thought South Africa was beautiful.

It is, Zola said, but you can't see it. I can't travel through it.

There was a man from Peru with an eagle feather. His name was Piero. This room—this space—was going to be Peru. Colleen had not gone to Peru in the end, had cancelled that trip and so was making the most of this Peruvian who had come to Larry Noyce's. Piero waved smoke over your face. You stood in front of him and he touched you on a shoulder with the feather to turn you around. Then tapped you again with the feather to say you're done, you can lie down.

They were all lying down. And Martha turned off the lights, although there was still some light shining from the floor in the kitchen, perhaps a lamp on the floor. Henry decided Colleen had never been with Keith in this house. It was always at her place. He heard Larry talking low. He had that white plastic orange juice container of what they were to drink. He was blowing smoke into the container. Then he poured out the brown liquid into a small glass and chanted like he was blowing through his teeth. He drank the liquid. He asked Piero to come forward. Piero knelt in front of Larry and took the glass. The South African woman, Zola, stood up. Henry was next. The drink tasted like a spicy malt. He saw Martha's face and she was worried. The silhouette of her pregnancy lit up by the floor lamp. You can rinse your mouth, Larry said. There was a residue like brewer's yeast, thick and sludgy.

Henry lay on a mat he had last used to go camping with Nora many summers ago. Martha sitting there. The pale light in the trees in the dark outside—Henry could see a roof—Colleen's. A half hour went by and nothing was happening. Others were moaning but his mind was clear. Oh well, he thought. A boring night of listening to the passion of others.

Then the chanting began.

He concentrated on Martha's silhouette. He was glad Martha had insisted on coming. Larry and the man from Peru, Piero, sang a rhythmic chant from the Amazon. Larry is not a shaman but he has been working with one for years.

Henry felt a second jawline. A transparent jaw or one made of see-through cartilage. It was peeling away from his jaw. If he held his hands up over his head the arms felt foreshortened. Panels of colour shifted like brilliant wallpaper. Now, an image of a tiny dark-leaved plant, sort of like an alfalfa sprout with its pod head of a seedling. This is the origin of life. It was welcoming and Henry asked it a question.

How can I do a better job. How can I be less false and more honest and do better.

What you are doing is the way you must do it. We all do it this way.

The chanting subsided and the panels of colour drifted over one another. There were little clicks and Henry felt like he was in a temple. I'm conscious and in control and enjoying the feeling of peace.

The chanting resumed. You think this is the real life? Yes, he said. A dimension shifted away to reveal another slide of the universe. A giant amber necklace hovered in front of him, a raised knob of amber pointed towards its own centre. The misery of the world is worth it. All will be forgiven and Henry understood that death is normal. Don't treat illness. Dying is not an issue. Life is teeming and joyous and everywhere and of the same fabric.

He closed his arms that had been wide open to receive the chanting. Then he threw up in a bucket. Martha, he understood, was holding his shoulders. He floated into sobriety. It must be over. That was powerful and moving. A real acceptance of what one is and what is out there. We are all one thing.

Then the chanting returned and he had to lie down again.

He had been peering into the cellular level of the cosmos, but now the cosmos approached him. It marched into him, a vastness took over and he was no more.

He hooked into himself again. Awareness. It alarmed him, knowing he had no longer existed. But there was a sound of little flutes and chimes. They were the most beautiful sounds he'd ever heard and a candle was lit. A light came on. The silhouette of a pregnant woman. A man said he'd been trying to quit cigarettes for thirty years. There was a plugging in of a kettle.

Where's Larry?

Martha: He's gone over to Colleen's to rest.

I need to talk to him.

Wait until he's ready.

39

It was really something, Martha said. The way he conducted things. I mean, I think Colleen saw something. Silvia too.

Henry: Everything Larry said about it is true.

Henry paid a visit. He walked down to the lightkeeper's door and knocked on it. Hello, he said. And he told Larry what was happening between his son and Colleen.

Have a seat, Larry said. Yes, it makes sense. I did not know this until just now. Colleen told me.

Well word's gotten out. But the word is the father. I know you've been nothing but kind. I know you are not at fault. However with the ceremonies and Colleen here it doesn't look good.

Larry Noyce closed the book he was reading. There's an old saying, he said. Don't let the dead bury the living. I'm hoping you've recovered from what happened to you in Afghanistan.

I'm converting the power of past experience into positive outcomes, if that's what you mean.

Use the ladder given to you, Henry. But then discard the ladder. Don't hold on to the ladder.

I feel like I've come here for you but you are unconvinced.

I see the trouble. I've talked to my son. But I can't stop the trouble. I love it here and I have a duty here. Perhaps you've found a duty.

To protect you.

He walked home. He liked how the house sat now on the land. He realized Larry would not move. He's had fish dumped in his car. What next. They will burn him out. Baxter and Emerson probably talked about that at the dump. While he was falling into the incinerator they were drinking and planning to torch a house.

He told Martha he needed to sit on the roof for a few minutes.

He climbed the ladder to his new roof and sat down against the chimney. The old lighthouse. He looked out to sea and waited for the problem to reach him. The knowledge was in the sea. Baxter and Emerson had begun with high stakes. Baxter was a retired police officer, he knew about evidence and motive and suspicious behaviour. He understood what it meant to cut the brake lines of a game warden or throw a dead pig in a well. The men would return safely to a torched house. To cultural thuggery. The men would wait until the boy was out. They'd allow the American to visit Colleen and lug two gallons of gasoline in a container exactly like the one the boy used for hitchhiking. The boy often went to the Copper Kettle with Justin King and Baxter would discover that routine. They'd wait for an empty house. And this is where Henry worried about variables. Perhaps the American no longer visits Colleen or is crafty with his excursions and they are surprised when he answers the door. Please come in I was meditating with the lights off. He sees their gas can and they act impulsively. They'd make sure there was nothing handy around him when they grabbed him by the neck and armpits and kicked him between the legs and carried him to the bed to smother him. A panic sets in but also an appreciation of how successful their movements are. Until they get him on the bed and then things even out a little. The pillow wasn't going to work. Something deep in the man would come out of him that they weren't expecting. So there's a struggle that creates a scene that isn't pretty to come onto. The men will know this and, before leaving, they douse the floors with gas and open up the woodstove and kick the fire into the room. Leave the door open for ventilation and that is what raises the alarm. The lightkeeper's house on fire. They throw the gas can in the field next to the burning house. The boy returns to police officers and a dying fire and no service for a pumper truck. Forensics will comb for evidence and discover the gas can in the field and notice a lack of forcible entry. It's difficult with scenes of domestic violence—you'd be surprised at how much calamity there is. And everyone knows they were at each other's throats for years ever since the divorce really and the boy do like a good fire.

But the boy does not know enough about killing to kill his father. That was something the police would not know.

Henry climbed down from the roof and John and Silvia were over. He asked them about it. He painted the picture as he saw it if everything all went perfectly wrong.

I didn't know you were the intervention type, John said.

These are my hundred people.

40

On one of the last days before the birth he thought he'd take the dory out and then beach it on the main shore and get John to help him lug it home in his truck. Martha asked him to be careful. That made him think. He said to her, I'm being selfish. I'm buttoning up rooms and you're about to give birth.

On his way down to Kingmans Cove, he saw Colleen Grandy in her front garden. It was still summer but even before September comes you can feel fall in the air. The fall comes after a rain, she said. You can feel the cold in your feet in the evening when you walk around the garden. I have a garden here that is just white flowers because I have no lights out here and the white helps.

Henry: The way to being selfish in a good way is not to be lonely.

Colleen: No, the way to be selfish is to be happy.

And he knew that if he did nothing, he might not see her again. He knew, from Afghanistan, that high spirits can lead to death. Keith in prison while Colleen's own father is responsible. A remote chance but could he make it even more remote. She would stop answering the phone. A year might go by—he and

Martha busy with the baby. Rick arrives and puts a call in for Leonard King. The front-end loader rumbling down the road. Rick zips through the picture window with a chainsaw. Leonard guiding the bucket of his loader into the house and the men step through the open side of the house while a slow ambulance arrives without a siren. An hour later the bucket of the loader is removed, and sitting in the bucket is a very big woman wearing a white bedsheet torn in the centre like a poncho. They manage to lift her into the back of the ambulance. Colleen Grandy.

Henry had to make this possibility even more unlikely.

I'm just going out for one last row, he said to Colleen. Before we head into town.

Oh my god the new arrival!

He rowed out and heard the whales. He searched for a black arch, a bump that rides over the surface like black thread sewing the fabric of the sea. There was a lot of krill too, these tiny crustaceans the whales use their baleen to sieve. When the tide pushes in to shore the outward lip of a wave shovels billions of little shelled insects up onto the dark beaches. This was probably what made the whales stay so late. The seasons are all out of kilter now, Silvia had told them. The northern ice was melting early and plenty of icebergs were calving from Greenland, including a large peninsula of ice that was almost a country of its own, and that too collapsed into great chunks of icebergs this summer that no one had seen before—long, flat bergs that floated past the harbour. The rest of the country reported scorching temperatures that blew off all previous records and cooked wheat in the fields and dried up shallow reservoirs in northern inland provinces, but this coast grew colder and the sea surges from hurricanes tore out the slipways that had stood for a generation.

Silvia knew about this environmental change. It was what she worked at on a computer in a lab. She had told them once at dinner about the winter that had snapped into this cove early and trapped the whales. This entire cove had frozen over in a thin sheet of ice and an ice breaker had to be called. Whales, Clem had told them, used to walk on land and then thought better of it and returned to the oceans. It was in one of his illustrated books. And here they were, trapped by the very forces they had rescinded. Henry was a mammal who had chosen the land side and was imagining them imprisoned in a sea he had once called Pakistan, as passive as evolution is, even though people dramatize evolution as a force when really it is as unemotive as water flowing downstream. A beaver under a frozen brook. Evolution is a force as conscious as gravity.

I am not beholden to evolution. He stood up in the boat. Look at me, I volunteered to be in a family. To adopt, adapt and improve. And look at me. He sat down again. He turned the boat around. He had to get to Martha.

He heard the snort of a whale and a plume above the water. A whale heading for him. He knelt in the bottom of the boat, unaware that people from small places will romanticize their virtues and begin stories to one another about rural events like whales that have difficulty with ice. We're all very modern people though, so let us push through this difficult thing as simply as possible.

The whale was still beneath him. The long white pectoral fin that looks like an arm. It rose to meet him and hit the side of the boat. The boat rose and lurched sideways and Henry caught himself from falling in. He grabbed the oars. A bad smell and then the dorsal fin sliding past. The whale looked shocked. There was an eye.

He rowed quickly to the main beach where John and Martha were waiting with the truck. Then he slowed down and gathered his breath, three hundred feet from shore. Had they seen that. Yes, they had. John was making arm gestures. That was something.

The swell as the sea narrowed to the main beach. The waves curling and breaking in long trails. He stood up again in the boat. To look at these waves. What John was doing was telling him not to come in.

He sat down again and rowed in. He felt a swell beneath him and rode over it. The boat sank into a trough. A wave gathered itself together behind the dory and he timed it and the dory rose and he paddled through the wave and the wave surfed him in and he kept the dory straight. The speed he achieved, he heard the sizzle of surf beneath him, and then the wave passed through him and he was low and up above the transom a wave mustered itself high and treacherous. Instead of running under the dory and bulling him, it rained down into the boat. It twisted the boat sideways and Henry was in the water. He was under. And he swam further to avoid hitting an oarlock.

He surfaced and saw John and Martha and gave them a thumbs-up. He dragged himself ashore as John found the painter and pulled the submerged dory in.

Martha: What were you thinking?

And Henry embraced her.

LATER, AT HOME, Henry: I noticed John didn't dive in for me.

When you went under, Martha said, he took out his wallet and handed it to me.

He keeps it in his left pocket, Henry said. That's where his dad kept it.

Silvia said it was because you weren't making any noise. It was probably a teenager, young and goofy, and you were just sitting out there. It couldn't hear you.

41

She tucked her hair behind the back of her shirt, before bending over the bathroom sink.

Martha: I was up at six.

Henry: So was I.

Martha: You were just turning over.

The doctor said they should come into town. It could be any day.

So they had driven in and were staying at Martha's. They took walks around the hill and listened to a busker who had a green hat on the ground. City life. Henry put in a five, just to see how a piece of paper money falls into a hat.

They ordered in food. There was still lots of evidence of Tender but it didn't affect him as strongly as he thought. He had grown used to the company.

He put a call in to Rick Tobin.

He said Rick I know what's going down. Rick said what do you mean. About Colleen. About what could happen.

Henry you're a good man but just keep your nose out of this and we can keep on being friends.

Rick you know I can't do that.

Then that's a problem for me, Henry. You're causing me a problem.

He hung up and turned to Martha. I don't know what else to do.

Go see him. Face to face.

He's in Alberta.

Go today. Go right now.

I'll go later.

Perhaps later is too late. Go for twelve hours. Hang the expense. Do all that you can, quickly, and get back here for me. Then you will have done your best.

She was checking availability on all the major carriers. You're in luck, she said.

He phoned Rick again and told him he was flying out there.

I don't have time. I'm snowed under here. I don't need to hear from you. This is not your area of expertise.

We're making it so.

HE'D BE BACK AT FIVE in the morning. Silvia was coming over. And he flew, he hoped, for the last time in his life. It was a very expensive ticket. He settled in to enjoy it. He was going to have a child and a house and a woman and he needed the cove to be secure. Colleen has a point and Rick must hear it.

He rented a car at Edmonton airport and drove straight to the work site in Fort McMurray. He hadn't been there in six months. He talked to Ryan Allen on the gate and Ryan phoned in and got him a visitor's sticker. He drove down a paved road that turned to mud and parked outside the trailers that were arranged in a star pattern. Rick's head at a phone. That's how he'd looked when Henry called him six hours ago.

How's Jamie Kirby?

He's driving a cement truck in Fredericton.

So, Larry Noyce.

You know it takes twenty minutes for me to think of what I feel or know about a thing. That man you're asking after has to speak out loud for twenty minutes to get to his conclusive thought.

I don't think that's your criticism of Larry Noyce.

I've never tallied up a list of renovations on that guy.

But you know some people might act on your behalf.

No one's going in without a written estimate.

Some men do work for cash under the table. No taxes. No paperwork.

I can't talk to you now. Where are you staying.

THEY MET AT MAZAJ on Franklin. This was where John's team ate chicken and pizza. Henry, for some reason, wanted his shoulders to be seen. He called Martha. She was good. Silvia was with her. She felt fine.

I love you, he said.

Don't miss that flight. Exert every ounce of will you have and then relinquish responsibility.

I'm not entirely happy with how things might go down here, but I'll be on the plane.

Rick bounded in, his tool belt on and a meter in his hand, his phone was ringing. But he easily found Henry and slid into the booth.

Sorry I'm late. We had to insert a build-up beam.

I ordered you chicken.

Good. That's about all you're ordering for me.

This is not a question of honour, Rick.

Honour is all I've got.

You have to adapt, Rick. You have to change your way of thinking. Do you love Colleen.

It has nothing to do with Colleen. I've thought that much.

So it's vanity.

You've got some nerve, Henry. After all I've done for you. Why can't you be on the other team?

I thought about it. It was my first thought, Rick. And then I thought of a superior response. You see it all comes back to Tender. What is the most dangerous thing you can do to yourself right now. If Colleen runs off.

Why can't you let me do something shitty?

Then Rick told him a marvellous story. About love. The ladder that love is. Love has a door quality to it, Henry. It pushes and pulls. It gives and gets. I know I'm not giving. I'm giving money but I'm not present. I don't know why I can't be present. You've decided to commit yourself to Martha.

It began deliberately, Rick, but do you know what happened? I love her. That's a ladder I climbed. And Rick, Colleen told me something. She said I had a hundred people. You're one of my hundred people, Rick.

And the boy?

So you know about the boy.

I have no stress on my foundation, Henry.

Rick you're the one who'll live with it. An act like that is a triggering event. I'm living with it. I know what it's like to live with that. I'm asking you not to make a mistake with your own life. Let go of the ladder.

What are you talking about, Rick said. What kind of act do you have in your head? You'd think I'd get involved in a criminal matter? In violence?

You're allowing the line to remain undrawn.

Henry I have one word for you, one word that will take care of that man: immigration. Importation of an illegal substance. Call me a rat—now I have to go. Guy on the crew is getting married. Been seeing his girlfriend for twelve years and he's only twenty-five.

42

He flew home and turned around to look at the airplane and the tarmac. That was it for flying.

He checked his messages and jumped in a cab to Martha's. The house she shared with Tender. Silvia was on the couch, still asleep. He got in the covers with Martha. She stirred. It's done, he said.

In the morning Silvia made breakfast and got her coat and said if there was anything just ask. They had an appointment with the doctor in the afternoon. It's funny, Martha said. To be a patient at the hospital where I work. All was well and stable. They just had to go home and wait.

I know you're not comfortable here in this house.

It's not that bad, he said.

We could stay at a hotel and order room service and watch television and walk around the headland every day.

No let's stay here until the baby comes. This is where the baby should be.

Martha: I want the baby in Renews.

John and Silvia brought over dinner. And they walked. He

made a call to Wilson Noel. Nothing seemed to bother Wilson Noel unless you burned down his land. Then on the third morning she said this is it. And they drove in and parked at extended parking and walked into the hospital and the nurse examined her and said she should come back in a couple of hours. They took the elevator back down to the parking lot. On the way to the car she said, I don't care if they think this is early it hurts too much.

She was in labour all day and he helped her in the bath. He rubbed her shoulders and, just as the sun was setting, the contractions became heavy and fast. Henry watched for movement and calmed her and used a face cloth to stroke her. He could see the shape arrive, that something was pushing out and before this shape there was a curtain of matter that bulged. He waited for this bulge to part and allow the baby through. The curtain stretched further and larger and was quite strange. He urged Martha, along with the nurse, to push and she did and this curve of orange matter ballooned out further as though it were the insides of Martha, she was being turned inside out. A ridge appeared in the curtain and then the most remarkable thing—the brow and hollow of a set of fiercely closed eyes, the bridge of a nose and a lip. The entire face, a shoulder. The little person was rotated by a set of hands and then she slipped out. The nurse had been replaced by a doctor who had wheeled in on a chair with an assistant carrying a lamp on a trolley and the doctor—his name was Dr Mahmoud—held the baby and attached an orange clip to the umbilical cord and the baby was placed on Martha's belly. She held the little person and the baby was wrapped up in a pink and blue towel, the cord snipped and the baby transferred to a stainless steel area of scales. The weak neck and the eye drops and a preventative needle in the foot and the little face with red hair turning away while Martha had some stitches. Forms needed information.

Do you have a name for the girl.

Yes, Henry said. We certainly do.

Martha and the baby stayed in the hospital overnight while he drove back to Martha's. He bought a slice of pizza at Venice pizzeria which was just around the corner from his first apartment when he went to trade school with John Hynes and Tender Morris. He walked down to the house where the apartment used to be. They had removed it now and returned it to a full house. They had a family here, they needed the room. The little stove, the sole sink in the bathroom, all of the things he did for one person. He saluted this old life with the slice of pizza and turned back to Military Road.

He followed the road as it bent down to the harbour and then found himself at the war memorial. He looked up at the men there, one with a telescope, one with a gun. One is a woodsman and one a fisherman. I have been all these men, he thought. And yet, what is above them. He stepped back to stare and realized the fifth figure wasn't a man at all, but a woman. She is holding a torch and a sword. A grateful people to honour its dead.

HE LEARNED HOW TO wrap the baby in a blanket and place her in the car seat and they took the elevator down to the main lobby. They both felt it astonishing that they were being allowed to take this infant away from the machinery of the world and become responsible. Henry carried the baby through the automatic doors and out into a small ring of people standing just outside of the painted white line. A man in a wheelchair with a portable IV unit was smoking. They were all smoking. You could smell the cigarettes and instinctively Martha called out, Gangway—brand-new human being entering the world.

They got in the car and turned onto the main road to the highway. They were on the arterial now back out to Tender Morris's house with Tender Morris's girlfriend and Tender Morris's baby. There were cars ahead of him and behind him and passing him and in the distance he could see the ocean. He knew the ways of a foreign country better than he knew himself, he realized. He clicked on his indicator and slowed and turned off onto the gravel shoulder.

What's wrong Henry.

It's a lot of pressure, Martha. The driving this fast.

It's okay. You take your time. Why don't we just drive to my place in town.

He looked at the face in the car seat and the face stared back at him.

You're going to be all right, he said.

Epilogue

He woke early and clipped his daughter into the car seat and drove
north. The car was American but it looked and ran like a European
car. It had leather wraps stitched on the wheel. It was a slow drive
and that allowed you to take in things, though it was foggy. But he
enjoyed driving through communities that were only half there in
the mist, as though they were docked along the road.

We'll see if they have crab in Bay Bulls, he said. His daughter
knew how to stretch her neck over and see him in the rear view
mirror. She was one happy kid.

He drove down the neck of land to the old fishing town of
Bay Bulls that still had a good active harbour. The gulls were
circling over the cup of the harbour and you knew the trap skiffs
were in. His daughter had fallen asleep now and the water tower
loomed out of the fog and he stopped the car on the gravel beside
a telephone pole that had yellow plastic collars over the guy wires
keeping the pole from falling in the high winds. He said to his
daughter, I'm getting a length of that plastic collar. He closed the
door quietly and heard the doors click behind him and the key
was still in the ignition for he wanted to keep the music on, to

keep her asleep. He turned and looked at the car, his daughter in the back seat, and somehow his powerful stare caused the doors to lock automatically. The windows were wound up. But he heard the radio. An announcer was on now, gravely discussing a meeting for seniors in Aquaforte, the meal a choice of flipper or dressed pork. Takeouts available.

One window, his daughter's window, was down half an inch. He pulled at the gap. He tried all the doors. The radio was playing and she was leaning against one of the padded wings on the car seat.

I'll be right back, he said.

He walked into the woods and looked for a straight stiff branch from a hardwood. There were alders. He tore off a branch and then peeled the small branches off this and trimmed the end with his pocket knife and walked back up to the car. He pushed the thin end of the branch through the window and threaded it across the chest of his sleeping daughter to the other window where the branch started to bob from its own weight and he aimed it for the door latch and had to aim it high to make allowances for the arc of the branch to droop down to the door latch. He hit it and pushed and the door latch moved.

His daughter's eyes opened at the sound and took in the branch and the fact the car was stopped and no one was inside the car. Her father was not in the driver's seat. He knocked at the window and waved. He pulled out the branch. He walked over to the other door and opened it and unclicked his daughter and she reached up to his neck and tugged herself out of the car seat. He called to her. Tender, Tender. Even though this was not her name and not one of the dozen names they both called her. It was his private word, not to name her, but for her to have a memory of the name—a happiness as she held on to the neck of this man raising her.

THEY DROVE INTO Bay Bulls and slowed as the houses started straight out of the edges of the pavement and the turns were tight. He drove out to the wharf and parked beside a yellow concrete guardrail and his daughter said click. And he unclicked the seat straps and carried her out of the back seat and down onto the concrete wharf. It smelled of fish and diesel fuel and the sea was opaque like the eyes of a grandfather, rheumy, he guessed.

They walked over to a trawler that was hauling crab pots and there were three fishermen in the hold smoking. They were younger than he was. He was happy to see young people working.

Can I get some crab? he asked.

They told him he had to go to the office in the plant.

He carried his daughter up to the plant and asked for the office. There were forklifts swivelling with their reverse beeper disabled because they were always in reverse and civilians, you could tell, never walked into the plant. With his daughter in his hands he had all the help he could get and numerous ways to the office. He took a composite of them and ended up opening a white door and through a hallway past some washrooms and a kitchen and then a lunch room with eleven men with their hardhats and their lunch boxes open, quietly eating sandwiches and soft drinks even though it wasn't even ten in the morning. They pointed to a door and he took a set of stairs and inside his head he was making a dotted line through a blueprint of the plant, realizing he had taken the direct opposite corner to where the plant office was. But his daughter was fascinated and made the sounds of the machines and conveyor belts and crawled over his back to catch a glimpse of some bright blue tractor working inside the building. The girl had never seen such a big and very clean machine on wheels inside before and you could tell she was taking that in.

The office was full of women laughing at a big story and when he walked in they finished up the story, some had various parts of the story that were important. They filled in these parts while walking back to desks and by the time one of them asked him what he wanted they were all sitting down and looking at monitors and typing and perhaps a bit shy.

His daughter wanted on the floor and he put her down and she lay on the hard industrial carpet, her arms wide, staring up at the bars of fluorescent light. Go Daddy, she seemed to say.

Is it all right if I trade her in for ten pounds of crab?

We're not processing today. If we were processing little girls.

What day are you processing little girls.

This one we'd never let her near the floor would we girls.

She's already been across the floor operating that big blue forklift. She's been up and down bagging pallets of shrimp.

The woman he was mainly talking to pressed a button and on a monitor her voice went through the building, ten pounds of crab to the office.

They took the easier exit. Because they had not come that way, that's how they had surprised the women in the middle of a good one. He had the child in one arm and the box of crab in another. It had just been processed and the claws were big and orange and pink and the shells nubbly and flash frozen. It is not a freeze that lasts long, so once they thaw it's almost as if they were fresh. In fact he's never had fresh crab, freshly boiled, and can't imagine it tasting better than this.

THEY DROVE BACK the way they came. But then he saw the turnoff for Kingmans Cove and thought to go there. The girl made him do things like that, it was good to have even a one-year-old with you to make you more active in the world. The road was worn here. The previous winter had frozen and washed away crumbs of pavement and the grade was making inroads into the road.

But the valley was a blanket of green. There was no sign of the fire the boys had started. It was like goats were taking care of this valley. It reminded him, at this distance, of the valley near Kabul that Tender had brought them to. He couldn't remember the name.

He took up a salt beef container and carried his daughter into the green. Blueberries. He picked a bucket as his daughter nudged rocks and peered at the ants moving their white eggs. He stared over at Fermeuse and the spirited horse with his neck to the ground. It took no time to fill the bucket.

He turned the car around and drove back to the main road. The car made a slurred sound and thump and they ran over something like a firehose. He slowed and looked back and there was a dark shape on the road behind—it hadn't been there when they came in. He put the shifter in reverse, the car sounding like a tank.

I'm just going to get out and check what that was, he said to his daughter. He pressed the window button down and then pulled up the handbrake and got out. It was a beaver. A big clean beaver, a gorgeous pelt on him and his mouth was open and his two yellowed curved teeth that were fused together, the size of his little finger. He was dead. Henry looked around. There was no family that he could see. He got a stick and touched it. He didn't like to leave it there. His leathery feet.

He took his daughter out and got the keys and popped the trunk. He opened a tarp and lifted the beaver by his tail and laid him on the plastic by the bucket of berries. He left the trunk open, for he saw another power line. This time he walked into the woods with his daughter and pried off a collar of the yellow plastic from a guy wire and put his daughter back in her seat and shoved the plastic collar on the floor below the front seat. He was going to saw off sections to use on his oars to prevent them chafing in the oarlocks.

They drove home and he saw the trunk lid lift up and down in the rear view mirror. He'd forgotten to close it. The beaver was an inch away from his daughter. The thickness of the seat padding between them, even though the idea of a trunk made it feel further away from the back seat than that. The flapping trunk awoke a thought in him that the beaver might not be fully dead.

They drove into the driveway and Martha came out and stood there. She had missed them.

I have something to show you, he said.

You make it sound sinister.

He was nervous. He lifted the trunk lid and looked in. The blue bloodied tarp and the shape of something that had been on it. But the beaver was gone.

You got blueberries, Martha said.

The bucket of berries was staring up at them. He had forgotten them.

Yes, he said, Kingmans Cove is alive with them.

Note

While there are communities in Newfoundland named Renews, Fermeuse, Aquaforte, Bay Bulls, the Goulds and Kingmans Cove, I have altered their geographical shape and inhabitants for the purposes of this story. No one should read this novel as a roadmap or ethnographic study of the highways and folkways of the southern shore.

Acknowledgments

I'd like to thank Nicole Winstanley and Helen Smith for editing this book. Shaun Oakey helped me clarify many cloudy passages. Karen Alliston found solutions to many inconsistencies in the narrative. David Ross I thank for the production edit.

While writing this novel I read a poem every day that is on our fridge. The poem is "Love" by Czeslaw Milosz. I'd like to thank Alayna Munce for putting this poem at eye level.

Thank you to Christine Pountney and Lisa Moore for commenting on early versions of this manuscript. I extend my appreciation to Michael Crummey and the Burning Rock for advice on scenes and images and plot.

I would like to thank the generosity of the University of Toronto's Massey College and Memorial University of Newfoundland's Department of English which both offered me terms as writer-in-residence. I'd like to thank John Fraser and Larry Mathews for their hospitality while overseeing my stays, respectively, at these two places of learning. The residencies bought me time which allowed me to rewrite this book.

For assistance with the dialogue, I'd like to thank Ken Babstock, Ben Basha, Gerry Brake, Rick Clarke, Charis Cotter, Eva Crocker, Stephen Crocker, Sue Crocker, Garfield Crowley, Jean Dandenault, Juliette Dandenault, Claudia Dey, Gillian Frise, Les Gover, Michael Helm, Craig Hewlett, Holly Hogan, Wayne Hynes, Don Kerr, Doris Meade, Michael Redhill, Laura Repas, Ray Robertson, Andrew Rucklidge, Karen Solie, Bart Szoke, Esther Wade, Boyd Whalen, Tom Whalen, Kathleen Winter, Leo Winter, Paul Winter, David Young and the rest of my hundred people.

Excerpts from this novel have appeared, in different form, in *Walrus*, *Reader's Digest* and *Sharp*. I thank the editors of those magazines.